# AN ALL-CONSUMING FIRE

## Book 5: The Monastery Murders

## Donna Fletcher Crow

**Verity Press**

Verity Press an imprint of Publications Marketing, Inc.
Box 972
Boise, Idaho
83704

ISBN: 978-0-578-17166-1

Cover design by Ken Raney
Layout design by booknook.biz

This is a work of fiction. The characters and events portrayed in this book are fictitious or used fictitiously.

Published in the United States of America

# Praise for the Monastery Murders

*A Very Private Grave*

Like a P.D. James novel *A Very Private Grave* occupies a learned territory. Also a beautifully described corner of England, that of the Northumbrian coast where St. Cuthbert's Christianity retains its powerful presence. Where myth and holiness, wild nature and tourism, art and prayer run in parallel, and capture the imagination still. All this with a cinematic skill.

A thrilling amateur investigation follows in which the northern landscape and modern liturgical goings on play a large part. The centuries between us and the world of Lindisfarne and Whitby collapse and we are in the timeless zone of greed and goodness.—Ronald Blythe, *The Word from Wormingford*

With a bludgeoned body in Chapter 1, and a pair of intrepid amateur sleuths, *A Very Private Grave* qualifies as a traditional mystery. But this is no mere formulaic whodunit: it is a Knickerbocker Glory of a thriller. At its centre is a sweeping, page-turning quest – in the steps of St Cuthbert – through the atmospherically-depicted North of England, served up with dollops of Church history and lashings of romance. In this novel, Donna Fletcher Crow has created her own niche within the genre of clerical mysteries.—Kate Charles, *False Tongues, A Callie Anson Mystery*

*A Darkly Hidden Truth*

In *A Darkly Hidden Truth*, Donna Fletcher Crow creates a world in which the events of past centuries echo down present-day hallways—I came away from the book feeling as though I'd been someplace both ancient and new. Donna Fletcher Crow gives us, in three extremely persuasive dimensions, the world that Dan Brown merely sketches.
—Timothy Hallinan, *The Queen of Patpong*, Edgar-nominated Best Novel.

With *A Darkly Hidden Truth* Crow establishes herself as the leading practitioner of modern mystery entwined with historical fiction. The historical sections are much superior to *The Da Vinci Code* because she doesn't merely recite the facts; she makes the events come alive by telling them through the eyes of participants. The contemporary story is skillfully character-driven, suspended between the deliberate and reflective life of religious orders in the UK and Felicity's "Damn the torpedoes, full steam ahead" American impetuousness.

Her descriptions of the English characters read like an updated and edgy version of Barbara Pym. *A Darkly Hidden Truth* weaves ancient puzzles and modern murder with a savvy but sometimes unwary protagonist into a seamless story. You won't need a bookmark—you'll read it in a single sitting despite other plans.—Mike Orenduff, 2011 Lefty Award Winner, *The Pot Thief Who Studied Einstein*

*An Unholy Communion*

A truly great mystery that had me guessing throughout the entire book. It was full of twists and turns and I learned a great deal of new information about the occult and spiritual warfare as well. The author most definitely did a lot of research and, although this book is a work of fiction, has included much fact so that it is not only a fun read but also a learning experience.—Alicia, *"Through My I's"*

Erie feelings, strange happenings, premonitions and unexpected occurrences mark the many events depicted within this well researched, documented and crafted novel. When all of the clues, the pieces and the final reveal come together you will not believe who is behind everything.—*"Fran Lewis's Book Reviews"*

Ingeniously plotted by a master of contemporary suspense, *An Unholy Communion* weaves Great Britain's holy places and history with an intricate mystery that will keep readers guessing to the very end. An exciting book that will keep you engrossed in the characters as well as life in England. A wonderful series.—*"Vic's Media Room"*

*A Newly Crimsoned Reliquary*

Skillfully builds tension from one peril to another, leading to a thrilling climax and satisfying denouement. But more than just a mystery, Crow weaves in rich and colorful details of English church and political history.—Donn Taylor, *Lightning on a Quiet Night*

If you like *Midsomer Murders, A Newly Crimsoned Reliquary* will be a comfortable read to sink into. Especially for the reader who loves centuries of English history. Perfect to read while on your vacation flight to the UK.—Mary E. Gallagher, *Gallagher's Travels*

A thoroughly enjoyable read from beginning to its suspenseful end. I could barely put the book down.—Janelle Watkins, *The SceneinTO*

A worthy addition to *The Monastery Murder Series*. Highly recommended.—Jeff Reynolds, *Sleuths and Suspects*

A really enjoyable, fast-read. It's obvious the author really knows her stuff. Great book.—Dolores Gordon-Smith, *The Jack Haldean Mysteries*

Thus with fire untrowed and thirling flame
the soul of a lover is burned.
It gladdens all things and heavenlike sparkles.

Richard Rolle


Almighty and most merciful God,
kindle within us the fire of love,
that by its cleansing flame
we may be purged of all our sins
and made worthy to worship You
in spirit and in truth;
through Jesus Christ our Lord. *Amen.*

Book of Common Prayer

# Timeline

1300(?)-1349 Richard Rolle

1340(?)-1396 Walter Hilton

Late 14th century *The Cloud of Unknowing* written

# Characters

Felicity Margaret Howard—Ordinand, Community of the Transfiguration

Father Antony Stuart Sherwood—Church History lecturer, Community of the Transfiguration

Family members:
    Cynthia Howard—Felicity's mother
    Andrew Howard—Felicity's father
    Jeff Howard—Felicity's older brother
    Charlie Howard—Felicity's brother
    Judy Howard—his wife
    Gwendolyn Sherwood—Antony's sister

Film crew members:
    Harry Forslund—Director
    Sylvia Mountbank—Producer
    Joy Wilkins—Presenter
    Fred Deluca—Main Camera
    Lenny Taylor—Lights, gaffer
    Tara Gilbert—Make-up
    Simon—Best Boy electric
    Pete Petrosky—Python wrangler
    Mike—Grip
    Savannah—Best boy grip
    Gill—Caterer

Film Resource:

Father Paulinus—Ampleforth monk

Sir Royce Emmett—Royal Academician

Monica—Pickering castle guide

Father Peter—Hampole priest

Father Theobald—Ampleforth archivist

Dr. Samuel Dedinder—Psychologist


From College of the Transfiguration and local community:

Father Anselm—Superior of the Community of the Transfiguration

Corin Alnderby—Ordinand

Stanton Alnderby—Corin's father

Elsa Alnderby—Corin's mother

Nick Cooper—Ordinand

Kendra—Youth worker at St. James Centre

Alfred—Assistant groundsman at Community of the Transfiguration

Melissa Egbert—Journalist

Father Douglas—Vicar, St. Saviour's

Father Sylvester—Sponsor, St. James Centre


Police:

Sergeant Mark Silsden—West Yorkshire Police

Inspector Tracy Birkinshaw—North Yorkshire Police

Police Constable Leonard Craig—Helmsley Beat Manager, North Yorkshire Police

Detective Inspector Nosterfield—West Yorkshire Police, Huddersfield

Police Constable Wendy Smith—West Yorkshire Police, Huddersfield

Sergeant Scott—Nottinghamshire Police, Southwell and
   villages
Police Constable Perry Crawford—Nottinghamshire
   Police, Southwell and villages

Youth from St. James Centre:
   Flora—Mary
   Joaquin—Joseph
   Syd—Melchior
   Dylan—Caspar
   Shaun—Baltasar
   Tanya—Narrator
   Balram—Narrator
   Habib—in choir
   Aisha—his sister
   Drue—Flora's little brother
   Ralph—Shepherd
   Eddy—Shepherd
   Babs—Angel

# THE FLAME IGNITES

C. 1320
Near Thornton-le-Dale, Yorkshire

*A puzzled line furrowed Joan's brow as she thought over her brother's written instructions to her yesterday. Richard wanted her to give him two of her tunics? She was to bring them to him at the little wood near their house? This made no sense. Of course Richard, her adored brother, could have her tunics. It meant sacrifice for the daughter of a family with straitened means, but she would gladly give him anything in her possession. But whatever could he want them for? And why must she take them to him so mysteriously in the wood? Why didn't he just walk in and take them himself?*

*Richard had always been her favorite brother, and she his favorite sister, he had said so many times. She had been so proud when, at the age of 13, Richard had been sponsored by Master Thomas de Neville to be educated at Oxford University. Of course, she missed him dreadfully during his absences, but there were always the long vacations to be looked forward to. And now here he was, home for a full two months before he returned to Oxford for his final year.*

*And then, who knew what great position the world would hold for one with such an education and such a patron? Perhaps an administrator for one of Master Neville's various* properties, or perhaps a church position in one of the livings of his patron who was the Lord of Raby? Or politics—a fine position at court... The possibilities were unlimited for one so brilliant and handsome as her brother.

Joan turned to the heavy wooden chest at the foot of her bed and began removing her tunics. The green one was her finest, but Richard's note had been specific: one white and one grey. Pity the grey one was a bit frayed around the hem, but if Richard meant to give it to some poor woman living in the woods—and that was doubtless the answer to the puzzle— then it would make little difference, or she could offer to hem it for her herself. Yes, she had best take her sewing kit with her just in case. Still shaking her head over her brother's whim, Joan gathered her bundle into her arms.

The woods were fresh and sweet, filled with birdsong. Golden patches of sunlight filtered through the leafy branches overhead. Joan loved the woods, but today the strangeness of her task made her shiver in the shade. "Here I am, Richard. I came as quickly as I could, although I find it passing strange —" She broke into the small clearing where they had played as children, then stopped abruptly, startled to find her brother on his knees, his face raised to heaven, a shaft of sunlight making a halo around his head.

"Joan. You are good. I knew I could count on you." His blond hair still shone golden even as he moved through the shadows to her and took the parcel from her hands. "Ah, good. Perfect." He held her tunics up. "And father's rain hood, did you remember that? Ah, yes. Thank you."

And then, even while she was looking around for the poor woman he undoubtedly meant to aid and was thinking she should have brought a basket of bread and cheese as well, he did the unthinkable.

With one sharp, ripping tear, Richard pulled a sleeve from her grey tunic. "Richard!" She held out her hands in protest. One more tug and the other sleeve was off. And then the buttons from the white tunic. "No!" Her protest echoed around the small clearing. Buttons were a precious commodity. Especially such fine bone as those. "What do—"

He held up his hand for her to be patient and went behind a tree. In a few moments he emerged from the shadows wearing her white tunic next to his skin, the grey over it like a scapular and their father's rain hood like a monk's cowl. Why was Richard wearing this mockup of the traditional garb of a hermit? She could take no more.

"My brother's gone mad! My brother's gone mad!" Joan fled from the woods screaming and sobbing.

# CHAPTER 1

## *O Sapientia*

"You're going to be a movie star! Oooh! Can I 'ave yer autergraph?" Felicity struck a pose.

Antony frowned. "It's a documentary for the televison. And I'm only doing the historical background." For all his understatement, however, the gleam in his eyes showed how pleased he was for her support, in spite of the nagging voice inside his head that told him he was sure to make a dog's dinner of it.

"Well, I think it's as good as being a movie star." Felicity leaned over and gave him a peck on the cheek—which made his eyes shine ever brighter. "After all, it's the Beeb even."

Antony held up his hand. "Not so fast. It's an independent company who hopes to sell it to the BBC."

"How can they miss with you in it?"

Antony wasn't sure whether or not Felicity was teasing. After all, he had been the second choice for Studio Six, brought in at the last minute when Father Paulinus, an Ampleforth monk who was the acknowledged authority on the English Mystics, died so suddenly and tragically. And it all came at such an inopportune time with Christmas next week and then—

"You're sure it will be all right—my being away—with all you have to do?"

"Handling my mother, you mean?" Felicity grinned. "We'll be fine. Really. Once I convince her she isn't putting on a royal wedding. She brought this DVD of all the weddings— Charles and Diana, Kate and William and all the rest—I forget who all. I tried to tell her we're getting married in a monastery." Felicity threw up her hands.

After waiting a moment to let her frustration subside, she continued with a sigh. "But, my love, you're off on location early in the morning and I really should get back to Mother. Who knows—she might have taken it into her head to order a truckload of white roses while my back was turned." She paused. "Although I think she was muttering about lilies being 'more spiritual'. I didn't want to hear, really."

Felicity leaned toward him and Antony took his soon-to-be-bride in his arms.

Even after the door of his lecturer's lodgings at the college closed behind her, he watched in his mind's eye as Felicity strode down the dimly lit path through the chill December night, across the grounds of the Community of the Transfiguration, her long blond hair swinging behind her, toward the big iron gate and her bungalow across the street. In less than a month they would be living in that little cottage as man and wife. For probably the millionth time he breathed a prayer of thanksgiving that he hadn't taken vows to be a monk before this maddeningly wonderful woman came into his life and turned his world upside down.

But oddly, the words of gratitude turned to a heartfelt plea for her safety.

Felicity's anxiety increased when she entered the cottage and found her mother on the phone. "Well, several hundred, I should think. Beef Wellington would be lovely. And perhaps lobster?"

Felicity made emphatic gestures that Cynthia should end the call, then forced herself to speak in a level voice when she obeyed. "Who were you talking to, Mother?"

"Oh, just chatting with the caterer, darling. And it's a good thing, too. She had some very odd ideas, I must say. Cold meats and boiled potatoes. Really, can you imagine? And what are eggs mayonnaise? Do we really have to offer a vegan option? I didn't realize your friends were quite so eccentric."

"You honestly don't need to bother yourself about all this, Mother. Everything is perfectly well in hand. It's going to be a fork buffet for one hundred people. Period. I told Suzette to plan whatever was appropriate." Cynthia opened her mouth, but Felicity hurried on. "She was recommended by the bishop's wife, Mother. She knows what they do at English receptions."

"One of the royals had beef stroganoff. It was on the DVD."

Felicity sighed. It was going to be a very long Christmas holiday.

"I was thinking a harpist for the reception. But maybe a string quartet would be better?"

"No, Mother."

"No?" Cynthia nodded. "No, you're right. The harp will be best."

"I mean no music. Not at the reception. The hall is too small and we want to be able to talk to our guests. We've hired a choir for the wedding mass. That's the special music we want."

Cynthia was speechless so Felicity took the opportunity to change the subject. "When do the others arrive? Do you have their itineraries?"

Now Cynthia was in her element. Ever the efficient lawyer she had her family's schedules at her fingertips. "Jeff will come up from London when he can get away from the office—so fortunate that McKinsey transferred him to their London office. And Charlie and Judy fly into Manchester on New Year's Eve."

Felicity nodded. That was her brothers accounted for. Might as well get on to the elephant in the room. "And Dad?" She held her breath. When she was a little girl and played brides her tall, handsome father had never failed to walk her down the imaginary aisle, even humming the Wedding March for her. And he always lifted the net curtain or lace tablecloth that was serving as a veil at the moment and gave her a peck of a kiss on her waiting cheek. But would he be here for the real event?

"Did I tell you he's ditched his doxy? I'm sure you can count on him to show up in time to walk you down the aisle." Felicity wondered just how rehearsed her mother's offhand attitude was. She so hoped her parents would make another attempt at putting their wobbly marriage back together but at this point least said was undoubtedly best.

"Darling, are you quite sure about having Judy for your matron of honor—or whatever they call them here? She is six months pregnant, you know."

"Chief Bridesmaid. And of course I know. That's why I chose empire-waist dresses for my attendants."

"The rose pink is a lovely color, dear. But mail order?" Cynthia shook her head. When Felicity didn't respond she went on. "And about your dress—I understand not having a strapless gown—even though it *is* the fashion—being in a monastery and all that." She made it sound like a prison, Felicity thought. "But it's not too late to have some beading added."

"Mother—" Felicity made no attempt to keep the threatening note from her voice.

"Just a few pearls? A sprinkling around the neckline, darling? It would be so lovely with your skin."

"I'll wear the pearls Father gave me for my sixteenth birthday." Felicity closed that topic.

So Cynthia reverted to her earlier subject, "Well, I think it's very loyal of you to have your sister-in-law and Antony's sister. But only two attendants? You know, darling, this English tradition of using children for attendants—it's really quite charming and it isn't too late. There must be little girls at that church where you work. I was looking at some dresses online. Of course you don't remember Charles' and Diana's wedding —it was before you were born—but the children were absolutely adorable. Here, I can find it on the DVD—" She reached for the television remote.

Felicity didn't know whether to laugh or scream. "I have to study, Mother." She marched down the short hallway to her bedroom and shut the door none too quietly on the still-talking Cynthia. In truth, she did have that pesky essay on Richard Methley's Latin translation of *The Cloud of Unknowing* to do, but she certainly wasn't going to tackle it now. Felicity flung herself on her bed and pulled the pillow over her head.

She had relaxed just enough to emerge from under her pillow when the community bell began to ring. Ah, perfect.

Now she could avoid her translation work without feeling guilty. She thrust her feet back in her shoes and hurried down the hall. Cynthia looked up from the wedding planner spread out over the coffee table. "Oh, good, I just wanted to ask you—"

Felicity forced herself to smile. "It'll have to wait, Mother. The bell is ringing for evensong. It's *O Sapientia*, so I don't want to be late." She pulled a coat off the rack by the door.

"I have no idea what you're talking about but I would love some fresh air." Cynthia likewise took a jacket off a hook and they went out together into the dark of the December evening. "Could you possibly slow down just a teeny bit, darling? This hill is steeper than it looks."

Felicity slowed her long-legged stride fractionally. "I keep telling you high heels are totally impractical here, Mother. I don't want to be late. Nor do I want you to break an ankle," she added almost grudgingly.

Cynthia was panting when they reached the level area in front of the community church. "Now can you please explain to me what's so special before we go in?"

Felicity could see Corin and Nick, two other ordinands who hadn't yet departed for the Christmas holiday, approaching from the dormitory, so she knew she had a minute or so before the service began. "*O Sapientia* is Latin for Wisdom. The week before Christmas we chant one of the 'O' Antiphons each evening at evensong. This is the first one, so it's special."

Cynthia's confused look told Felicity her explanation had gone over her mother's head, so she tried again. "The 'O' Antiphons are ascriptions for the Messiah from the Book of Isaiah. Um, names for God, praising his qualities."

"Yes, dear. I do know what an ascription is." Cynthia sounded slightly miffed.

Felicity forbore replying that she *had* asked. "Oh, good. Well, they've been used since the early church. There are seven of them—one for each day of the last week of Advent. It's a lovely way of keeping track of time."

"Oh, something like an advent calendar." Cynthia gave a satisfied nod and smiled. "Remember, I always bought the ones with chocolate in them for you?"

Felicity did remember, with an impact so strong that for a moment she could taste the chocolate on her tongue. For once her smile for her mother was unforced as she led the way into the vast Romanesque church. Candles flickering behind the purple-draped altar cast wavering shadows on the rounded arches of the chancel and behind the stalls of the choir.

Somehow the penitential seasons of Advent and Lent were Felicity's favorite times in the church year. Counter-cultural though it was—or perhaps because it was counter-cultural—she had come to love this time and found that there was nothing else like it for relieving the frenzy of the run up to Christmas. The somber pageantry, the minor key hymns, the solemn reminders of the fleetingness of life and the need to prepare for the eternal always spoke to her at a deep level and then made the celebrations of the festive seasons that followed even more joyous.

She had found it hard to adjust when she first came up from London to study in this college run by monks on a remote hillside in Yorkshire. What could possibly be more unconventional than spending the week before Christmas praying in a monastery? Especially for the thoroughly modern American woman she believed herself to be. But she had learned a deep appreciation for this very uncommon experience. And an even deeper appreciation for the church history lecturer who had taught her the value of tradition by his quiet example.

Now her heart leapt as she spotted Antony sitting in the front row of the nave. Stepping as quietly as she could across the stone floor, she slipped into the row beside him with Cynthia following close behind her. Felicity flashed Antony a quick smile that she hoped didn't show the lingering strain of her time with her mother. But there was no time to sit because the procession was entering. The black-robed monks, their hands folded in front of their grey scapulars, filed into their place in choir behind the processional cross and, since this was a solemn evensong, a white-robed thurifer swung a thurible emitting a cloud of spicy incense. The precentor and succentor, in purple copes, took their places on opposite sides of the choir and pronounced the opening sentence anti-phonaly:

"Our God shall come,"
"And shall not keep silence."

Felicity knelt with the others for the general confession, feeling squeezed between her mother and Antony, although, in truth, there was plenty of room. She and Cynthia had come to new understanding when they had been thrown together in a perilous situation just a few months earlier. She had hoped that this time of being together before her wedding would be a final healing, but her expectations were fading fast. Felicity mouthed the words of repentance, then caught herself up short when she realized she was thinking only of her mother's need to ask forgiveness for following "too much the devices and desires of our own hearts..." Did she need to repent of that herself?

She was still attempting a somewhat reluctant self-examination when the words of the collect penetrated her consciousness. It was one she especially loved because it encompassed both meanings of Advent, of preparing for Christmas and for Christ's second coming as well.

"...who at thy first coming sent a messenger to prepare thy way before thee: Grant that at thy second coming we may be found an acceptable people..."

Determined to try harder, she struggled to make her smile sincere as she helped Cynthia find her place in the prayer book for the readings.

After the New Testament reading the priest censed the altar while all stood for the highlight of the service. Choir and congregation chanted:

"O Wisdom, coming forth from the mouth
    of the Most High,
reaching from one end to the other,
mightily and sweetly ordering all things:
Come and teach us the way of prudence."

Felicity felt her tension drain away and her breathing slow as the rhythms of the service continued. During the next seven days they would complete the list of appellations: O Adonai, O Root of Jesse, O key of David, O Morning Star, O King of Nations, O Emmanuel, each one building the intensity and longing of O Come, O Come, Emmanuel. Now her smile for her mother was relaxed. Yes, a better way to mark time even than chocolate.

At the end of the service Antony gave Felicity's hand a quick squeeze before he departed into the shadows. He had sensed her stress easing during the service and for that he was grateful, but at the same time he felt his own anxieties mount. Tomorrow he would face rolling cameras in front of an audience of professionals. This would be a far cry from the classroom where he was so comfortable. And he felt woefully unprepared.

It had been several terms since he had lectured on the mystics and his classroom notes would need considerable polishing to get them up to production standards. What a pity that Father Paulinus's notes had been burnt in the freak fire that killed him. Antony shuddered. What a terrible way to die. And how odd that there should be an electrical fault in such a well-maintained monastery as Ampleforth.

Antony started to run his hand through his hair, then stopped himself—he hadn't done that for ages. He mustn't let himself do it on camera. After all, it was a tremendous honor to be asked to take Paulinus's place and he certainly didn't want to let anyone down. Fortunately Father Anselm, the Superior of their community, had already faced the cameras yesterday, explaining, in his poetic way, the distinctive mystical fervor that developed in the north of England in the fourteenth century. In his winsome way Anselm had clarified the highly personal and intimate relationship with God experienced by the mystics. This, so very unlike the more rigid intellectualism of the scholastics who ruled the Church and universities at that time.

Antony had been invited to Anselm's book-lined office to observe the interview and he could still see it sharply in his mind.

Anselm had given the camera a gentle smile and mused in his soft, almost ironic voice, "No one has ever been a lukewarm, an indifferent, or an unhappy mystic. If a person has this particular temperament, mysticism is the very centre of their being. It is the flame which feeds them."

Joy Wilkins, the twenty-something presenter, had wrinkled her forehead beneath her sleek blond fringe and asked a rather vague question about the theology of mysticism.

Again, Anselm's slow smile, emphasized by a twinkle in his eyes. "Mysticism is a temper rather than a theology, a complete giving of oneself to God in contemplation of Him, seeking unity with Him.

"The mystic is somewhat in the position of a man who, in a world of blind men, has suddenly been granted sight, and who, gazing at the sunrise, and overwhelmed by the glory of it, tries, however falteringly, to convey to his fellows what he sees."

Antony shook his head and stared at his stale notes. It was all perfectly true. But how was he to convey all that to, hopefully, several million viewers through the cold facts of history and biography? Why had he ever agreed to do this? It hadn't seemed that he had an alternative when Father Anselm asked him to take on the challenge. But now a dozen excuses filled his mind.

Well, at least Richard Rolle was a good place to start. Not only was he the first of the English Mystics, but he was also one of the most fervent. Rolle had even titled his crowning work *Incendium Amoris*, The Fire of Love. And the producers, it seemed, could do no better. The television series was to be titled "The Fire of Love".

Antony forced himself to focus on the page before him:

Born into a small farming family and brought up at Thornton-le-Dale near Pickering, Richard studied at the University of Oxford. He left Oxford at eighteen or nineteen—dropping out before he received his MA.

Antony smiled to himself. At least he was all right there. They were to begin filming tomorrow in the woods beside the Beck, the pretty stream that ran through the village of Thornton-le-Dale, reportedly one of the most picturesque villages in England—although how picturesque it would be in mid-December, Antony was unsure. But at least he could tell the story of Richard's unorthodox entry into the life of a hermit; he had recounted it often enough for his students.

Then they would move on to Pickering. It sounded like a rather grueling schedule to him, but apparently the producers were determined to work around the Christmas holiday. It would set Antony his paces to keep ahead of them. He turned to the filing cabinet under his window to dig out his information on the Pickering church.

He switched on a table lamp and as the light streamed across the lawn outside, a movement in the garden caught his eye—a furtive motion that struck him as uncharacteristic of any of the monks or the few students still there during the Christmas holiday. Surely no one else would be about in the gardens at this hour, though. He had heard the bell for Compline when he settled at his desk so all the gates would be locked. The peace of the Greater Silence reigned over the grounds.

He was turning back to his file when the world exploded. A loud bang was followed by balls of fire hurled against his window and sizzling on the stones of the building. Antony flung an arm protectively over his face and staggered backward.

# CHAPTER 2

"Fireworks?" Still dazed, Antony had rushed out into the night, but before he could summon the emergency services on his mobile, Alfred, the weekend caretaker, arrived on the scene with a fire extinguisher.

In the light of Alfred's torch Antony surveyed the pile of spent tubes and cartons that had been piled in the flower bed beneath his window. Fortunately the ground was too damp for the dormant plants in the border to catch fire, but black smudges showed on the stones of the building even in the dim light.

Antony shivered as the image of erupting flames replayed in his mind, making him think of Father Paulinus's fiery death. He shuddered. Was someone trying to warn him not to go ahead with this project? Nonsense. Why would anyone possibly care? Just a prank, surely. There would be fireworks everywhere for Christmas Eve in only a week. Some local lads undoubtedly thought it a good laugh to stir up the monks a bit.

But Antony was the one left shaken by the escapade. How would he ever be able to focus on his notes now?

The grey stone spire of the Pickering parish church lanced the midmorning mist, drawing Antony up the path winding through the churchyard grave stones as the events of the past few hours swirled in his mind. After the alarms of the night before he had risen early that morning: it was an hour and a half's drive to Thornton-le-Dale, on the edge of the North Yorkshire Moors. Even in a winter early morning the village, believed to have been Rolle's birthplace, maintained its chocolate box charm with the Beck flowing full in front of the thatched cottages lining the street.

For the first scene the director had positioned him at the edge of the woods assuring him that the early morning sun and the mist swirling through the bare branches gave just the atmosphere they wanted. It had required several takes to get a wrap, most of them due to Antony's nervous gaffes and once by the director's editing. "Cut! Wait. 'Leafy' has to go." He pointed at the bare branches ringing them.

Antony had salved his conscience with the argument to himself: Well, all right, we didn't know for certain what month Richard made his dramatic gesture, even though his self-robing was most likely during his long vacation from Oxford which would have been in the summer. But at least the other details and his sister's response, if not her name— Antony had added that detail for the sake of smoother storytelling—were recorded history. Richard had ministered to the nuns of Hampole for many years, and they had written down his story with loving care shortly after his death.

Now the entire film crew had moved on to their next location, Pickering church, and Antony looked up at the spire piercing the sky. That tower had been built a hundred years before Richard's birth after its predecessor collapsed. They were on solid ground now, and Antony hoped he wouldn't be required to blur the history too often for the sake of dramatic imagery.

"Sorry, you can't go in there. We're filming." An officious young man with a clipboard barred the door.

"I'm, um—" what was he? Did he have a title in this foreign world he had been catapulted into? "The history," he finished weakly.

The young man eyed Antony's black cassock, probably thinking it was a costume, and ran his eye down the list of names on his clipboard. "Father Antony?" Antony nodded. "Right then. Go in quietly."

Fortunately, the hinges on the door had been oiled for the occasion so he was able to comply. The stone floor was covered with coiled black cables running to cameras, microphones and the strong lights beamed at the ancient wall paintings. Although Antony had been here many times, he was captivated anew by the scenes covering the walls of the nave in the spandrels above the Gothic arches. He looked up at St. George, in full armor on horseback, slaying the dragon with a lance thrust down its throat while George's horse trampled the dragon in spite of the serpent's tail encircling one of the steed's legs. This had always been his favorite. Keeping well out of camera range and stepping carefully, Antony walked on up the aisle surrounded by the great cloud of witnesses hovering there: St. Christopher carrying the Christ-child; John the Baptist at his beheading; the Virgin Mary, crowned as Queen of Heaven; St. Edmund, martyred by a dozen arrows for refusing to renounce his faith...

Antony took a seat in the choir. He smiled at the American flag hanging just beyond his left shoulder, marking the plaques commemorating England and America's alliance in the Great War. Felicity would like that. He made a mental note to tell her. But for now he turned his attention to the proceedings in the nave. Sir Royce Emmett, RA, an expert from London in medieval church art, was telling their future viewers about the frescoes. "These paintings would not have been considered unusual in the fourteenth century. In those days nearly all church walls were covered with biblical scenes and depictions of the saints. The paintings were there as an aid to worship to help the largely illiterate congregations understand religious stories.

"*Biblia Pauperum*, the poor man's Bible, they were called." He pointed at St. Edmund. "The scenes of martyrdom, so frequently depicted, helped people in the Middle Ages face the closeness of death in their everyday lives."

The expert strode back down the nave, careless of cords and cables, obviously confident of being followed by camera and crew, to take his stance before the depiction of the Descent into Hell. "This is perhaps the most striking painting in the church." He gestured upward and one of the cameramen obediently zoomed in on the wide open jaws of a fiery red dragon, swallowing people in his sharp-toothed jaws. "A warning to the would-be sinner, yes, but, surprisingly, this is not a painting of damnation.

"It is actually a message of hope. Christ is there, pulling souls from the very jaws of the dragon. And," he pointed to the next scene, "notice the rays of sunshine emanating from the risen Christ to tell us that, even in the darkness of Hell, he represents the light of the world. All very encouraging to the medieval mind which readily accepted this as fact."

"Cut. That's a wrap." Harry Forslund, the director, strode

forward and clasped Sir Royce's hand as the crew offered a smattering of applause. The director's smile softened the severity of his close-cropped black beard. "Thank you, that was superb. Just the right tone."

The rest of the chatter was lost to Antony as a plump young woman with luminescent pale skin and red, full lips scurried toward him bearing her make-up kit. "Oooh, you've been biting yer lips 'aven't you?" Tara Gilbert shook her mop of magenta-dyed hair.

Antony's impulse to apologize was cut short by her application of gloss to his lips. She stood back and observed him through narrowed, kohl-lined eyes. "Len, can we get some light over 'ere?" She tugged at her black sweater pulling it tight over her voluptuous figure as if preparing to be in the spotlight herself.

Lenny, in charge of the lighting crew, obediently flipped a switch on his magic panel and the chancel was flooded with light. Tara considered her handiwork, standing alarmingly close to Antony, then backing away and observing him with a creased forehead. "Mm, just as I thought. The lights wash you out." She produced a pot of blush and a large brush.

Antony started to protest, but she forged ahead with her work. "Don't worry. I won't make you look painted. Just restoring your natural color—what there is of it. Naturally pale, aren't you? It looked good in the woods earlier—suited the mist—but 'Arry's sure to want more definition indoors."

Antony shut his eyes and let her get on with it. His more serious concern was whether he had chosen the right spot for his narration. The church furnishings were, of course, relatively modern. The 1876 renovations had also removed the whitewash covering the medieval paintings, judged to be "too popish" by an earlier generation. But Antony wanted to be as close as possible to the site of the actual scene of the events he would be relating. That is, if they were in the right church at all, of course. Scholars did suggest others, but Antony felt they were on good ground here in this historic church.

Would the lady of the manor have had a stall in the choir? Or a pew in the nave? The choir seemed more likely, since the only nave seating offered in most medieval churches were stone seats against the wall. But Antony's dithering was cut short as Tara snapped shut the lid on her make-up box and melted into the shadows. The crew bore down on Antony with Harry Forslund barking directions for sound readings, test camera shots and adjustments to the lighting.

Joy Wilkins, the series presenter, gave an off-camera introduction which Antony couldn't hear, then all attention turned to him. He knew he was perspiring, spoiling Tara's careful ministrations. He took a deep breath. "After fleeing from the woods in his cobbled gray and white hermit's robes, having failed so miserably to gain the support he had hoped for from his sister, Richard Rolle's one thought was undoubtedly to get away from parental influence. He was underage and could have been dragged back home. His primary concern must have been to find himself a patron and likely his mind turned to John de Dalton, his father's former squire."

Telling himself to ignore the intruding eye of the camera, Antony concentrated on trying to picture the young man in his mind, the confusion Richard must have been feeling in spite of his certainty over his calling, the fatigue and hunger after his three mile trek to Pickering from Thornton, the relief of finding sanctuary in the protection of the church...

"Did Richard take a seat in the manorial pew by mistake?

Was it divine guidance? Or was it a calculated move on his part to gain the attention of the lord of the manor? All we are told is this:

*When Lady Dalton entered the church for the vespers service her servants were horrified to find a scruffy hermit occupying their mistress's place. They moved forward to throw him out. '"No! Wait,' she ordered. 'I will not have this holy man disturbed at his prayers. I can pray as well in another seat.' And so she did.*

*"When vespers was over her sons, who had joined her for the service, looked more closely at the unconventional holy man.*

*"'Richard!'*

*"'What, do you know this man?' the lady asked.*

*"Dalton's sons declared him to be William of Rolle's son Richard, whom they had known as a fellow student at Oxford.*

"The following day Richard donned a surplice and, without asking anyone's leave, sang the office of Matins. Rolle's official biography says that he obtained permission from the officiating priest to preach a sermon, although since he was unordained and unlicensed, how he managed that is a puzzle. The adoring nuns of Hampole recorded, however, that the resulting sermon was of such virtue and power that all present were moved to tears.

"Richard Rolle achieved his goal of gaining a patron. John de Dalton invited Rolle home to dinner. Although it seems that Richard made a poor guest because when the meal was ready he could not be found. He was eventually located meditating in a broken down old building and persuaded to join the feast. Afterwards Dalton gave Rolle a cell in his house and provided him with a proper habit and food instead of sending him back to his father.

"It's perhaps helpful to understand that in the fourteenth century many men and women chose personal sanctity as a career just as today they might choose medicine or law. Hermits were part of the established social order and it was a matter of considerable status to have a hermit ensconced on one's property. Lady Dalton was known to take large parties to visit Richard after dinner.

"This patronage turned out to be a somewhat mixed blessing for Richard. His cell in the manor house was surrounded by so much hubbub that he found it nearly impossible to concentrate on the life of intense meditation he wished to undertake. And Lord Dalton was less than generous—he fed Richard on moldy bread."

When the "Cut" command came Antony felt reasonably pleased with his contribution. He hadn't tripped over the cords or any of his words or made any awkward gestures—so far as he was aware. But Harry Forslund wasn't so easily satisfied. His mouth was set in a disapproving line framed by his dark beard. At least the problem was apparently with the unexpected shadows on the scene, not with Antony's recital.

At the director's order Lenny adjusted several light angles and Fred Deluca rolled the main camera smoothly over the rough stone floor for a test shot. After several more technical adjustments, including having the well-endowed Tara apply a layer of loose powder which made Antony sneeze, they repeated the process. Unfortunately, this time Antony did fluff his carefully prepared narrative, requiring a retake.

When the third take ended Antony's sigh of relief was cut

short by Pete Petrosky from the sound board, "Sorry, we got a buzz in the background on that last bit." He pulled his headphones off, shaking his head.

"Okay, once more then we'll break for lunch," Harry barked. "Now get it right."

Perhaps it was the promise of lunch that produced the required results. The smiles of relief when Harry pronounced it a wrap were universal. "Catering van, boys and girls—no sneaking off to the pub. One hour. Assemble at the Castle."

Antony felt Harry's orders called for a salute.

In spite of the weak winter sunshine, it was hardly picnic weather but the ravenous crew, gathered around the catering van parked in the street beyond the church yard, didn't seem to notice. The warmth of the large cups of lentil soup and steaming pasties made up for the chill in the air. Antony was wondering if he could slip off and ring Felicity when Sylvia Mountbank, the producer, approached him. "Well done, Father. We do appreciate your filling in for us on such short notice."

Antony looked up at her tall, broad-shouldered figure and mumbled something about being glad he could help while wondering how true that was. He asked her about other films she had produced. Sylvia pushed her brush of curly brown hair behind one ear and, between bites of pasty, told him about the series on the Pre-Raphaelites she had produced last spring. Antony would have like to hear more but Sylvia turned abruptly to toss her empty pasty wrapper in the bin. "You'll have to excuse me. Have to go exercise Zoe. Poor thing wanted to chase the ducks in Thorntondale Woods, so she's been in the car all morning."

Antony was still trying to puzzle this out when Fred Deluca, the slight cameraman in tight jeans and bulky jumper explained. "Her Golden Retriever. Topaze—Zoe for short. Something of a mascot to everything our Sylvia produces. Beautiful animal and very well-mannered. Except where ducks are involved, that is. Hope you like dogs. Pretend you do when you meet Zoe any road. It's probably written in your contract somewhere."

"Have you done a lot of work with Sylvia?" Being neutral on the subject of dogs, Antony felt it just as well to move on to another topic.

"Sylvia's produced just about everything I've done since I joined Studio Six—nine years ago, now. We're a small company. Aim to do high quality and sell to the big boys." He shrugged his slim shoulders. "It works pretty well. Harry and Sylvia know their business and work together like silk most of the time—unless they're having the odd domestic, that is."

"Domestic? You mean they're married?"

Fred shrugged again. "Near enough, anyway. Met at RADA what—twenty years ago? Came up through the ranks together."

"Isn't The Royal Academy of Dramatic Art for stage?"

The characteristic shrug again. "Can't all be Gielgud, can we? That's where I got my technical training, too. Absolute tops. Not RADA's fault some go over to the dark side and take up film." Fred downed the last of his soup and finished his flapjack in two bites. "Well, see you in church, as they say— except it's the castle. Operating Ginger on that hill's going to be no small challenge, I can tell you."

"Ginger?" Was this another canine mascot Antony had yet to meet?

"Camera. As in Fred and Ginger. Because she's such a smooth mover. Want a ride up in the van? It's a pretty steep walk."

Antony knew. He had clambered up the arduous slope more than once. "Thanks, I will." He followed Fred to the parking lot and the white van with the Studio Six logo on the side.

Fred had unlocked the passenger door and started around to his own side when a sharp exclamation made Antony turn. He arrived at the back of the van to find Fred swearing at the door which hung slightly ajar.

"A break-in?" Antony asked. "Are you sure you locked it when you stowed your equipment?"

Fred swore again and shook his head. "Mike's job—the grip. I've warned him to be careful. Everything in there's valuable—" He swung the door open and leapt inside, even in his agitation stepping carefully around the equipment. "He was probably distracted by Savannah. I knew taking on a nubile redhead as his Best Boy would lead to trouble. But our Harry likes them young and—" He sketched a generous hourglass gesture with his hands and began sorting through the equipment.

"Is everything there?" Antony asked after several tense moments.

"Seems to be. At least Ginger looks fine. I'll have to check with Lenny about the lights."

"Does he load his own equipment?" Antony wasn't certain about the hierarchy of crew positions.

Fred nodded. "Part of Len's job it is. Gaffer—head of electrics."

Antony frowned at the odd term. "They used to use a gaff —long pole—to adjust lights in a theatre," Fred explained.

"Where is Len?"

"He went on ahead with Tara." Fred smiled. "Time for a

smoke and a quick grope behind the parapet. Out of hearing of the sound engineer, so to speak. Pete gives new meaning to the term python wrangler. Or at least he'd like to where our Tara is concerned." Fred slammed the door shut and went around to the driver's side.

Antony got in the van, still trying to make sense of Fred's words. "Python wrangler?"

"Sound technician—because they spend so much time pulling cables. But in the case of Peter..."

"But I thought you said Tara and Len..."

Fred gave a bark of laughter. "Just a bit of fun. You spend too much time in that monastery of yours, Father."

Rather wishing he were there at the moment, Antony shook his head at the apparently seething dynamics of the crew. And the odd titles. He had enough trouble keeping simple identities straight, never mind the convoluted relationships and esoteric terms.

Fred took the van up the precipitous, narrow road in low gear. The gravel parking lot behind the castle held space for two coaches—both reserved for studio vehicles today, although the castle would not be closed to other visitors. Antony was surprised to see several children playing on the grassy hillside, then realized they were on Christmas holiday.

Fred had just begun unloading Ginger when a spiky-haired, stockily built youngster arrived. He introduced himself as Mike, the grip, and the ripely plump red-haired woman with him as Savannah. Antony couldn't help thinking that Savannah's curvaceousness must give rise to plenty of sniggers when she was introduced as Best Boy. The three crew members set about efficiently moving the equipment onto dollies and wheeling it along the path to the castle.

In what seemed to Antony like record time the equipment was in place and Harry Forslund, his stocky figure planted in a commanding position, was issuing clear orders. At least Antony could relax now and observe the proceedings. Sylvia had scheduled a castle guide for the presenter to interview for this bit of the footage. Antony supposed he didn't really need to stay for the afternoon, but no one suggested he should leave and he was finding the filming interesting. The better he understood the over-all project, the better he could do his part.

Apparently Sylvia agreed, because when she spotted him standing apart from the general activity she called him over to join them at the gatehouse. "Monica, I want you to meet our expert on the Mystics, Father Antony. Father Antony, this is Monica, chief guide here at Pickering Castle."

A few minutes of small talk followed until Sylvia got them back on track. "Joy, why don't you run Monica through your questions?"

The presenter commented on the excellent condition of Pickering Castle. "Yes," Monica's smooth dark hair swung across her cheek as she turned to survey the fine curtain wall circling the hilltop, enclosing the bailey. "We're so fortunate to have the castle preserved so well. For most of its life Pickering castle afforded accommodation for the king and his retinue when he visited the north. In the king's absence it provided a local power base. The great thing is, Pickering was never sacked."

Antony turned from the interview to walk across the wide, green inner ward of the castle, quiet now except for a few scattered visitors. In earlier times this open bailey area would have been crowded with rooms where the king's household slept, ate and worked. Stone foundations still marked the locations of the various halls and lodgings. He crossed the small bridge at the foot of the motte and climbed the stairs ascending the large earth and stone mound. Once crowned with the King's Tower, this would have been the heart of the castle and its last resort in case of siege. From this vantage-point it would have been possible to survey the surrounding valleys for many miles to watch for approaching enemies and to command all parts of the castle at the same time.

Looking back toward the gatehouse Antony saw Fred, with Ginger gliding gracefully on her dolly, moving along the path toward the bridge over the inner ditch. Not wanting to be caught in any long-distance shots, Antony descended the stairs to the base of the two-story Coleman Tower, which Harry apparently had chosen for the background for Monica's interview. Antony took up a position well behind the camera and crew to observe the interview.

"William the Conqueror built the mound and the first castle which was constructed of wood. The inner stone castle was built in the thirteenth century as defense against the Scots. The outer curtain wall and towers were built in 1323— likely at the very time Richard Rolle was living in his hermitage nearby. It's little wonder he complained of the lack of peace and quiet."

Joy responded, filling the pause left by the guide. "Yes, it's believed to be quite likely that the Dalton Manor house was near the castle so life would have been a bustle, wouldn't it?"

"John de Dalton, Richard Rolle's first patron, was an important man—if not to say self-important." Monica turned her shy smile on the camera. "Dalton was bailiff to Thomas, Earl of Lancaster, and served as constable of Pickering Castle, bailiff of the liberty of Pickering, and keeper of Pickering Forest. That means Dalton would have been directing the building of the stone wall you see all around you." Fred swung Ginger to pan a long expanse of wall.

"Which then successfully kept out the invaders?" Joy prompted, although she certainly knew the answer.

"Not the wall, no. When Edward II launched a campaign against the Scots in the summer of 1322 Robert the Bruce invaded northern England. He burnt the town of Ripon and installed his army at Malton, just eight miles south of Pickering. When Bruce's men began ravaging the surrounding countryside Pickering took action, not arms.

"The town of Pickering promised to pay the Scots a sub-stantial sum and gave up three hostages as pledge. Both town and castle were saved from pillage. The interesting thing for our story is that Dalton was so disliked that the population offered him to Robert the Bruce as one of the hostages."

"If Dalton indeed fed Richard Rolle moldy bread as we are told I can certainly understand that," the presenter concluded with a smile. There followed a voice-over, urging viewers to join them for their next episode which would focus on the life and work of the mature Richard Rolle—work which changed the course of English spirituality.

As Joy was speaking, Fred began backing across the bridge, panning an ever-wider view of the ancient walls and towers surrounding them. Ginger followed Fred in a smooth glide. He paused at the point that the bridge met the path, just where the railing ended and the sheer walls of the ditch plunged downward to repel any attacking enemy that might get inside the curtain wall.

At first Antony thought Fred was angling for a trick shot

of the motte structure looming above him. It wasn't until Sylvia screamed that he realized cameraman and camera had pitched headlong into the defensive trough.

# CHAPTER 3

Everyone surged forward to line the edge of the precipice. Then all stood speechless for a moment, taking in the tangle of limbs and equipment. A loud groan let them know that at least Fred was alive.

Harry Forslund jabbed numbers on his mobile. The broad-shouldered Mike, whose primary responsibility was maintaining the structure that supported the delicate camera, was first to descend the grassy slope. He set about pulling the camera off Fred—whether out of concern for Fred or for the camera was unclear.

Sylvia backed down the precipice on her hands and knees and arrived before her more cautious husband. Producer and director helped their cameraman to his feet—or rather foot because Fred gave a sharp cry of pain when he placed his left foot on the ground.

A maintenance man rushed from the visitors' centre with a ladder and shoved it against the wall of the ditch. The insistent, rising and falling scream of an ambulance siren reached them from far below in the town, silencing for a moment the excited buzz of chatter around Antony. He stepped apart from the crowd, thinking. What a strange accident.

Ginger was such a well-maintained piece of equipment, Fred such a careful technician and Mike almost a mother to his electronic charges.

The unlocked van—had someone tampered with the wheels of Ginger's dolly? For what possible reason? Could this be sabotage or were Antony's own nerves making him paranoid?

Antony continued to ponder as he drove back toward Kirkthorpe. He hated the thought of worrying Felicity— especially when she had so much else on her mind. But he very much wanted to talk to her about his concerns.

And what would happen to the filming now? Sylvia had set a tight schedule, undoubtedly dictated by budget constraints for their small company. But Antony's concern was more personal. He and Felicity were to be married in just eighteen days, on the Eve of the Epiphany. Then the honeymoon. He smiled in spite of his worries. And let his mind drift.

Honeymoon, yes. He came back to the issue at hand. He did not want a delayed shooting schedule to mean that he and Felicity would spend their honeymoon on some windswept Yorkshire moor with him answering Joy Wilkins' leading questions while Harry Forslund barked orders.

Outside Leeds Antony came to a roundabout and shifted gears, making him think how much he enjoyed driving, even in the somewhat dilapidated community car. When he and Felicity were married he must see what he could do about getting their own vehicle. And Felicity would need an English driving license. The exam was beastly hard to pass. He recalled having to take his three times—at considerable expense of money and nerves. But he had no doubt that Felicity would sail through with her usual élan.

He had just exited the M62 toward Huddersfield when a glance in his rearview mirror made him frown. How long had that green mini been behind him? Definitely through the roundabout. Before that? On the M1? He couldn't say for sure. Then he gave a shake of his head. Silly. It was no secret where he lived. If anyone wanted him they would hardly have to follow him surreptitiously to the Community of the Transfiguration.

Then he wondered just how comforting that thought was.

He was careful, however, to notice that no one followed him into the community parking lot. And a few minutes later as he walked up Nab Lane toward the bungalow he scanned the parked cars to be certain no suspicious vehicles lurked in the shadows.

"Antony!" Felicity flung herself into his arms and planted a welcoming kiss full on his lips then pulled him forward into the tiny sitting room. "Don't be cross," she whispered. "It was Mother. She insisted. And I had to keep her busy."

Antony gave an indulgent smile and shook his head at the sight of a fully decorated, brightly lit Christmas tree filling the far corner of the room and extending almost to the middle of the carpet, completely blocking access to their one comfortable chair. "I know it's still Advent—" Felicity began.

Antony tightened the arm he had around her waist. "Don't worry, we've had *O Sapientia.*" He had suggested to Felicity and she had agreed that, when married, they would run their home on the same liturgical principals as those that governed the church. Advent would be Advent—a time of somber reflection to prepare for the feast to come. December

Seventeen, which was yesterday, was the traditional day for greening churches and a relaxing of restraints.

He smiled more fully. "And it is beautiful."

He started to suggest they sit in the glow of the colored lights but was preempted by Cynthia bustling into the room. She brushed his cheek with her lips, undoubtedly leaving a smear of scarlet lipstick. "Our blushing groom returns."

"It's the reflection of the lights," he muttered.

"Isn't it beautiful!" His enthusiastic future mother-in-law continued. "Felicity said not before Christmas Eve, but I knew that was nonsense. Everyone has decorations up so I was certain she had just misunderstood."

Antony opened his mouth to explain that a strict Advent observance was hardly a universal English custom, but rather to his surprise, Felicity spoke up. "I didn't misunderstand, Mother. It's just something Antony and I agree is important. The less society attends to such things the more important it is for someone to set an example. When the whole world's going mad someone needs to keep their head."

Antony was amazed at Felicity's passionate speech. He had been afraid he might have forced his way of thinking on her, even though that had been far from his intention.

But Cynthia ignored her daughter's protest and swept on. "Besides, it's so dismal here. Dark by 4:30 in the afternoon. Don't you get depressed?"

Antony shook his head. How could he possibly explain the wonderful coziness of coming in from the cold and dark on a winter's afternoon to a fire on the hearth and tea in the pot?

At least Felicity understood. He had barely registered her slipping from the room before she returned, bearing a tea tray. The fire on the grate was only electric, but it served.

Felicity poured out a steaming cup—with milk and two sugars the way he liked it. "Now, tell us all about your first day of stardom." She settled into a corner of the sofa and beamed at him.

"I think I got through it all right. It was just an introduction to Richard Rolle."

"Who will the series cover?"

"Just Richard Rolle, Walter Hilton, and the author of *The Cloud of Unknowing*."

Felicity frowned her outrage. "Only the men? What about Julian of Norwich and Margery Kempe?"

"They came slightly later. I think Harry is hoping for a second season. I wish him luck." Antony answered lightly, but he couldn't help recalling the dangers they had encountered exploring the homes of those women while seeking the community's missing icon.

Antony was thankful for the knock at the door which interrupted his disturbing memories. Felicity uncurled her long legs from under her and went to answer it. She returned a moment later with two of his students in tow, Corin Alnderby and Nick Cooper. Since Nick was from South Africa it was expected he would be staying in college over Christmas break, but Antony was surprised to see Corin who was from north Yorkshire. Felicity ducked into the kitchen to fetch more tea cups while Antony pulled two folding chairs from the cupboard.

"So what brings you lads out?" Antony asked when all were settled.

"Just come from St. James." Corin explained, tossing back the shock of blond hair that perpetually hung in his eyes, a gesture that made him slop the tea Felicity had just handed him. Antony nodded. Students from the College of the Transfiguration worked in a youth centre in Kirkthorpe on Wednesday afternoons.

"We met Father Anselm outside the church and he suggested you," Nick added.

"Me? For what?" Antony frowned. He wasn't sure he liked the sound of this.

Corin sloshed the tea from his delicate cup again. In spite of the fact that he was a graduate theology student, Corin's tall, rangy figure always reminded Antony of a half-grown colt. And his enormous hands and feet looked like he would be far more comfortable on his native farm on the Yorkshire moors than serving at an altar. Corin could be awkward, even difficult, but there was no doubting his enthusiasm. "The Epiphany pageant. In the Quarry Theatre. For the Youth Club."

Antony had heard some time ago that the monks planned to reopen the long disused Quarry Theatre at the back of the community grounds. It was considered a good way to reach out to the wider population and to raise awareness of the monastery. As long as the productions mounted there were on appropriate themes it could even be considered a tool for evangelism. Perfectly laudable, but—"In the dead of winter?" Antony asked.

"The yobs—er, I mean young people at the centre are dead excited. They already have a committee of volunteers to clear the stage of debris. And Kendra who does music at the centre will lead a sing-song," Nick added. His horn-rimmed glasses reflected the lights of the Christmas tree.

"But it's so cold!" Everyone jumped at Cynthia's outcry. Sitting as she was in the overstuffed chair obscured by decorated branches it was as if the tree had spoken. "Absolutely frigid. Sub-Arctic," she embroidered her theme.

"We thought bonfires. In barrels. For warmth and light. And lanterns around the stage—like theatres used before electricity," Corin added.

"And Father Anselm approved this?" Antony felt weak in the face of such energy.

"Like I said. He sent us to you."

"But why?" Antony wasn't sure he wanted to know.

"He said you're involved with a telly production, so you'd be able to advise us."

Antony held up his hand, shaking his head forcefully, but Felicity came to the rescue. "Stage work is really quite different from film. Actually I've had quite a bit of experience in that line from my days in ballet."

"Oh, darling, you were so lovely." The tree spoke again. "Remember all those years of *Nutcracker*? And then *La Sylphide*? What a shame you gave it up."

"I grew to nearly six foot," Felicity reminded her mother almost under her breath.

But their visitors, fired with a vision for their project, carried on. "We might even be able to get a real camel. A family near our farm rescues circus camels," Corin said.

"And I found a llama farm near Harrogate who definitely rents out their animals for events. They would be a lot closer than transporting a camel from the North Yorks Moors," Nick added. "Of course, sheep should be easy to get."

"It sounds like an awfully big project. And we don't have much time to pull it together." Antony appreciated that Felicity was trying to bring a bit of sanity to the discussion, but her use of the pronoun "we" worried him.

Just then his phone rang. He slipped around the corner to the kitchen to answer it. As he feared, Sylvia reported that filming would have to be delayed at least a day. Fred was under strict orders to keep his foot elevated for twenty-four hours and it would take Mike most of the day to repair Ginger's dolly. Fortunately, the camera had survived the fall, probably because she landed on top of Fred. But the broken wheel whose shaft had caused the accident would have to be replaced. This was a rare occurrence, so Mike would have to go to London to get a new one. If all went well they could plan on picking up the schedule Thursday morning.

When Antony returned to the hallway Felicity was showing their guests out, promising to meet them at the Quarry Theatre in the morning. Cynthia gathered up the used cups and tactfully retired, leaving the soon-to-be-married couple alone. When the kitchen door clicked shut behind Cynthia Felicity and Antony grinned at each other, turned off all the lights except those on the tree and snuggled into a corner of the sofa.

"Maybe there's something to be said for putting the tree up ahead of schedule," Antony said after a very satisfying lingering kiss.

"Mmm," Felicity replied and pulled him toward her again.

Antony would have liked to continue in the euphoric atmosphere for the rest of the evening, but he did need to bring Felicity up to date on the days' events.

Felicity was enthralled. She wanted to know all the details about his interview and the various members of the crew. "Maybe I could go with you one day. I know Mother would find it fascinating."

Antony liked the sound of that proposal better before

Felicity added the last sentence, but he gave an "Um-hum" of agreement. He still needed to tell her about Fred's accident and the broken dolly. If anything devious was going on he certainly didn't want her involved.

But Felicity brushed off the idea of anything nefarious. "Well, accidents do happen. And you said yourself the stone walkway was rough. Fred probably hit a rock and just snapped the shaft on that wheel. You aren't thinking it was cut or anything are you?"

Antony admitted there had been no such suggestion.

"Well then," Felicity turned in his arms for another kiss. "What a good thing that you have a day off tomorrow. You can help me with this mad pageant idea."

Antony laughed. "At least you admit it's mad. And I'm happy enough to have the time to brush up on Richard Rolle's process of contemplation. I don't know just how much information Joy—or Sylvia—whoever makes those decisions —will want but I need to be ready with a concise answer if she asks."

"That's good then. So stop worrying." She ran a finger along the furrows in his brow.

"It's just that we need to be through with Rolle at least before Christmas because I have to be off to Blackpool." He paused. "Felicity, are you sure that's all right? You know I'd rather spend Christmas with you."

"Of course it's all right. You need to be with your aunt." She shook her head. "Her first Christmas without Edward in sixty years. I can't imagine. Do you think we'll ever be married that long?"

Sometime later—considerably later than he had planned, actually—it was so easy to lose track of time—Antony left the cottage with a small smile on his lips, the glow of the Christmas lights seemingly following him out into the misty December dark.

The great wrought iron gates of the community were swinging shut behind him when a sharp noise made him glance over his shoulder. He frowned at the sight of a little green car parked beside the curb. Surely not the same green car that had seemed to follow him back from Pickering?

# CHAPTER 4

*Nowhere had Christianity been embraced with greater warmth than in England, and nowhere was there a more fertile soil for mysticism... This new departure of mysticism—as a separation from Scholasticism—is embodied in Richard Rolle, who represents the protest of the heart against intellectual scrutiny...* Antony rubbed his hands together briskly to warm his fingers, then picked up his pen to resume the notes he was making from a little-known nineteenth century German writer.

Perhaps he should have taken the book back to his room to work. He hadn't realized quite how thoroughly the chill had penetrated this north side of the library. He glanced out the window looking out over the community's back garden. The grass was still green and a few faded blossoms clung to the rose bushes in the borders. But little heat emanated from the radiator under the window.

Still, the cold could be a prompt to help him focus; a counter to the warmth of Richard Rolle's passion derided by the German Horstman who suggested that Rolle is *quite as excessive on the side of feeling as the Scholastics on that of the intellect; indeed, he is all feeling, enthusiasm, inspiration, unrestrained by reasoning or any exterior rule, without method or discrimination.*

Antony shook his head. That was his challenge, to make sense of Rolle's poetic right-brainedness in a way that wouldn't sound either dull or demented to modern, secular viewers. And yet Rolle was not without structure in analyzing his road to contemplation and his experience of the mysterious presence of God. As with all the mystics, Rolle underwent the classic three-step process of Purification, Illumination and Contemplation...

"We need to be going." Antony started at Felicity's voice. He hadn't heard her footsteps. "I brought your scarf and cap. I knew you'd forget." She held them out to him. "Although it actually feels warmer outside than it does in here." She shivered, making the bobble on her red knit cap bounce.

A pale winter sun broke through as they walked hand-in-hand, along the path to the back of the community grounds. For just a moment Antony recalled the day last February when he and Felicity had run along this same path fleeing what they had been led to believe was his certain arrest for murder. How long ago that all seemed. How could so many life-changing events have been crammed into less than a year? He squeezed Felicity's hand through their gloves.

Her question brought him sharply back to the present. "Who was your fellow researcher? I didn't think the community took guests the last week of Advent. Aren't the monks in retreat?"

"What? What are you talking about?"

"That man reading in the next stall. Didn't you see him?"

Antony thought. There were five individual study carrels in that wing of the library, each stall completely enclosed with floor to ceiling stacks of books. The Community of the Transfiguration was ever a place of scholarship. People came from around the world to read in their library. Little surprise, then, that there would be another reader there. Except for the fact that the community was, as Felicity suggested, closed to visitors at the moment. And that his fellow reader had been surreptitiously quiet. Antony's brow furrowed.

Felicity, however, looked around with carefree pleasure. A lemon-yellow sun shone on drops of moisture clinging to still-green leaves on the bushes lining the path over the hill. Birds chirped as they hopped from branch to branch pecking at the bright red berries. So different from the Decembers of her childhood in Idaho where one fervently hoped for snow to cover the winter-brown grass and bare branches. "You know, this pageant thing might work. If they hold it in the early afternoon and then offer mulled wine in the Common Room afterward. Everyone will be past the Christmas party rush so it could be a really welcome thing for starting off the new year."

"Maybe," Antony's tone showed that he wasn't convinced. "I suppose it could be a good teaching moment for people no longer accustomed to celebrating the Epiphany. In medieval times it was a bigger celebration than Christmas."

They passed the monks' cemetery where row on row of brown wooden crosses with little A-frame roofs marked the passing of faithful, holy lives lived in this community over the past century and a quarter. Felicity paused briefly at the cross marked, Dominic, *REQUIESCAT IN PACE.* Dear Father Dominic. Such a brutal end to a life dedicated to love and peace, but his murder had brought her and Antony together. "Thank you," she whispered before moving on.

On the back side of the hill the path descended by way of

stone stairs set into the hillside. Here the overhanging tree branches were bare and the fallen leaves and autumn rains had produced a slimy pulp over the already mossy steps. "First thing will be for Corin and Nick's work crew to clear these stones off. Public safety and all that." Felicity pulled a notebook from her pocket and jotted a note. "Maybe we could get tiki torches to line the stairs. That would add safety and just think how dramatic it would be!"

At the bottom of the stairway they came out from under the tree branches onto the wide floor of the quarry. The weed-and-bracken-covered basin sloped gently downward toward the sheer stone wall that had produced materials for the manor house and outbuildings in the nineteenth century when the property had been a gentleman's country estate. In front of the rugged backdrop a low stone building had been erected with a flat concrete roof that apparently served as a stage in earlier days. She considered the logistics. "People would have to bring their own chairs. We could set the holy family scene on the stage..." She looked back at the stairway they had descended. "But I don't think we could get a camel— or even llamas—down those steps."

"I wish you'd quit saying 'we'," Antony objected.

Felicity gave him a quick hug. "Don't be a grouch. I know you can see the possibilities. It could be really wonderful."

Antony frowned, but after a moment he pointed across the quarry floor to a grassy bank curving away from the stone wall. "The slope looks gentler over there. I suppose a path could be cleared for the animals. But I don't really recommend it," he added hastily.

Further contemplations were interrupted by a cheery "Hulloo!" And two familiar figures came around the corner of the stage, the tall Corin towering over the shorter, stockier Nick.

Felicity strode through the knee-deep growth and followed the lads to the back of the flat stone structure. Nick disappeared inside the open doorway, then stuck his head back out the window opening. "This is great space in here for storing props and such—well, will be when we get it cleaned out. These stone walls and the cement roof are pretty much water tight. Want to come in?"

Felicity hesitated. There wasn't much that put her off, but there would certainly be spiders lurking in there. "That's all right. Thanks." She scrambled up the steps leading to the floor of the stage instead. "This certainly feels solid enough." She looked around.

"Do you figure we'll need a sound system? Or will the rock walls of the quarry provide the necessary acoustics?" She asked. Almost a hundred years ago these rock walls had rung to the sound of actors' voices proclaiming "Murder in the Cathedral." Felicity added her voice to that of the thespian ghosts:

"Unbar the doors! Throw open the doors!
I will not have the house of prayer, the church of Christ,
The sanctuary, turned into a fortress....
The church shall be open, even to our enemies. Open the
     door!"

Antony, still back at the foot of the stairs, applauded. Felicity gave a satisfied nod. Right then. Acoustics good.

"Kendra said she could get whatever we'll need in the electronic line for the music." Nick had come out of his burrow and joined her on stage. "It won't be elaborate. Just a narrator and the audience singing familiar things like 'We Three Kings'."

Corin also joined them. He pushed back his blond shock with a fierce jab that expressed the agitation he was suppressing. "I rang my dad this morning. He's none too excited about my not coming home for Christmas." His frustration came out in a cross between a sigh and a growl. "So much pressure being an only child. If I had six brothers and sisters like some—" He shot Nick a half-amused look, "They'd be glad to be shot of me."

"Hey," Nick objected. "My family loves me." Then he smiled self-deprecatingly, "But of course, my brothers are glad enough to have me out of the bedroom."

Corin returned to the subject at hand. "Still, I haven't given up on talking dad into loaning us some sheep."

"'Maybe if you went home for Christmas he'd more amenable to your bringing a truckload back," Felicity suggested.

Corin shook his head. "It's more than just a few sheep or one holiday. I'll probably go for Mum's sake, but it's..."

"His dad's, um, well—difficult," Nick tried to help.

Corin shot is friend an ironic look. "Difficult I could handle. He's fixated. I'm supposed to follow in his footsteps. Be a sheep farmer." He shook his head. "He's sure this 'priest thing', as he calls it, is a passing fancy."

Felicity nodded. The source of Corin's moodiness was clear, but she could sympathize with the father, too. "That probably means he has a deep love for the land and wants to pass it on to his son. I can understand that."

This time Corin made no attempt to suppress his growl. "Love doesn't enter into it. Grasping control is more like—not wanting the farm to go to my great, great something grand-father's line. There was some silly family squabble about a hundred years ago and he's still living it."

"So maybe it would be best not to bother your father about sheep for the pageant," Felicity suggested.

"I don't know. I think in some strange way he might be flattered. Show him his world can be important to mine." He shrugged and executed one of the swift mood changes Felicity was becoming familiar with. "I can but hope."

Antony, who had wandered a way across the weedy expanse during that exchange, spoke from beneath the stage, "If you got the sheep early they might be able to graze down some of this undergrowth." Felicity wasn't certain whether Antony was being helpful or ironic but was glad enough to leave the uneasy subject of Corin's family problems, although she could sympathize. Her mother hardly understood her calling.

Glancing at the notes she had been jotting in a small notebook Felicity shared her thoughts about tiki torches along the path, which Corin and Nick heartily endorsed, "Yes, and we could line the rim of the quarry with torches, too. That would be brilliant!"

"And be sure any publicity advises the audience to bring their own chairs," she added.

"And blankets." Yes, this time Felicity was certain Antony was being ironic. Talk about sub-subliminal humor.

But he had a point, in spite of her enthusiasm, she had to admit that the cold was penetrating. Abandoning her center stage stance she descended the stairs and linked her arm through Antony's. "Right. Time for a pot of tea. I really should buckle down to writing my essay. Why don't you bring your books over and we can have a cozy afternoon with our heads in the Middle Ages."

Abandoning Nick and Corin to continue their scheming, Antony and Felicity strolled back arm-in-arm, chatting about their work: Antony's script on Rolle's time in Hampole and Felicity's essay on the medieval practice of translating religious works written in vernacular English into Latin. "It seems so backward," she mused, "until one considers that Latin was the *lingua franca* of Europe in the Middle Ages, so a work appearing in Latin meant it could travel anywhere. For those with the ability to read, that is, of course."

Antony nodded. "And it gave the work literary respectability. It was also considered a way of preserving a work's orthodoxy—keeping it out of the hands of the *hoi polloi* who might be more likely to run to heresy than an educated Churchman."

"Right. One hopes."

"Let's stop by my room. I'll get my books on Rolle. And I have a volume on some *Cloud* translations you might not have seen—they talk about Methley's translation into Latin."

"Great! It would feel good to make some really solid progress this afternoon," Felicity agreed.

It sounded like a good plan, but when they entered the bungalow Felicity was met with the astounding sight of her mother in the middle of the sitting room floor surrounded by satin, lace and ribbons. "Mother, what on earth?"

Cynthia triumphantly held up a small basket covered in white satin and dripping with lace, ribbons and rosettes. "For your flower girl, darling. Isn't it absolutely perfect!"

Felicity couldn't decide which was more staggering, the concept of the mother whom she had almost never in her growing-up years seen without her nose in a law tome, suddenly turning her hand to frilly crafts, or the image of incorporating such ornamentation into their wedding. "Um, are we having a flower girl?" She said weakly.

Cynthia ignored her daughter's response. "And I thought we could gather the petals ourselves. I noticed there are spent blooms still on the bushes in the monk's rose garden. I'm sure they wouldn't mind and it would be so much more romantic than just having the florist supply them." She rootled around in her piles of furbelows and produced a satin pillow covered with lace, ribbons streaming from each corner. "For the ring-bearer. What do you call them here? Pageboy, is it? Won't he be darling?"

"I'll put the kettle on." Felicity turned from the room.

# CHAPTER 5

The afternoon did not turn out to be the cozy twosome Antony and Felicity had envisioned. It took much of the afternoon and far more pastoral skills than Antony knew he possessed to calm Felicity down and to convince Cynthia that since there were no available small children in their near connections it might be a bit impractical to add to the wedding party at this late date, but that her creations could be used as decorations for the reception.

With mother and daughter reconciled—for the moment —Antony turned to his still-rough narration notes. "Um, I wonder, would it be too much of a bore if I went over these with you? I'd really appreciate some feedback before I face the camera."

"Oh," Cynthia jumped to her feet and pulled a piece of paper off the notepad by the telephone. "A woman named Sylvia called." She held the note out for Antony to peruse.

"Oh, good. We're filming tomorrow. That means I do need to get this script in shape."

Felicity squirmed beside him. "I'm sorry, Felicity. I forgot —you need to work, too. I'll be quiet."

"No, no," Cynthia insisted. "Felicity can work best at her

desk." She waved her daughter away. "You stay right there and read to me. I'd love to hear it. This is really very exciting. I do hope the series will make it to American television. I get BBC America, you know."

Antony's skepticism about Cynthia as a sounding board faded when he reminded himself that she was probably exactly Studio Six's market target—intelligent, vaguely interested, with no more than a casual church background. "Thank you. I'm afraid you're rather coming in on the middle of the story, but I thought I'd begin with just a line or two to remind viewers what the first episode had been about." He picked up his paper. "Having abandoned his university career and ensconced himself in an uncomfortable hermitage under his patron John Dalton, Richard Rolle gave himself with youthful passion to the process of mystical contemplation. After four years and three months Richard reached the pinnacle of the mystical experience which he described as *Canor* or song.

"With a burning soul Richard experienced what he termed 'songful love'. He heard, he said, 'spiritual music—the invisible melody of heaven.' With all-pervading holy joy Richard was caught up into the music of the spheres and joined the choral dance of the soul around God."

Cynthia blinked. "I'm afraid you lost me there. What does that mean?"

Antony looked back over his notes. He'd been right to accept Cynthia's offer. Her woman-on-the-street reactions were exactly what he needed. He marked through the last sentence. "How would it be if I just say: Rolle is the most musical of mystics, and where others see or feel reality, he hears it. Melody was his normal form of prayer. His life was set to music—sunny and carefree."

Cynthia considered, then nodded. "That's better. He does sound the most complete innocent, though."

"Yes, I suppose he was. At least at that stage of his life. It was a glorious time for him, though—a shining vision that stayed with him and instructed the rest of his life. One gets the feeling that Richard found a great deal of *fun* in his life with Jesus."

Antony returned to his script. "But Richard couldn't stay in his hermitage by the manor house and enjoy visions of Divine love for the rest of his life. Now the challenge was to put this great gift to work: apply the love to the world around him, share the vision with others."

"Oh, good. Getting practical, is he?"

Antony cocked an eyebrow. "I'm not sure I'd go that far. Of this part of Rolle's life we have only scanty information. We know that he traveled from manor house to manor house for his living, conversing with people in a desire to help them, but this mission effort does not seem to have met with much success, or to have lasted long."

Antony looked down at his notes. When he had these smoothed out he would have to make some attempt to memorize the main points. He hadn't really realized this undertaking was going to be so different from university lecturing. "As often happens after one experiences the heights, Richard now experienced the depths. He lost patrons and friends, his writing was rejected, living was difficult, and he was restless.

"And he apparently struggled with his chastity. He records having temptations and the nuns of Hampole who wrote his biography record that a young woman loved him 'in good love not a little'."

Antony looked up. "Should I take that bit out?"

"Goodness no! It makes him sound almost normal. Pity we don't know more. What did he say?"

"Nothing more on the chastity issue. He records that he felt that his plans had failed, his labor was lost, and he was of no use to anybody. The very noises of the world gave him a headache."

"So what did he do?"

"He refused to give into his funk." Antony glanced at his notes. "Richard returned to the joys of contemplation. When his enemies tormented and defamed him he said he fled to God and sheltered under the shadow of His wing. The fire of love banished the power of the adversary."

"Nope, too lala. Cut that."

Antony grinned and pulled out his pen again. "Sylvia should put you on the payroll." He considered for a moment. "How about: Now, freed from doubt and renewed with spiritual energy, Richard was free to get on about his ministry and be of comfort to those in spiritual or physical need, especially to the weak, the neglected and the poor. Having come through his own dark night of the soul he was undoubtedly better equipped to serve others."

"Sentences too long. You need to give yourself a chance to breathe and your listeners to follow your drift."

Antony tried again.

Cynthia gave a satisfied nod.


The next morning Antony chose to drive the A road eastward rather than take the more efficient, but far less scenic, motorway. Past Dewsbury and Wakefield the winding road led through a patchwork of farmland. He had allowed himself plenty of time to take a small detour through Kirkby since he would be telling the story of Margaret of Kirkby before the camera later in the morning. Even though the industrial revolution had changed the peaceful farming community of Margaret's day beyond all recognition he hoped seeing its location would be instructive. Outside the village the road became narrower, more curving and the hedgerows lining the way higher. Antony encountered little traffic other than a few farm vehicles entering from the occasional driveway or field.

Less than an hour's drive brought him to the tiny village of Hampole which was really little more than a cluster of houses. Father Peter, priest from a nearby parish, his cassock blowing in the breeze, was waiting for Antony at the end of a narrow, wooded, lane. Antony leaned across the seat to open the door for him to get in the car, but the priest waved him onward. "Two more vehicles to arrive, I'm told. Don't want them to miss the turning, it's easily done." So Antony continued on to the village green where Mike, Lenny and the other technicians were setting things up for the days' shoot.

Antony found Fred sitting in a canvas chair under a winter-bare tree, his wrapped ankle elevated. "Are you all right?"

"I'll do. Got Ginger repaired, that's the main thing." Antony quizzed him in more detail about the accident, but couldn't learn anything of seeming importance.

A short time later the last vehicles rolled up and parked at the top of the lane. Tara approached, make-up kit at the ready. Harry began barking directions and everyone jumped to attention. Except Fred who more hobbled. Father Peter was first to come under the camera's gaze. As the local expert he directed attention to a broken, stone gatepost in an over-grown field and a few scattered stones. "I'm afraid that's all that remains of the medieval priory where the prioress invited Richard Rolle to come be their spiritual director in 1340."

Father Peter walked across the rough ground, followed by Lenny, who had temporarily abandoned his lighting panel to Simon. With a camera balanced on his shoulder, a mic on a boom and a heavy power pack slung over his shoulder, Lenny stooped to get close-up shots of the stones as the narrator continued.

"St. Mary's was a Cistercian nunnery, very small and probably very poor. And life would have been uncertain. Here in the border country it would have been exposed to the back and forth forays of the Scots and English armies. At any moment the nuns might have to flee before a raid, and their lands were constantly ravaged. Although Hampole was not on a direct battle line of the Scots wars, it would have received fugitive nuns from other sacked nunneries.

"Richard came to live in a cell on the grounds of the nun-nery. Here he could maintain his solitary life of meditating and writing and also serve as spiritual adviser to the nuns. It was here that he wrote his masterpiece *The Fire of Love.*"

Now it was Antony's turn. At Harry's direction he took his stance under the bare branches of the tree in the centre of the tiny green. "And so we come to the story of Margaret Kirkby who was a young nun when Richard came to Hampole. Perhaps through the influence of Richard, who served as her spiritual director, Margaret left the community and became an anchoress. She lived in a sealed cell attached to the side of a church where she spent her days in prayer, meditation, writing and reading, and counseling those who came to her window for guidance. This was a fairly common practice in those days and some scholars think Margaret's actions might have influenced Julian of Norwich to take up a similar life a generation later.

"We are told that Richard was wont to instruct Margaret in the art of loving God. Richard has been called 'the English St. Francis' and some suggest that Margaret was a friend and inspiration to Richard such as Clare was to Francis."

Having set the stage, Antony could now abandon his memorized text and take up the narrative style he so preferred for his lectures. He knew the producers would use most of this narration as voice-over with robed actors pantomiming the action as he described it.

*His head filled with heavenly music, Richard was going about his joyful task of preparing for the Maundy Thursday service the parish priest would be celebrating for the sisters when the messenger arrived. Mud-spattered and drenched with the early April rains, the man squelched his way into the tiny church.*

Antony followed his own words with pictures in his mind, the dripping rough cloak, the mud-caked boots leaving prints on the stone floor of the church. *"Ye the priest friend o' our holy woman?"*

*"And what holy woman would that be, my good man?"* Richard was shocked by the man's rough appearance and abrupt approach, but all were welcome in the house of God.

*"Our Margaret o' Kirkby. Ye are. I've seen ye at 'er window."* It was more an accusation than an identification.

*"Yes, I am."* Richard had no thought of denying it in spite of the man's tone. *After all, if he had ridden twelve miles from*

Margaret's cell in this weather it was little wonder he looked like a drowned rat.

"Ye need t' come."

"Come? Now?" Richard held his hand out to indicate the prepared altar. He had only to fill the basin for the foot wash-ing. "Father Ailred will be here soon. We are about to celebrate our Lord's institution of Holy Communion."

"Sick unto death, she is. Thirteen days now, not able t' utter a word. Ye'd be best to make 'aste if ye care t' see 'er in this world."

Richard turned instantly to fill his scrip.

Again, Antony saw it all: the tall, thin figure in hermit's garb, carefully placing the needed objects in a small leather pouch: a crucifix, his beads, prayer book and most important of all—a reserved host from the tabernacle.

His inward songs of burning love seemed but a distant echo as Richard rode through the grey drizzle. Lord grant that he be not too late. No man could enter the cell of an anchoress, not even her spiritual director, so Richard took up his familiar position outside her window. The window was small, but low enough for the anchoress to be able to converse with her visitors sitting down. The heavy woven drapery kept the chill winter winds out as well as providing for her privacy. "Margaret? It is I. I've come to bring you the comfort of our Lord."

Her low moan told him that she was still alive. "Pains and prickings" his summoner had described Margaret's sufferings and, indeed, he could hear the rustle of her tunic as she thrashed about on her straw-filled mattress.

Even as Richard prayed for Margaret's healing he was aware of the rich interplay of love and death, sickness and *healing. He lifted his soul and was caught up into the music of heaven.*

*"Richard? Is that you? Have you come to me?"*

*"Aye, to plead for your healing. In this world or the next, as our Lord sees fit, but I would leif it be in this world as I can ill spare my soul friend."*

*He did not hear her move, but he felt warmth surge through him as she clasped his hand resting inside her window.*

*"I have brought the body of our Lord. Are you able to partake, Margaret?"*

*"Aye, let us keep the feast."*

*They shared the sacred meal, then Richard heard Margaret yawn and felt her head droop against his shoulder leaning on the window frame. Richard shifted his body to provide more support and returned to his customary internal prayer.*

*Margaret slept thus for only a short time when suddenly an acute convulsion seized her. Richard cried out at the violence of the attack and tried to hold her, fearing she would injure herself.*

*The seizure woke her and she proclaimed, "Gloria tibi Domine." Glory be to thee, O Lord.*

*Her voice faltered and Richard finished the verse she had begun, "Qui natus es de Virgine," For Thou wast born of a Virgin. Together they continued on through the Compline hymn.*

*Margaret now seemed fully recovered so Richard gave her a final blessing and admonition, "Now thy speech is restored to thee, use it as a woman whose speech is for good."*

*A few days later Richard returned to her cell and he and Margaret shared a meal at her worldside window. As had happened before, Margaret relaxed and became sleepy. She fell asleep leaning against Richard.*

*This peaceful scene was shattered, however, when Margaret's convulsions returned. Richard was alarmed. She became seemingly mad as she was shaken by extraordinary ferocity. Richard struggled to hold her but in spite of his efforts she slipped from his grip. The fall shook her out of her sleep.*

*Appalled that he had let her drop, Richard apologized, then gave the promise that remained her security. "I give thee this word of comfort, that as long as I shall remain in this mortal life you shalt never again suffer the torment of this illness."*

*And Margaret was healed.*

Antony paused for breath. Throughout his recital the camera had rolled and Harry remained still, although Antony suspected much—if not all—of the footage would wind up on the cutting room floor, even though it was recorded history.

He finished the story with a quick summary. "Later, however, in September of 1349, the seizure returned—all the same symptoms except that Margaret could still speak. She sent for Richard, and a horseman rode off to Hampole.

"The messenger returned with the news. Richard Rolle was dead. He had gone out from his hermitage to minister to victims of the Black Death that was raging in Yorkshire and so had met his death.

"The messenger made careful inquiries and, truly, Richard Rolle's promise had held. Margaret's illness had not returned until shortly after the hour of Richard's death."

Joy Wilkins, her sleek cap of blond hair shining above the red muffler wound around her neck, stepped forward to ask Antony about Richard Rolle as a writer.

"Rolle was perhaps the most prolific English writer of the

fourteenth century. He has been called 'the father of English prose.' He had remarkable versatility and ease, whether writing in Latin or English, in prose or verse. It is said that he could give cogent, even inspired, spiritual guidance verbally while continuing to write in his mellifluous Latin."

Antony paused and considered whether he should continue. Then, looking straight at the camera, he took a breath. "But ultimately, it is his passion, the fire of his love that shouts through the ages, singing through eight centuries, 'Fall in love with Jesus—burn with love for him, be overcome with his sweetness, sing his praises.' Richard Rolle was a great mystic because he was a great lover."

"Cut." Even though Antony had been expecting it, Harry's bark was startling. Unfortunately, the command was not followed by the comforting "wrap."

"Lunch," though, was almost as welcome a direction.

Antony, however, would have little time to enjoy the delights of the catering van. Harry Forslund strode across the green, his heavy eyebrows knit. "Right, lad. Cut it in half next time. What do you think we're making—a blooming saga?" He stumped off shaking his head and muttering about academics. Just before he reached the catering caravan he tossed back over his shoulder, "But keep that last line. It has sex appeal."

Sylvia approached with her clip board. "Excellent information, Father Antony, and I do like your narrative style, but I've made a few notes." The notes extended to three pages and Joy, whom Sylvia invited to join them, had more.

After lunch, of which Antony managed time for about three bites, the pale sun stayed firmly hidden behind a looming cloud bank, requiring Lenny to set up more lights for the afternoon's retakes. The expedited version of the story was declared a wrap just before darkness descended mid-afternoon.

Antony heaved a great sigh and felt his shoulders relax as he started the engine on his borrowed community car and turned on his headlights. He wasn't sure whether his relief was for the fact that he had completed the first segment of his assignment without totally embarrassing himself or because he now had a weekend ahead free of make-up, cameras and shouting director. Or was it because they had gotten through the day without a major mishap?

Looking back, Antony realized he had been metaphorically holding his breath in fear of another accident and had been keeping firmly at bay the deeper, dreaded question of whether Fred and Ginger's fall had truly been an accident.

Now as Antony drove along the nearly deserted country lane he slipped a CD of Advent carols into the player and sang along with the hymn, "Come, Thou Long-Expected Jesus, born to set thy people free..."

The headlights played on the hedgerows as the narrow road curved up the side of a hill. Felicity had asked him to come to the bungalow for supper and, free from the worries of filming for two whole days, he could relax and even give some thought to Cynthia's plans for their wedding. Antony smiled. He had a greater indulgence for his American mother-in-law-to-be than Felicity had for her own mother. Antony could sense Cynthia's vulnerability under the protective shell she had built up over the years and he was aware of her desire to make up for the time she had lost with her daughter by being so distant throughout Felicity's childhood.

And Antony was aware that he and Cynthia had the same

goal: They both wanted to make Felicity happy. Although, Cynthia's way of going about it was counterproductive at the least. Felicity and her mother had made great strides forward last Easter when Cynthia had confessed her own pain and guilt over the death of Felicity's brother that had precipitated Cynthia's withdrawal from her family. But there were still years of mother-daughter bonding to be made up. Perhaps he could help as something of a mediator. Or at least bring a bit of perspective to Felicity's brittleness.

At the foot of the hill the road straightened out and Antony could speed up. He returned to his hymn, "Dear desire of every nation, joy of every longing hea—"

Seemingly from out of nowhere the glare of headlights from an oncoming car caught Antony full in the face. His eyes dazzled, causing him to fling up a protective arm even as he jerked the steering wheel to the left and slammed on the brake.

Antony's car rocked and the rear end slewed crazily. A sickening crunch of metal made his stomach clench. He gripped the steering wheel as the impact sent his little car into a spin. With a thud it came to an abrupt stop that made his head snap. Then silence and dark.

# CHAPTER 6

Antony's eyes flew open just in time to see the tail lights of the other car fading to dim red dots as it sped away over the crest of the long hill. Where had it come from? He was certain there had been no approaching headlights as he drove down the hill. Could it possibly have borne a resemblance to the car that seemed to follow him a few days ago? There was no telling. His heart pounding so hard he thought his chest would explode, Antony struggled to clear his thoughts and remember what had happened. But it had all happened so fast. Had he been preoccupied, too absorbed in his own thoughts to avoid danger rushing at him? Yes, he had been thinking about Felicity and singing along with his CD... He suddenly became aware of the music still issuing from the steeply raked dashboard:

By Thine own eternal Spirit
Rule in all our hearts alone;
By Thine all sufficient merit,
Raise us to Thy glorious thr—

Antony extended an unsteady finger and stabbed the

player into silence, then flicked the key to turn the engine off, but left the headlights on. He did not want to be engulfed by the total darkness of the English countryside.

He took a deep, unsteady breath. He needed to think clearly in spite of the fact that his head was spinning and his pulse racing. No, he was certain he had not been guilty of inattentive driving. That car had not been approaching normally. So where had it come from? Could it have entered from a farm track? In spite of the dark, Antony had been aware that the hedgerow lining the eastern slope of the hill had given way to intermittent bushes on this side of the slope. In such an open area surely he would have seen the lights of a vehicle approaching even from the side.

Had it been resting in a lay-by and just pulled onto the road at that moment? Right into Antony's path? But if the collision had been due to mere inattention on the part of the other driver, how had he reached such a furious speed so quickly? And why had he sped on?

Surely the other driver had felt the impact of metal on metal as Antony had.

Antony unsnapped his seat belt, pulled a torch from the glove-box and, unsure that his legs would support him, opened his door. In spite of his wobbly knees he forced himself to stand up. The cold winter air sent shivers over his body but did wonders to clear his head. He turned to focus on the task at hand.

He needed to see the extent of the damage. The speeding car had clipped his right wing, spinning his front tires into the drainage ditch running alongside the road. Holding to the side of the car for support and moving slowly over the uneven ground, Antony shone his light on the sadly crumpled wing.

He bent down, braced his feet on the firmest ground he could find, and tugged at the deepest crease. It moved only a fraction, but that was enough to keep it from rubbing against the tire.

Standing upright again he observed the bonnet. The impact had knocked it askew, but thankfully, the engine appeared to be unscathed. And thank goodness the community were careful about such matters as keeping up insurance. What Father Anselm would say about the damage to a community vehicle, however, Antony couldn't imagine. And how would he get to the rest of his filming appointments? CT, as the Community of the Transfiguration referred to itself, owned three people carriers as well as this little runabout to enable them to transport the community or student groups to pilgrimages such as the annual national gathering at Walsingham, but Antony would hardly have the nerve to ask to borrow one of them. Especially after this.

He moved forward and squatted down to examine the depth of the ditch. Perhaps two feet? Stepping into the trench for a better assessment he was instantly ankle deep in muck the tall weeds had obscured. Would the weeds give his tires enough purchase to back out? He shone his torch on the steep wall of the ditch and his heart sank. It didn't look like there was anything for it but the delay, cost and inconvenience of having to ring for a breakdown lorry.

Or should he ring the insurance company? Or even the police? He shuddered, thinking of his past run-ins with D I Nosterfield. Not that the West Yorkshire police would send out a Detective Inspector for such a small incident. Where was he even? If he rang 999 would the emergency services come from Dewsbury in West Yorks or Doncaster in the south? Was it even an emergency?

Antony sneezed explosively and realized that he was standing in water over his shoes on a chill winter evening. Whatever he did he wanted to get help fast. But first, he should preserve the record for the insurance company. He wouldn't want a skeptical adjuster accusing him of tangling with a telephone pole and then claiming hit and run. He pulled his mobile from his pocket and did his best to get photos of the car and the scene.

Then, pulling his feet from the mire with a squishing sound, he scrambled up the bank, soaking his cassock in muddy water to the knees, and made for the relative warmth of the car.

Back in the car he considered. Did he have a duty to ring the police before moving the car? Surely there was nothing the police could do now. The hit-and-run vehicle was long gone and Antony could give no kind of a description. He had seen nothing but blinding lights. Of course, the other driver was at fault for leaving the scene of the accident—and for causing the accident by driving in the wrong lane. He was probably guilty of driving over the limit, but there would be no proof of that. Celebrating at a holiday party. That had to be the answer.

A simple accident. No one would have caused that collision on purpose. If Antony hadn't instinctively jerked aside the crash would have been head-on. No one would knowingly put their own life in such jeopardy. And what could possibly be the purpose?

Antony heard the chug before he saw the lights. Then, from a field ahead a Land Rover rounded a clump of bushes and turned onto the road toward him. Antony jumped from the car, waving wildly. When the headlights caught Antony the driver braked and rolled down his window. "Ee, ye'r right mucky," the farmer observed.

"Um, spot of bother. I wonder if you might be able to help me get my car out of the ditch?"

The farmer pushed his cap back and scratched his head. "How'd ye manage that?"

Antony sighed. "It's a long story. If you could just—"

The farmer nodded. "It's yer lucky day." He jerked a thumb over his shoulder. "Tow rope in the back."

Less than an hour later Antony all but staggered into Felicity's bungalow after pausing only long enough to pull his shoes off at the door.

"Antony, where have you been? You're so late! I've been ringing and ringing your mobile, but it must have been turned off. You're white as a sheet." She looked at his muddy clothes. "What on earth?"

He opened his mouth to answer, but before he could get a word out Felicity threw her arms around him and engulfed him in an enormous hug, muddy cassock and all. "Oh, I was so worried! I kept thinking about that accident with the camera and thought what if something had fallen on you?"

He pulled back fractionally and managed a grin. "You mean, what if I weren't able to walk down the aisle in two weeks?"

"Or ever." She clung to him with a desperation he wouldn't have imagined from his fearlessly independent Felicity.

Before he could reply Cynthia entered from the sitting

room. "Antony! You're a mess. Get out of those wet clothes this instant. Felicity, let go of him and go put the kettle on."

A few minutes later Antony was wrapped in a warm blanket, sitting at the kitchen table with a mug of hot tea laced with plenty of sugar—just the way he liked it.

The lawyer Cynthia's reaction was immediate when he concluded his account. "Call the police. You really should have done it before you left the scene. Or you could have stopped at the nearest police station on your way home."

"I'm glad he didn't—he'd have been even later."

Cynthia ignored her daughter. "At least you had the sense to take pictures. It's important to preserve the record. And I suppose it would be possible to unearth that farmer if you need a witness."

"He wasn't a witness. He came along much later," Antony said around a swallow of tea.

"A witness to the fact that it happened where and when you say."

Felicity jumped up to get Antony's phone and look up the non-emergency number for the West Yorkshire Police. A short time later Antony, now fully dressed, was opening the door for Sergeant Mark Silsden whom he hadn't seen since the summer. On that occasion, the shocking death of a former student had set in motion events leading to an alarming encounter with the forces of evil. Now, as Antony ushered Silsden into the sitting room he hoped that seeing the sergeant again wouldn't bring those alarms back to Felicity. She was already worried enough over what must be nothing more than a series of accidents.

Felicity served another round of tea and Antony told the

facts in as straightforward a manner as he could, struggling to keep any alarm out of his voice for Felicity's sake.

Silsden recorded it all in his notebook. "And can you please send those pictures to this address?" He produced a small card with his e-mail address on it. Antony nodded. "But you can't give any description of the other vehicle?"

Antony shook his head. "It was dark and it all happened so fast." He stood. "The community car's out front. You'll want to see it."

"Aren't you going to tell him about the camera?" Felicity insisted.

"I don't see why. They can hardly be connected," Antony protested. Still, he obediently sat down and gave Silsden a brief account of the accident at Pickering Castle two days ago. Then stood again.

"And the fireworks," Felicity persisted.

"They were just fireworks. Some local lads having a laugh."

"It could have started a fire. Someone could have been hurt."

Antony made quick work of the story, then led the way to his car.

He returned in a few minutes. "There. Duty done."

"Right." Felicity kissed his cheek. "And that had better be the end of it. I want an 'all is calm, all is bright' Christmas."

"Could Christmas in a monastery be anything else?" Antony hoped the kiss he returned to her held more assurance than his voice.

# CHAPTER 7

Felicity and her mother were still sitting at the table nibbling toast the next morning when Felicity saw Antony walking down the lane. Not bothering to put on a jacket she dashed out into the crisp morning. "How did Father Anselm take the news?"

He returned her hug and gave a rueful grin. "He wasn't amused. All the hassle of dealing with the insurance and seeing to repairs will fall to the community."

"Mm, yes, unfortunate for them. But I am thankful you don't have to do that."

They were still talking about the downside of car ownership as they walked into the kitchen where Cynthia was just concluding a phone call. "There, that's taken care of."

Felicity's heart sank. What had her mother done now? Please don't let her have hired a DJ for the reception. "What's settled, Mother?"

"I hired a car. You'll need transportation for the rest of your filming, won't you?" She looked at Antony.

"Yes, but—"

"Well then, there it is. And," she beamed at her daughter, "we'll be able to get around when Antony's gone off to his family for Christmas. We need to visit florists and bakeries and photographers—" She reached for her wedding planner. "I've got a list. We don't want to have to be taking buses for all that."

"Mother," Felicity took a deep breath. How many times had she told her mother it had all been arranged? "My friends—"

Antony cut her off before the argument could escalate. "Thank you, Cynthia. That's enormously thoughtful, but I'll have to sign on your contract in order to be able to drive."

"No, no, that's not necessary. I'll drive you. I've been longing to see these fascinating places you're always dashing off to and I've never seen a film crew at work. It must be thrilling."

"Not really. It's mostly cold and boring. Especially when I make a dog's dinner of it. That's terribly kind of you, but I'm certain you have better things to do with your time."

But Felicity disagreed. "Mother, that's brilliant. I'd love to see the behind the scenes bit. It will make watching the finished programs even more fun."

"No, really—" Antony began to protest but was cut off by a knock at the door.

Felicity sprang to answer it. "Oh, Nick and Corin. I forgot they were coming by."

The young men were glowing from their walk in the crisp air and their exciting news.

"We spent all yesterday afternoon at the St. James Centre —" Nick began then paused to rub the steam off his glasses.

"You can't imagine how chuffed the youngsters are about the pageant," Corin continued as he sank his lanky frame onto the chair Felicity indicated nearest the table.

Nick perched on the edge of the folding chair Antony pulled from the cupboard. "We thought we'd have five or six show up. There were nearer twenty. I can't imagine how we'll find parts for all of them."

"Not to mention costumes," Corin added.

Felicity laughed. "I'm not sure what the English expression is, but at home we'd call that biting off more than you can chew."

"Yeah, we say that here, too. But my mate Phil Davies would tell me I've sat down to eat an elephant." Corin grinned at her and Felicity realized how charming he could be when he wasn't being difficult.

Nick nodded. "Maybe we didn't quite think this through before we started. But we're into it now."

"True. You can't disappoint the kids," Felicity agreed.

"Goodness, I'd have thought your monks would have more costumes than you could use." Cynthia bent over the table with a freshly filled teapot.

"What are you talking about, Mother?"

"Well, you know—all those white robes they wear in church. I'll bet they have enough for a whole angel choir. And the fancy cape thingeys like those purple ones they wore a couple of nights ago. Perfect for the wise men."

"They're called copes, Mother." But maybe Cynthia did have something there.

"That's brilliant, Mrs. Howard," Corin said.

Nick looked to Antony. "Do you think they'd let us use vestments?"

"Isn't Brother Sylvester the advisor for the St. James team?" Antony asked.

Nick nodded. And Antony smiled at the irony—Tall, pale blond, bone thin Father Sylvester—the quietest monk he had ever known, sponsoring the St. James Centre. Perhaps it was a discipline—or even a penance?

"Sylvester would need to get permission from Father Nicholas—he's the sacristan. If Father Anselm has given permission to use the Quarry Theatre, I expect Father Nicholas will approve. No actual liturgical vestments, of course, but you won't be asking to use chasubles. Cassocks, surplices and copes should be all right."

"And how are you coming along with clearing the weeds?" Felicity asked.

"We've got a crew coming to work in about an hour. Alfred said we could use his tools and he'll even meet us at the quarry to get everything organized."

Felicity was impressed. "You really are doing a great job." She picked up a sheaf of papers from the counter. "Here's the narrator's script I've put together. It's pretty basic, mostly scripture. I expect the actions and carols to do the real storytelling."

Corin and Nick read over the sheets she handed them. "That's brilliant."

"Yeah, really good. Will you be the narrator?"

"Certainly not. I'll direct a couple of rehearsals if needed, but one of your local youth needs to narrate. It'll be much more authentic." Felicity didn't add that the pageant was scheduled for the day before her wedding so she just might have a few other things on her mind. She hurried on before they could protest. "Now, we'll need to work out a rehearsal schedule." She glanced at the calendar hanging on her wall. "Um, how about the Saturday after Christmas for the whole cast? That would be a week before the pageant. Then again on Monday. Of course you'll rehearse your principals separately.

That should do it if it's going well. You won't be able to get your cast of thousands together when families are having their own celebrations."

Corin shook his head, making his mop of hair swipe his forehead. "Some hope for most of those kids. It would be a good start if they even had families. Never mind doing a Christmas dinner."

Recalling their earlier conversation on that fraught subject Felicity asked, "Will you be going home for Christmas, Corin?"

"Yeah." He ducked his head in a gesture of uneasy submission.

"And taking me with him for moral support," Nick added.

"And to wrestle with the stupid sheep. Surprisingly enough Dad agreed to let us use some. Even offered to truck them over the day before the pageant."

"That's wonderful!"

"Well, I think Mum made him do it."

"Still, it's a start at reconciliation," Felicity urged. "So your parents will be here for the pageant?"

"First thing they've come to. Mum's wanted to but Dad always said they couldn't leave the farm. Stupid sheep again." It was obvious Corin tried to make light of it, but Felicity could tell how much the divide with his father bothered him. Perhaps the pageant would help build a bridge.

"So when are you leaving?"

"Tonight. After Lessons and Carols. Assuming my old banger will make it over the moors." He nodded at his companion. "Nick here has a solo. So we've got to get the major clean-out work done on the theatre today—"

"That's why we were hoping you could, er—" Nick started strong, then faltered too.

"Of course we'll help you." Felicity startled at Cynthia's voice. She didn't even realize her mother was still in the room.

"We?" Was Cynthia really volunteering to spend the afternoon slogging through the cold and wet pulling weeds in an abandoned quarry?

Apparently she was. "This sounds like the most marvelous project. And I'm sure you can use the help. All hands to the deck. Isn't that what you say?"

Felicity nodded weakly. If she could just get her mother into suitable footwear they might both enjoy the walk. And the outing would just possibly take Cynthia's mind off dreaming up ever-more-elaborate wedding plans for one morning at least.

An hour later, with Cynthia appropriately clad in a pair of Wellington boots and an old Barbour coat Antony borrowed for her from the mud room in the monastery, Felicity, Antony and Cynthia carefully descended the stone steps into the quarry, with a cacophony of voices calling them forward from the Quarry floor. Felicity could almost picture how it would all look when the way was alight with the tiki torches Nick had informed her they had located. She was pleased to note that already the stones were clear of moss and the worst of the weeds cut back from the path.

But when she emerged from under the overhanging winter branches onto the floor of the quarry Felicity stopped short at the scene of chaos before her. She hadn't remembered the area being quite such a jungle. What were they thinking? They wouldn't have it cleared if they worked full-time from now until Epiphany.

And the chances of their getting much accomplished

today didn't look hopeful. Nick and Corin seemed to be giving conflicting orders to a motley gaggle of young people: Some appeared to be squabbling over the tools the community under-gardener was trying to dispense, others were using hoes and pruning shears for mock sword play and another small group hung back near the stage where a couple of the older boys were smoking.

The whole project was doomed to disaster before they started. Felicity was wondering if she should suggest to Antony that he give Corin and Nick some direction when Cynthia strode forward with her arms extended as if she would embrace them all. "My, isn't this delightful! How good of you all to come."

A ringing silence met the commanding American voice that had been honed in two decades of courtroom debates—most of which she had won. Cynthia took a step aside toward the pair dueling with secaturs. "How lovely that you have such excellent equipment to work with." She turned to include the two with hoe and pruning shears. "I wonder which pair of you can clear a patch of that hillside first? Father Antony, why don't you oversee the competition?" She gestured toward the sloping back area that would provide excellent viewing for their audience.

"Alfred, dear—that is your name, isn't it?—do you have more of those long-handled things? I'm sure Antony could use another team or two." Felicity watched open-mouthed as everyone acquiesced to her mother's orders.

The gape turned to a gasp, though, when Cynthia clutched her arm and propelled her toward the group lounging against the wall of the stage. "Thank you for being so patient and not grabbing at the tools. Actually, I think you'll do much better working with your hands anyway since you seem to have chosen the stage area. Felicity will show you where to set to work cleaning out underneath. We'll be needing to use that area, so be sure you get it good and clear."

Before Felicity could protest Cynthia glanced at the cigarette butt at the feet of the tallest, hooded youth. "I know you won't want to leave that litter there. I'm sure Alfred can give you some trash bags. Better ask him for a whole box— you're sure to find lots of trash under the stage."

Cynthia turned toward Corin who was looking rather desperate as he attempted to show a pair of small girls how to wield rakes, leaving Felicity facing five pairs of sullen eyes. She gulped. Then took a deep breath and gave the most overtly sullen boy a level look. "Hello. I'm Felicity. What's your name?"

She held her breath, having no idea how she would proceed if he refused to answer. He took a long draw on his cigarette, then blew the smoke out slowly, returning her stare. She knew if she had been closer to him he would have blown the smoke in her face.

After a measured silence he dropped the fag and ground it with the toe of his boot. "Syd."

"Good." Felicity was afraid she showed all too clearly how relieved she was that he deigned to speak to her. The ice was broken. She turned to the smallest boy, thin and shivering in a threadbare hoodie. "And you?"

"Drue."

Good, that was progress. "Drue, would you please go ask Alfred for some trash bags?"

Drue looked at Syd for instructions. Syd raised one

shoulder in a languid shrug. Drue gave a jerk of a nod and set off on his mission.

A hollow-eyed girl in a jacket too small for her stood next to Felicity. "I'm Tanya, Drue's sister." Wisps of straw-colored hair hung below her knit cap.

"How nice. I have brothers, too." Felicity hoped that would at least show a willingness to form a bond. She turned to the dark-haired boy and girl on her right.

"Habib," the boy said. "My sister, Aisha."

Felicity greeted them, trying to cover her surprise that youngsters with Arabic names would be involved with the St. James Centre. Of course, one of its goals was to promote community integration, but that noble goal often fell far short of its vision. Surely they wouldn't be here if their family were Muslim extremists, so she needn't worry about stirring up political tensions by involving them in a Christian celebration.

Drue returned with the requested trash bags and a box of disposable gloves. "Health and safety," the youth explained when Felicity asked what the gloves were for. Surely everyone would already be wearing gloves in this frigid weather. But maybe not. Young males seemed to be universally impervious.

"Right, you hand out the gloves." She directed before pulling a trash bag from the roll and confronting Syd. "You might want to start by putting your fag ends in there." Without waiting to see whether or not he obeyed she handed one likewise to Tanya. "You, too. We're here to make it better, not worse."

Hoping she wasn't pushing her luck too far, but not knowing anything else to do, Felicity led the way around to the back of the stage. She was relieved when the sound of feet trampling in the weeds told her they were following. She halted, though, at the gaping door of the stone structure. The open hollows of door and windows looked like sockets in a skull and she could only imagine what the black interior held. For all her fearlessness Felicity had a horror of spiders. Especially spiders in dark, enclosed spaces. "Er—it's going to be too dark to accomplish much in there. You lot go on and get started just inside," she indicated where the winter-white sun penetrated the darkness just beyond the openings. "I'll see if Alfred has some torches."

"Never mind, I'll go." Tanya, following at the back of the group, had already spun around.

Felicity gulped. "Right then. Forward. Be careful, though. There may be nails, rusty tins—who knows what?"

"Snakes?" Alisha's voice was small beside her.

Ah, Felicity would much rather think of snakes than spiders. "Oh, I doubt it. But they'll be harmless if there are. If you see a snake I'll catch it for you and you can chase your brother with it. I did that once when I was about your age." Felicity could feel the group's respect rising. Now, if she just didn't blow it by going hysterical over a spider.

"And everyone be careful not to bang your heads." The shorter ones of the group would be able to stand upright, but Felicity feared she and Syd would be in danger of grazing the tops of their heads. Just inside the door she dropped to her hands and knees and began thrusting an old newspaper tangled in other trash into her bag.

Tanya returned with two torches which Felicity suggested Tanya and Syd use with their groups so they could begin working further back under the stage. For a time her little crew worked steadily, each filling their bag with weeds, broken bits of crockery, various decayed boxes and scraps of fabric and bits of junk. Felicity had no idea what some of it was, and figured she was better off not knowing.

She was just about to congratulate herself on the success of her mission when Syd gave a guffaw. "Rue, Habib, cum 'ere." He called them into the back corner. Sniggers and *sotto voce* comments that Felicity intuited were lewd remarks echoed through the low-ceilinged space.

Felicity had resisted leaving the relative comfort of the daylit area, but forced herself to plunge into the dark recess to investigate. It was no more than she had suspected. Syd had pulled discarded condoms over his gloved fingers and was doing an energetic shadow play for the amusement of his mates.

"Shall I help you clean this out, Syd?" Felicity held out her bag. The youths who hadn't noticed her approaching had the grace to look slightly abashed, although their amusement remained.

"I can take care 'uvit." Syd dismissed her offer of help.

She started to return to the air and light below the window openings when a squabble broke out between the girls working in the other corner.

"No, it's not right," Aisha protested.

"Shhh," Tanya gave a sharp warning.

"I won't—"

"What is it? Something I can help with, Tanya?" Felicity peered into the circle of light shed by Tanya's torch, hoping she could see what was causing the contention.

Tanya shifted the beam of her light. "No. It's nothing. We can handle it." Her deep-set eyes darted around as if desperate to find something to distract Felicity.

"That's fine, I'm glad to give a hand." Felicity dropped to her knees, trying to peer into what seemed to be an old cupboard against the back wall. "Can you shine your light over here, Tanya?"

The girl reluctantly obeyed. At first Felicity thought it was just another pile of cigarette butts in the corner. Then she realized these white, slightly cone-shaped butts didn't look like any cigarettes she had ever seen. She picked one up and sniffed, although she wasn't certain she would recognize marijuana if she smelled it.

She was spared showing her ignorance. "Yeah, they're joints. But the silly git who smoked them left some good weed. No sense in wasting it." Tanya thrust her trash bag behind her.

"You're probably right, Tanya. They shouldn't go into the trash." Felicity sat back on her heels. "Does anyone have a sandwich bag?" Sergeant Silsden might find this interesting. She couldn't help noting that the joint butts seemed much fresher than most of the decayed rubbish littering the Quarry Theatre.

The fact that they were clearing the space for a public event should be enough to discourage a recurrence of any illegal activity here, but she certainly wouldn't want to be bringing the St. James youth into contact with area druggies. Unless some of them *were* the druggies, of course.

# CHAPTER 8

"Comfort ye, Comfort ye, my people, sayeth your God! Speak ye comfortably to Jerusalem..." Nick's fine tenor voice carried to the curving ceiling of the Community Church, filling Felicity with anticipation for the coming season.

When the echoes of the organ faded Corin stood for the brief second reading. As his clear voice proclaimed Jeremiah's prophecy of the coming King Felicity marveled at how right this sometimes clumsy, contradictory young man seemed in the sacred service.

The service moved on to the next hymn, "The Lord Will Come and Not Be Slow." Antony was the reader for the third lesson, this from the prophet Isaiah. Felicity wondered if she would ever get over the prickles of pride she felt whenever she watched Antony performing his duties at the altar. She hoped she wouldn't; it was such a lovely warm feeling.

At the end of the reading the congregation stood again to sing the Advent carol "Hail to the Lord's Anointed" and the familiar service moved on through its set pattern of nine readings foretelling the birth of the Christ that was to come, each followed by a hymn or anthem. This was not the more familiar Festival of Christmas Lessons and Carols made famous by King's College, Cambridge, but a strictly Advent service that took worshippers through the Old Testament prophets up to the Annunciation by the Angel Gabriel to Mary. Accounts of the Babe in the manger and singing of familiar Christmas carols would await midnight on Christmas Eve, then continue for the full twelve days of Christmas.

Father Anselm led the community and their guests in the Advent Responsory following the ninth lesson and hymn. "My soul waits for the Lord; in his Word is my hope." When Felicity repeated the words with the congregation she became aware of a particularly resonant male voice behind her, but checked her impulse to turn around.

"Almighty God let not our souls be busy inns that have no room for You, but quiet homes of prayer and praise where You may find fit company..." Father Anselm pronounced the final collect and the organ boomed forth the recessional "The King Shall Come When Morning Dawns." The white-robed crucifer and thurifer led the readers and monks from the choir and Felicity turned to watch their progress down the aisle.

When she did she saw the man whose sonorous voice had so enriched the responses. She blinked to be certain. No, Corin had been a participant in the service. He was recessing with the monks. Besides, this man was older, more weathered. But the likeness was remarkable. The same blond hair droop-ing into his eyes, the same large-boned height and prominent nose and cheekbones. On second look, though, this man had none of Corin's rangy coltishness. This man exuded a self-assurance that had long outstripped any awkwardness he might have possessed.

"May the Daystar from on High shine upon you and fill

your hearts with joy as you await his coming..." Felicity wrenched her thoughts from the visitor to the benediction just in time to join in the final "Amen."

"Go forth in peace to greet the coming King!" Anselm pronounced.

"Thanks be to God." Again, the voice behind her boomed above the rest of the responses.

Felicity was still gathering her belongings when Corin approached. "Felicity, I want you to meet my parents. Stanton and Elsa Alnderby, Felicity Howard." Ah, so Corin was capable of displaying social graces when the situation demanded it.

Felicity held out her hand as she turned. So she was right that the man with the strong resemblance to Corin was his father. Now she looked at the small woman standing beside him. Elsa Alnderby seemed half her husband's size with rather mousy brown hair, but when the women shook hands a warm smile lifted the lines of weariness in her face and Felicity realized that Corin's intelligent blue eyes were his mother's gift to her son, whereas the father's were a much colder steely grey.

"How lovely that you could be here tonight," Felicity said. "But I'm surprised, I thought Corin was going home tonight." She didn't add that she was also surprised because Corin said his parents had never come to anything at the community, although the sixty-something mile drive across the North Yorkshire moors seemed practically next door to Felicity who still thought of distances in American terms.

"I'm so pleased, too." Elsa beamed at her. "I've wanted to see all this ever since Corin came here to study, but it's just so hard to get away from the farm. The beasts always need something."

"It's nice to know they put me ahead of the sheep." Corin's grin didn't quite hide the edge to his voice.

"Don't get above yourself. It's actually me they came for, you know." Nick gave his friend a sharp nudge with his elbow.

While Elsa Alnderby was telling Nick how much they had enjoyed his solo and how pleased they were that he could spend Christmas with them Corin explained: "I knew the rust bucket was on her last legs—well, wheels—but thought she'd do. When I went to pull her up to the dorm to pack this afternoon, though..." He shook his head. "Lucky the parents could come collect us."

Stanton gave a jerk of a nod. "Best be off now."

"Oh, must you go just yet? There's mince pies and mulled wine in the Common Room." Felicity beamed her best smile at Corin's father.

But her plea found a cold reception. Stanton shook his head. "Hour and a half drive across dark moors." For all the melody of his voice, Alnderby senior was apparently a man of few words. Their departure was delayed only briefly by Antony's arrival which made another round of introductions necessary.

"I'm so pleased to meet you, Mr. And Mrs. Alnderby. Corin is one of my most promising students. You must be very proud of him. I think he'll make a fine priest."

Elsa's warm response covered her husband's silence.

Felicity was still thinking about Corin's parents a few minutes later as she bit into the warm, flaky crust of a mince pie.

"So they call these mince pies?" Cynthia broke in on her

reverie. "Your grandmother always made mince pie, but it was nothing like this. It was a real pie," she indicated the nine-inch diameter with her hands. "And she poured this wonderful rum raisin sauce over it."

Felicity nodded. She could just remember the grandmother who had died when she was a child. Yes, there had always been mince pie at family gatherings at her aunt's home, but she hadn't thought of it for years. "Mince pies are a hallmark English custom, Mother. I think they're delicious. Why don't you get a cup of mulled wine to go with it? I'm sure you'll like that."

Cynthia's place at her side was taken by Antony. "What a surprise to meet Corin's parents." He picked up where Felicity's earlier thoughts had been interrupted.

"I really liked his mother. But I don't think his father was very happy to be here. He seemed to enter into the service, but I had the feeling he would rather be back on his farm."

Antony nodded. "Poor Corin, it must be hard with his father so determined that his son become a sheep farmer." Then he added, "And hard for Stanton, too, I suppose. It seems the land has been in their family for well more than a hundred years."

"That must be a lot of pressure on Corin, especially since he's an only child. It probably explains why he's so moody and rather awkward at times. Too bad he doesn't have an older brother to take the family land and leave him free for the Church in the old tradition."

"You're right, darling. This wine is absolutely lovely!" Cynthia rejoined them. "We must serve it at your reception." She took another sip then rushed on. "And while we're on the subject, I've been thinking about the cake. I know you said you wanted a traditional English wedding cake, but, darling, you can't seriously expect your brothers to travel all this way to be served *fruit cake.* You know Charlie doesn't like anything but chocolate. And what will Judy think? You know how beautifully your sister-in-law's family always entertains."

Felicity was delighted to see Father Anselm approaching. "Ah, Father Antony, how is the television series coming?" he asked.

Antony gave a vague answer, then presented his future mother-in-law to the Superior of the Community. It was hard to tell who was the more charmed by the introduction, Cynthia or the elderly monk, but they were immediately absorbed in one another's company as Cynthia enthused about her rapture of spending Christmas in a monastery and asked about the history of the community, then hung on every word of his reply.

Felicity could only shake her head in amusement as she watched. That was her mother in good hands. Now she was free to steer Antony into the corridor for a good night kiss thorough enough to put irritation with her mother, concerns about Corin's family and worries about the success of the pageant entirely behind her.

And she awoke the next morning still wrapped in the euphoria of that kiss and the thought that soon she would waken wrapped in Antony's arms.

Some time later Felicity picked up her hairbrush, wondering whether or not she should waken her mother for church. She had heard nothing from Cynthia's room and the community bell would be ringing soon.

She jumped when her door flew open and a fully dressed Cynthia strode in. "Oh, good, darling. You are awake. I was thinking you must have overslept." Cynthia took the brush from her daughter's hand and began brushing the long blond tresses with smooth strokes. "You weren't thinking of braiding it this morning, were you? It's so beautiful. Do leave it loose over your shoulders. Like an angel." Cynthia kissed Felicity's cheek, then pulled back and looked at her. "What a beautiful bride you'll make. Just the thought of it takes my breath away. I wonder if Antony has any idea what a lucky man he is?"

"Almost as lucky as I am, Mother."

The bell rang out across the crisp December air as they made their way up the hill. A pallid sun shone bravely turning the drops of moisture clinging to bare branches into chains of diamonds. On a morning like this Felicity could almost forget her exasperation with her mother. In fact, she renewed her determination to do so. This was the last Sunday of Advent. Only two days before Antony would be going to Blackpool to spend Christmas with his family. She couldn't let anything spoil this time.

She took in a deep invigorating breath. Yes, love, joy and peace. That was what the season was all about. And Felicity resolved to exemplify it. She took her mother's arm and they entered the purple-draped, incense-filled church together.

At the end of the service Felicity's warm glow of affability swelled to its fullest as they sang her favorite Advent hymn for the recessional:

Lo! He comes with clouds descending,...
Thousand thousand saints attending,

Swell the triumph of His train:
Hallelujah! Hallelujah!...
God appears on earth to reign.

Felicity didn't think her good will toward her mother could possibly rise any higher but then Cynthia topped it all by preparing a traditional Sunday dinner for the three of them at the Nab Lane cottage. Felicity gazed in wonder at the perfectly browned roast beef surrounded by Yorkshire puddings and a platter of three vegetables. She blinked, trying to remember when she had last eaten such a meal prepared by her mother. Throughout Felicity's growing-up years Cynthia was always entombed in her office, working on her latest legal brief, to be summoned forth at the last minute when Felicity's civil servant father had everything on the table and Felicity and her brothers were already gathered awaiting Cynthia's arrival.

"Mother, where on earth did you learn to cook like that?"

"Well, really, darling. I *can* read. And how hard is it? You put the beef on a pan and stick it in the oven. I did it when I first got up this morning. Can you believe you can just buy the Yorkshire puddings off the shelf here? And the veg come in bags ready to steam."

Felicity was still shaking her head an hour later when Cynthia had sent Felicity and Antony into the front room, insisting, over Antony's objections, that she would do the washing up. "I can't imagine what's come over Mother. But I hope it lasts." Felicity paused, deciding whether to mention the topic preying on her mind. "Dad won't believe it either."

Antony touched her cheek. "You're still hoping your parents will get back together, aren't you?"

Felicity hadn't quite realized how fervently she was hoping just that until Antony put it into words. Yes. She was fully aware of how much she wanted him to be here to perform his Father of the Bride role. But it was so much more than that. Antony's parents were dead. Her parents would be the only grandparents their children could have. Would they have a grandfather in their lives? And the whole family thing —that wonderful, messy, inexplicable conglomeration of people called a family. She didn't want hers to be forever broken. She didn't want to think of her mother growing old alone. She bit her lip, then merely nodded and opened a book.

A few minutes later she turned to Antony who had picked up his notebook and pen, but sat motionless, staring at the blank paper. "Writer's block?" She asked.

He sighed. "Tomorrow is our last day of filming before we break for Christmas. I need to get this right. People aren't going to be amused if I delay their Christmas hols."

"Where are you filming?"

"Rievaulx." It was a statement, yet there was a tone of doubt in his voice.

"Really? Which one of the English Mystics was there?"

"That's the problem. None, really. Aelred was their most famous abbot—the leading religious figure in all of England in the twelfth century. And he wrote profoundly influential books on spirituality at the request of Bernard of Clairvaux.

"But having said that, Aelred was not a mystic. He was an extremely energetic administrator. He constructed many of the buildings we see at Rievaulx today—you see my problem."

"So why are they filming there?"

"I think Harry, or Sylvia—whoever makes those decisions —likes the romantic look of the ruins."

"And it's up to you to make it fit into the story."

"Precisely. That wouldn't be so bad, I could quote from some of Aelred's writings or something like that, but Harry wants me to do an historical perspective piece. 'Make it an allegory of the age,' he said. 'Time of religious upheaval, Cistercian reforms, flowering of the monasteries, while at the same time Lollards planting seeds of the Protestantism that was to bring it all down.'"

Felicity nodded. "I can see that. It sounds like good drama. What's the problem? Can't you tie it in with Richard Rolle?"

"No, that's the easy bit. Ironic, really, because Rolle's reaction against scholasticism and his insistence on an individual relationship with Christ, even his unorthodox actions of robing himself and becoming a hermit without the approval of a bishop, paved the way for the rise of the Lollards half a century later."

Felicity closed her book, leaving her finger between the pages as a bookmark. "Um, Lollards. Remind me." Then she added, "Odd name."

Antony nodded. "Translates 'mumbler' from the Old Dutch. The term had been used on continental groups who combined pious goals with heretical belief."

"Were they heretics?"

"By the standards of their day. Today many consider them pioneers, martyrs, heroes. Like most things—depends on your viewpoint." He paused and grinned. "Would you forgive me if I said they were men of burning faith?"

Felicity groaned appropriately before he continued more seriously, "They believed in a lay priesthood, an individual approach to God and the primacy of the Scripture. They especially promoted making the Bible available in the vernacular. They were followers of Wycliffe who translated much of the scripture into English."

"So, nonconformist, but hardly apostate, then?" Felicity's observation was interrupted by Antony's ringing phone. She returned to her reading, but her attention was soon drawn to Antony's vehement protests.

"What? You can't be serious!... But it's Sunday... Surely an early start in the morning—"

"What is it?" She asked when he rang off.

Instead of answering her, however, Antony went to the kitchen to inform Cynthia. "I'm awfully sorry, but it seems I'll be needing your chauffeur services sooner than we'd realized. Harry says a dazzling sunset is predicted. The cameras roll in two hours. It's the exact image Sylvia wants for this scene and we might not have another for weeks."

Cynthia's response was immediate. "Oh, what fun. I'll get my coat."

Felicity had little choice but to attempt to match her mother's equanimity. "Don't worry, you can work on your script in the car," she reassured Antony who was taking his director's orders with anything but complaisance.

"Ready." Cynthia reappeared in the doorway wearing hat, coat, scarf, gloves and carrying a handbag the size of a small suitcase.

"Mother, we're going to north Yorkshire, not the North Pole."

"Best to be prepared, darling. Didn't your mother teach you anything?" Felicity gave her mother's attempted witticism a stiff smile.

A short time later, though, as the little car sped northward along winding, hilly roads and through little stone-built villages Felicity had to admire Cynthia's competent driving in response to the sat nav's instructions. The sky to their left took on the first tinges of pink and gold and Felicity began to suspect that the resulting footage might well be worth the Herculean effort of calling a film crew out unexpectedly.

They turned off the A road onto a narrow lane sunk deep between the rising field on one side and a stone wall on the other. Around another curve and Cynthia gave what Felicity at first thought was a cry of alarm, but then realized her mother was gazing in rapture at the magnificent ruined structure set against the wooded hillside beyond them.

The deepening colors of the sky were turning the golden stones to flames of crimson, vermilion, amber and topaze. Little wonder Harry Forslund wanted to capture this.

Fred, with Ginger on her dolly, and Lenny, wielding the handheld camera, were already at work catching the play of light on the ancient stones and broken arches as Harry barked orders at them.

Felicity smiled in amusement as the voluptuous Tara, her magenta hair now edged in bright blue, pushed Antony into a chair and began applying make-up with deft touches. Felicity's grin turned to a scowl, however, as the make-up artist's low-necked shirt gaped when she leaned toward Antony. The glare turned to a chuckle, though, when Antony closed his eyes. It took Tara only a few deft strokes of her brushes. "There, you'll do. Harry'll have my guts for garters if I delay you."

And she was none too soon. "Father Antony! Get yer cassock over here!"

Antony strode to the center of the green lawn to take his place before the towering Gothic arch at the west end of the ruined nave, gilded with iridescence. If only he could recall the words he had honed so carefully on the journey over. He took a deep breath and plunged. "This abbey was one of the most powerful centers of monasticism in Britain. At its peak in the mid-twelfth century it was home to 650 men, both monks and lay brothers." He gave a few carefully selected facts about the work of the abbey, wishing he could somehow convey a picture of the hive of activity these now silent chambers and fields would have been as the monks maintained their round of eight services a day and the lay brothers went about the labors that supported the economy of what today would be a major corporation.

"Cut!" Harry broke the flow just as Antony felt he was hitting his stride. "Enough of that. Get on with the drama. Where's the blood and guts? I have a series to sell to the big time. The BBC isn't interested in pabulum. If this doesn't fly I'll be directing kangaroos on the Australian outback.

"Give us more conflict. Gore. Danger. That's what sells." He pointed. "Over there. By Joy."

Antony moved to stand by the presenter whose cap of blond hair had been turned to a halo by the setting sun. "This is such a peaceful scene today, Father, but isn't it true that in the fourteenth century much of England was torn by religious strife that resulted in grisly executions?"

Antony tried to hide his bewilderment. What did this have to do with the English Mystics? Still, all he could do was try to make the best of it. He gave his prepared background about the Lollards then segued to answer her question. "King Henry IV passed the *De heretico comburendo* in 1401, which did not specifically ban the Lollards, but authorized burning heretics at the stake."

"Cut." Harry Forslund stormed forward in his bull-like way. "'Burned at the stake' doesn't do it. We've got a gibbet here, in case you hadn't noticed."

Antony turned to the structure behind him where Ginger's round eye was pointing. He stared, unbelieving, at the sight. A gibbet, indeed.

But why? What on earth was a gibbet doing here? An obviously newly constructed one that had no relevance to the history of the place. It must have been set up on Harry's orders. Antony shuddered to think what English Heritage would have to say about that.

All Antony could think of was to offer a weak protest. "Er—but really, heretics were burned at the stake, not hanged."

"And how effective an image would a pile of kindling wood be, I ask you? Think, man! A gibbet is a much stronger statement. It's all about making pictures in the viewers' minds. Pictures they will carry with them. Television is a visual medium."

Antony gazed at the stark black beams silhouetted against the winter sky, cutting a black gash through the glory of the sunset. The empty loop in the dangling rope swayed in the breeze, giving Antony a momentary feeling that it was swinging out toward him. He shuddered and stepped back. A powerful image, indeed.

# CHAPTER 9

Antony woke completely disoriented the next morning. Rays of the nascent sunrise struck the wall beyond his bed, making him startle. Flames? A heretic being burnt? He threw his covers aside, then realized he had been dreaming about the execution of William Sawtrey, the first Lollard martyr.

He had attempted to tell the story to the cameras as the blaze of sunset sank behind the Hambleton Hills last evening. But Harry insisted on his gibbet image, so Antony had mentally speed-read through his church history notes as if his files were in front of him. "Well, Sir John Oldcastle, a friend of Henry V's and Shakespeare's model for Sir John Falstaff, was a Lollard who led Oldcastle's Revolt—a widespread Lollard conspiracy, which planned to seize the King and establish a commonwealth.

"The plot was discovered. Sir John was condemned, hanged, and burnt—gallows and all."

"Well, there you are, then. Tell the story, man. That's what we're paying you for."

"But the execution was in London," Antony protested. Harry made an impatient gesture and Antony told the story.

And now here he was, without so much as a toothbrush,

in a farmhouse B and B just beyond the abbey. Again, at Harry's insistence. The whole crew was staying there. Well, Harry and Sylvia were in the B and B. Several of the others were staying in the small caravan that accompanied the crew to locations. And Antony suspected some had slept in their cars to save money, for all that Harry was paying them.

It seemed someone had failed to warn Antony that this was to be an overnight stay when the whole venture was set up in haste on Harry's orders that they were to capture the sunset and begin filming at the Terrace the next morning as soon as the sun illuminated it. In spite of the discomfort, though, of being caught out without his kit, Antony was glad they hadn't had to make the drive back through the dark last night and then set out again before sunrise this morning. Fortunately, the B and B had been able to accommodate Felicity and Cynthia with a room just down the hall.

Again, Antony puzzled over the fact that they were to begin filming at the Terrace. What place that scene would play in the story of the mystics he couldn't fathom, but it was Harry and Sylvia's film and as Harry reminded him, they were paying his salary, such as it was. Apparently Sylvia, as producer, had scouted the sites months ago and set the filming agenda. It remained for the rest of them but to obey.

Antony crossed the room to splash his face and swirl water around in his mouth at the sink in the corner. At least he had a comb in his pocket, but that was about the extent of what he could accomplish in the way of morning ablutions.

He clicked on the electric kettle sitting on the wide window sill. It had just boiled when a tap and soft voice at his door told him that Felicity would share his morning tea with him. Acutely aware of the dog-eared mien he presented, he blinked at her glowing appearance. After a good morning kiss he asked, "Goodness, how do you manage to look so fresh?"

She laughed as she added a container of long-life milk to her tea. "I'll have to say my mother is a wonder. She had everything in her bag—including an extra toothbrush they had supplied on the airplane."

"You know, Felicity..." Antony stopped. He wouldn't go there. Felicity would find her own way with her mother.

"Hmm?" She raised an eyebrow at him over her teacup.

"Er—uh, it looks like it's going to be a brilliant day. How about going for a walk? We've got at least an hour before the cameras roll."

"Sure. Do you have your script ready?"

Antony shrugged. "I'm not sure what I'm to do today. Just technical advice, I think. I understand Joy will be interviewing a local expert—descendant of the local great family, I think she said. Whatever that has to do with the Mystics I can't imagine. Seems considerably farther off-topic than the Lollards to me."

They finished their tea quickly and slipped down the stairs before Antony could be waylaid by Harry Forslund. They heard his booming voice and Sylvia's murmured responses as they tiptoed past their door.

"Oh, it's magical!" Felicity held out her arms to the awakening world. Overnight frost had limned every tiniest twig and branch of the vegetation bordering the lane to the abbey and the millions of tiny prisms caught rays of the dawning sun and made rainbows dance like fireflies. Woolly sheep baaed at them from the fields beyond.

"I'd been hoping for snow for our wedding, but maybe frost would be even more romantic." Felicity slipped her gloved hand into his and they walked on in silence as the radiance increased around them.

Although the abbey was closed on Mondays during the winter, Harry had made arrangements for one small gate at the back of the grounds to be left unlocked for the crew. Antony held the gate open for Felicity, then led the way across the frost-brittle grass to the foundation stones of the broken walls of the infirmary. "Let's just go around that way into the infirmary cloister," Antony directed her. "It would have been a marvelous medicinal garden in Anselm—"

His words were lost when Felicity gasped and shoved him to his knees behind a partially standing wall. "He's got a gun!" She hissed.

Antony followed her pointing hand to see a figure in a long black coat and hat standing in the arched alcove high up on the infirmary wall. A shaft of sunlight struck the end of the dark object he held raised to his eye. Antony froze.

Then he relaxed in laughter. "That's not a gun. It's a camera." He pushed himself to his feet and waved at the figure in the oversized niche. "Lenny!" Antony called and strode toward the cameraman. "This is devotion to art. What brings you out so early?"

Lenny held out the Leica with its long telephoto lens. "Well, you can call it art if you want to. I call it following orders. Although I can hope some of those sunrise shots might qualify as artistic."

Before Antony could reply Lenny jumped from the wall in something of a daring feat. "We'd best be heading back if we want breakfast before the action starts. This morning air has me ravenous." He took a few steps toward the exit then turned back. "Coming? Gill in the catering van does a killer bacon butty."

"We'll be along soon." Antony waved him away, then looked at Felicity. "Are you hungry?"

"Not yet. I didn't really get much of a look round last night. This is truly magnificent, isn't it? One forgets." Her head lifted to the soaring Gothic arches of the east end of the nave. As she walked across the frosty grass the morning sun highlighted the intricate molding of the arcade arches high above.

Antony pointed out the paired lancet windows of the clerestory, then suggested they take the path running along on the hillside beside the nave for an overview of the building. As they made their way down the length of the building from the higher elevation of the path Antony started to point out what a celestial effect it created to look through the high-vaulted arches linking the piers of the nave. But before he could give words to his thoughts Felicity grabbed his arm. "Ugh. Why don't they take that thing down?"

Not wanting to tear his gaze from the shafts of morning sun streaming through the open panels of the east window, Antony gave her a rather abstracted answer. "The gibbet? I'm sure Harry'll get rid of it later today. Probably too dark to take it down last night."

"But it's obscene." Antony felt Felicity shiver beside him.

"Shall we go back then?" He started to turn.

But Felicity took a step up the hillside toward the gibbet. "No, look. He's added something else. It looks like—"

Felicity's scream ripped the dewy serenity of the morning.

# CHAPTER 10

A slight breeze twisted the plump, nearly naked body dangling on the end of the rope. The morning sun made the white skin appear even more snowy than the frosty landscape. Wisps of black and lavender lace underwear cut like gashes across the pale form. Spikes of magenta and blue hair pierced the morning sky.

Felicity closed her eyes but the image was burnt into her eyelids. She shivered inside the blanket Sylvia put around her shoulders, her chill more from shock than from the icy air. Now all she wanted was to get back to the warmth and security of the B and B. And to her mother.

But she wasn't leaving without Antony. And he couldn't leave until Police Constable Leonard Craig, Helmsley Beat Manager of the North Yorkshire Police, had finished questioning him. PC Craig had arrived in record time in response to Antony's emergency phone call. Craig took one look at the situation and summoned backup from the Ryedale Station, but at the moment he was soldiering on alone. And doing so admirably against the odds, Felicity thought, since the entire Studio Six crew had arrived on the scene just moments after Craig.

So far the constable, with considerable help from Sylvia, had managed to keep the filmmakers from trampling over the scene in spite of the best boy's hysterical pleas that the body be taken down, Zoe's wild barking at the foot of the gibbet, and Harry's thundering demands to be allowed to carry on with his work. When his dictatorial approach failed, the director tried another tack, offering his crew's assistance. "We have two professional photographers here, Constable. Surely you'd like pictures of the scene of the crime."

"We have a forensic photographer on the way from Rye-dale Station, sir." Craig even managed a "Thank you," that somehow made his refusal sound more final.

"No! You can't just leave her there! It's indecent." Savannah, her red hair flying out like flames, tore from Sylvia's grip and flung herself at the gibbet. "How will I live without her?"

Sylvia summoned Fred to help her restrain their best boy and PC Craig turned back to Antony. "Now let me get this straight, sir. You and this young lady were out for an early morning walk when you spotted the body?"

"Felicity saw it first," Antony replied. "I approached the gibbet to be sure she was dead, but I didn't have to get close." He shook his head as if to clear the image. "The cold would have killed her if the rope hadn't."

"And you recognized her?"

Antony nodded. "Tara. She did the make-up. That's all I know. The others could tell you more."

"Did you observe any special relationships, Father? Did she have a boyfriend, for example? Or girlfriend?" His gaze followed the still-sobbing Savannah being sherphered toward the catering caravan.

"I wouldn't know about anything like that. But I wouldn't

have thought her affections would lie in that direction. Pete, the electrician—python wrangler in their parlance—rumor was he was attracted. But from what I saw it was all on his side."

"And how did she seem yesterday?"

Antony thought. "Very efficient. She was good at her job as far as I could tell. Harry was hurrying us to get the cameras rolling before the sunset faded, so she didn't do much work on me."

"She didn't seem to be upset or depressed?"

"I would have said maybe a bit keyed up. Excited. But I thought that was because Harry was yelling at us all to hurry."

The rest of the morning went in a blur: the arrival of the Scene of Crime officers, another round of questions from Inspector Tracy Birkinshaw, Harry's repeated rage when the officers began wrapping the abbey in what seemed like miles of yellow crime scene tape and moving the Studio Six crew beyond the barrier.

Felicity's last look back was the sight of Tara Gilbert's body being cut from the noose and lowered onto a white plastic sheet. Felicity felt she would never be warm again.

"Come on. A good soak in a hot tub for you, my love." Antony's arm around her had never been more welcome.

And that broke the tight control Felicity had been holding on herself. She turned her face into his shoulder and sobbed. He held her, gently rocking her and making soothing noises as one would comfort a child.

When the storm subsided, arms still around her, Antony directed her feet toward the lane that would take them back to the B and B. They got about six steps when Harry stopped them. "Up here, Father. Nothing like having a priest around when you need him, huh?"

Felicity looked around and saw that Harry had assembled the crew on the hillside, just above where the police were still working over Tara's prone body at the foot of the gibbet. "You'll know what to do." Harry motioned Antony forward.

Felicity was surprised. For all that he was directing a mini-series on a spiritual topic, this was the first Harry had shown of any personal religious feelings. But she was pleased. Of course it was the right thing to do.

Antony took a deep breath and stood facing the little group shocked and shivering on the hillside. A sob broke from Savannah, quickly muffled. Pete stood a little apart, his ashen face a frozen mask. "In the midst of life we are in the midst of death." Antony began. His voice wavered, but it quickly picked up a ring of assurance as he found the rhythm of the psalm, "Though I walk in the shadow of death, I will fear no evil, for you are with me..."

Then he signaled the beginning of the litany: "Lord, be merciful. From all evil," he paused and looked at Felicity.

She caught his eye and led forth with the response, "Lord, save your people." A few voices around her joined in uncertainly.

"From every sin,"

Now more voices joined Felicity's, "Lord, save your people."

"At the moment of death,"

This time the response was heartfelt, "Lord, save your people."

"Lord, look on our sister Tara. May she rest in peace where sorrow and pain are banished and may the everlasting light of your merciful love shine upon her through Jesus Christ our Lord." Antony made the sign of the cross and the meager service was ended.

Brief though it was, Felicity found that the words of comfort and the weak but resolute sun had combined to relieve the chill at her heart if not in her hands and feet. She turned to share that encouraging word with Antony when she saw Lenny approach Harry, carrying his camera. The men exchanged conspiratorial nods.

What? Was it possible Lenny had been filming that at Harry's direction? Could Harry be planning to exploit the grisly death of one of his crew members for his series? Surely she had mistaken the look she thought she saw pass between the men.

And yet... "Antony," she asked when he joined her. "Did Lenny join the prayers?"

Antony looked puzzled.

"Was he standing behind me, maybe?" She prompted. "I didn't really look around."

Antony thought for a moment, then shook his head. "I don't know. I don't recall seeing him. But I expect he was. Harry's orders for the crew to gather were comprehensive."

Felicity nodded, but she still wondered. Had the gaffer-cum-cameraman been standing at the back of the group, or had he been hidden in the clump of trees just up the hill with the telephoto lens of his camera recording every detail of his fellows' shock and grief? At Harry's orders?

At that thought a surge of anger drove the frozen lethargy from her. What was going on here? How *had* Tara come to her fate at the end of that rope? And why was she undressed? Had a lover rejected her so harshly she felt driven to make such a spectacular bid for attention? Or was it all the result of something far darker? Pete—was that the one Antony said was trying to make time with her—had she rebuffed him so harshly he snapped and did this to her? Maybe because she preferred Savannah's attentions?

"Ready for that warm bath?" Antony interrupted her thoughts.

She nodded and they started toward the lane. But again, they had taken barely half a dozen steps when Harry's orders stopped them in their tracks. "All right boys and girls. Twenty minutes. It's a shame about Tara, but the police have everything under control. No more we can do here. We'll finish today's footage from the Terrace."

"What? You can't! It isn't decent!" Savannah ran at him with her fists flailing.

Harry caught her wrists. "Whoa, there. It's what she would want. Tara was a pro. We'll dedicate the series to her memory." He handed the wildly sobbing best boy over to Sylvia who led her away once again with an arm around her.

"Right." Harry turned back to the crew. "Less than a mile walk around that way," he pointed to the curving road. "Or get in one of the vans. Twenty minutes." As an afterthought he added. "Sylvia will do make-up."

Felicity replayed the scene in her mind a short time later as the steam rose from the hot water pouring into the wonderful old-fashioned, claw-footed tub in the B and B's one bathroom. It had taken Felicity months when she first came to England to catch on to the fact that bathroom was a very specific term meaning the room where one took a bath. She had more than once been shown to such a room when what she was asking for was a toilet.

She sank into the blissfully warm water and leaned back, trying to sort out the dynamics of the interpersonal relationships she had witnessed. She wished she knew the crew better so she could have more idea of what was going on. Was Savannah that distraught at the sudden death of a coworker or friend? Or had there been something more to their relationship? How serious had Pete's attraction been? And had Felicity been right in thinking Tara was making advances to the spikey-haired grip—what was his name—muscular, looked like he lifted weights—Mike, maybe? She recalled Tara's unnecessary physical contact with Antony and wondered just who such behavior could have angered—especially if it had gone considerably further with someone else.

Well, all that was conjecture and no doubt the police would go over it all. Felicity pushed the thoughts away and reveled in the warmth penetrating her chilled limbs. She picked up the luxurious oversized bath sponge their hostess had thoughtfully provided and reached for the soap. How odd. There was no soap on the wire utility rack spanning the tub. Nor on the shelf beside the tub. She would just have to make do with rubbing herself vigorously with the sponge.

"Felicity, darling, are you still in there?" Cynthia's voice was accompanied by several sharp raps on the door. "What's taking you so long? Don't you want to watch the filming? I certainly do."

"Mother." Felicity sat up so quickly she splashed water out of the tub. Cynthia had slept in. She didn't know what had happened.

Felicity pulled on layers of her warmest clothes and was soon filling her mother in on the events of the morning as they walked toward the abbey. "Hanged herself? That little fat girl with the tacky hair?"

"Mother!" Felicity looked over her shoulder to see if anyone could have overheard them. In less tragic circumstances her mother's bald-faced observations might be refreshing rather than shocking. "She's dead," Felicity protested.

But Cynthia was unfazed. "That's a shame, of course, but she was up to no good."

"How do you know that, Mother? Just because you didn't like her hairdo?"

"What I didn't like was the way she rubbed her body against your intended. And you shouldn't have liked it either."

"No, I didn't. And nor did Antony, thank goodness. But do you think somebody killed her for that?"

"Rubbing somebody the wrong way, you mean?" Cynthia smiled. "Who knows? You never can tell about what people get up to." They rounded a curve in the lane, bringing the police vehicles and activity surrounding the gibbet on the hillside into view. "Oh, isn't that fascinating!" Cynthia strode ahead.

"Mother, I don't think the police—" It was hopeless. There was no curbing Cynthia when she had the bit between her teeth. And the thing that made it doubly irritating to Felicity was that she knew she was often just the same way herself.

Felicity was thankful that at least Cynthia did have the sense to stay well back behind the police line. Then she reminded herself that after all, her mother was a lawyer. She probably knew far more about protocol in such situations than Felicity did, in spite of her various encounters with danger in recent months.

The two women stood near the trees just beyond the

gibbet observing the white-suited officers going efficiently about their work photographing the scene, scanning the area for evidence and examining the body. At last Felicity heard Inspector Birkinshaw tell her crew they could remove the body. Felicity felt as if she should put her hand over her heart or somehow mark Tara's removal with respect as they zipped what had so recently been a lively young woman into a bag and two policemen carried her to the waiting vehicle on a stretcher.

The others packed up their equipment and departed leaving three uniformed Police Constables to guard the area and continue combing it for clues. Felicity would have been more than happy to turn her steps upward to the Terrace, but Cynthia was already moving toward the scene vacated by the forensics team. They were stopped several yards from the gibbet by the yellow tape barrier. Still, they were too close for comfort in Felicity's opinion.

In spite of her unease, though, she had to admit that there was a macabre fascination. Even as a child Felicity had been revolted by the horror videos her brothers watched, and yet many a Friday night she would creep down from her room and peek at their late night viewing with their friends. She felt the same mesmerized drawing now as she gazed at the tall wooden structure, the discarded rope coiled at its base, the sad hollows Tara's body had made in the long grass.

Then her gaze was drawn back to the rope. At first she thought she was seeing frost on the twined strands of hemp. But surely not. The sun had been up for several hours now. A cold winter sun, yes, but enough to melt the earlier frost from the grass. So what was the white film coating the rope?

Cynthia's attention, however had moved further afield.

She watched the police constables poking in the bushes and examining the nooks and crannies of broken stones around the abbey, then began a search of her own along the path. Felicity was happy enough to be moving toward the Terrace where she would find Antony with the film crew, so she turned away from the gibbet and hurried up the steep hillside to Cynthia. "Mother, what are you doing?"

"Nothing, really, I suppose. I just thought that if I had done something terrible to that girl I don't think I would have gone back through the abbey where those policemen are searching. It's too exposed, even at night. I would have headed for the nearest cover, which is these trees." She poked in the grass under a bush. "So I just thought I'd have a look. I know it's unlikely, but someone could have dropped something."

It made sense to Felicity and she began looking as well, even though all she found was an interesting stone, a gnarled stick and a discarded juice box. She wondered for a moment if the box could be a clue, but it was far too weathered. Probably a remnant of a months-ago summer picnic.

"Well, now, that's interesting."

Felicity looked at the white oval object Cynthia was holding up. "A rock?"

"No." Cynthia sniffed it. "Lemon Verbena. Very nice soap."

The white-coated fibers of the noose sprang to Felicity's mind. She knew what had glazed them. "Mother, don't touch it. I mean, put it back. I'll get the constable."

A hastily summoned PC Craig agreed that it was, indeed interesting. "Very sharp-eyed of you." He nodded at Cynthia as he drew an evidence bag from his pocket.

"I'm afraid I touched it," Cynthia said.

Craig asked her to stop by the mobile unit later and leave them a copy of her fingerprints, "for purposes of elimination," and the women were free to go.

But Felicity couldn't leave it at that. It was their discovery after all. "But, Constable Craig, what does it mean? Why would anyone rub soap on a noose?"

He frowned and raised an eyebrow at her.

"They did," she insisted. "I saw it. At first I thought it was frost on the rope—"

"Thank you, Miss Howard. As I said, you're very sharp-eyed. Don't worry. Our forensic experts will examine it all carefully." He nodded at Cynthia. "Ma'am," and turned back down the hill.

There was nothing for the women to do but move on. But Felicity couldn't let it go. What did it mean? Why would anyone rub soap into a noose? Her mind repeated the question.

And why such a dramatic execution—if that was what it was? Most murderers would want to hide their victims, not go to extreme lengths to publicize their foul deed.

It reminded Felicity of the ghastly medieval custom of putting the heads of executed prisoners on pikes in public places as a warning to future miscreants.

But what message could this hold?

# CHAPTER 11

The hill on up to the Terrace was steep, but they were already almost halfway up, so, walking at an angle, Felicity and Cynthia continued on their way. "Be careful, Mother," Felicity warned. "These leaves are slick underfoot. Best hold on to the tree trunks." Felicity matched her actions to her words as she felt her own feet slip. It occurred to her that if a villain had come this way last night he would likely have left a trail that PC Craig and his men could follow.

She looked around in hopes of spotting something, but the sodden leaves and winter brown weeds all looked the same to her. She was more than happy to leave it to the police.

"Oh, how charming!" Cynthia cried as she crested the hill. She grabbed a low-hanging branch from one of the trees bordering the rim and pulled herself onto the plateau beyond.

"Surprising, isn't it?" Felicity likewise hauled herself over the crest onto the level and stood beside her mother.

Cynthia turned her head one way, then the other, looking at the small neoclassical buildings at each end of the long sweep of leaf-strewn lawn. "But what are they?"

"Follies." Felicity looked at the round, dome-topped structure surrounded by classical columns to their right. "That's the Tuscan Temple." She turned to the far end. "And that's the Ionic Temple." Appropriately named, since a row of Ionic columns supported the classical portico of the rectangular building.

"But what are they for?" Cynthia persisted.

"I've only been here once before. I came with a group of ordinands last spring, but the most I remember is that they were built in the mid-eighteenth century by some great landowner to give his guests a nice day out. They would drive over here in their carriages to view the abbey and he gave them dinner in the Ionic temple. It's basically an elegant dining room. I'm afraid that's about all I remember."

At that moment Fred, pulling Ginger backwards on her dolly, emerged from the side of the temple and Joy Wilkins, her shining blond hair set off with her favorite flame-colored scarf, ushered a tall man in a tweed jacket between two of the Ionic columns and down the steps of the temple. They stopped at the bottom of the steps and Joy continued her interview.

"Let's get closer." Felicity moved forward. "Antony said Joy was going to be interviewing some local expert. I think someone who knew the family who owned this before they gave it to the National Trust. I know Antony was relieved he wouldn't have to be on camera today."

A small group of crew members stood behind Harry and Sylvia to the right of the camera, well out of range of Ginger's bright eye, but where they could hear, if not see, the interview. Felicity crossed the lawn to stand beside Antony. He slipped his arm around her waist and they exchanged smiles before Antony turned back to listen to the interview.

Felicity, however, gave scant attention to the speaker. She couldn't wait to tell Antony about her discovery that the noose had been soaped and to find out what he might make of that fact. But this was neither the time nor the place for that conversation, so Felicity considered the crew members around her. Had one of them stolen soap from the B and B bathroom and rubbed it into the rope hanging from the gibbet? If so, why? Soap was a lubricant. Felicity had used it herself when removing a tight ring from a swollen finger.

As it seemed so many things did lately, the thought triggered a long-buried memory. This one of helping her father with DIY tasks around the house. How often had she seen Andrew pick up a bar of soap and rub it on a sticking pipe to make it turn more easily? He called it his secret weapon.

For an instant she was eleven years old, on her hands and knees, her head under the kitchen sink helping her father. Her heart pinched so hard she gasped for a breath.

She gave herself a small shake and returned to the matter in hand. Would soaping the rope somehow make it easier to commit murder? Or had Tara done it herself, thinking it would make her suicide easier?

Felicity shook her head to clear the troubling thoughts and made a half-hearted attempt to listen to the interview. Even as the camera and its subjects moved away from her.

"Yes, that's right, Sir Charles Duncombe, Lord Mayor of London and the wealthiest commoner in England, bought Helmsley and Rievaulx in the late seventeenth century. His son Thomas built the Terrace half a century later. He lived at Duncombe Park," the speaker, his back to Felicity, gestured across the valley beyond the abbey. "This made the perfect vista for showing off his estates and entertaining his guests."

Joy led her expert to speak about the Picturesque movement in landscape gardening which was popular in the middle of the eighteenth century, as they walked toward the edge of the Terrace, leading camera and crew in procession. "Yes, the Picturesque was all the rage. Many gardens were created on those principles, but Rievaulx's design represents a new idea. Instead of the visitor being led from one garden feature to another, a series of thirteen views or stations were cut through the trees. The idea was to make it all appear the work of nature so one could simply wander the half mile of paths and at each clearing see the abbey from a different angle—rather like a giant piece of sculpture."

The speaker stepped toward one of the cuts in the vegetation rimming the plateau, inviting the camera to take full advantage of the panoramic sight of the abbey. As he did so he came into Felicity's full view for the first time and she gasped. Stanton Alnderby. Why was Joy Wilkins interviewing him about the history of the Terrace? Hadn't Antony said it was to be a descendant of the former owners? She must have misunderstood. Corin had indicated their farm was in this neighborhood. So Stanton must have an enthusiasm for local history. He did seem to know what he was talking about.

Joy's next question was lost on Felicity, though, as her mother's tug on her arm pulled her away from the view of the ruined abbey. "I've seen enough old stones for one day, no matter how picturesquely they're arranged. Let's go into the temple," she whispered.

Harry Forslund swung around with a warning look. Felicity put her finger to her lips and followed her mother more to keep her quiet than from any desire to leave Antony's side and the stunning view.

Once they were out of range of the microphones Felicity thought of arguing with her mother, but it was easier simply to follow up the wide steps and across the portico of the temple. "Ah, now this is lovely!" Cynthia stopped just inside the door, admiring the long banqueting table surrounded with Chippendale-style chairs and set with fine porcelain.

"Dishes are Chamberlain Worcester and the chairs were made to order for the room."

Felicity gave a little squeal of surprise as the speaker stepped from behind her. "Corin. Nick. What are you doing here?" Then she thought. "Oh, of course. You must have come with your father. I was so surprised to see him. He seems to know his stuff. Do you share his passion for local history?"

Corin made a dismissive gesture. "I love the views of the abbey, even if I find all this beyond indulgent," he waved a large hand at the pair of ornate velvet and gilt settees against the wall, "but Nick wanted to see the sights."

"Sure, blame it on me." His dark eyes sparkled behind his glasses. "But I wouldn't mind being served a light meal here."

Corin bowed. "Roast meat with sauces, wine and beer, followed by fruit, tea and coffee. With cream and sugar, of course. I believe that was the standard menu. Thomas Duncombe had a kitchen built below to ensure flawless service for his guests."

For someone who professed little interest in the history, Corin seemed to have the details down, Felicity thought, but Cynthia spoke, her neck craned to look at the ceiling. "It's magnificent. Who are they?"

Corin glanced upward. "Apollo and the Muses in the

middle. I don't remember the others." He stopped and turned suddenly as if he felt he had said too much.

Felicity was confused. Corin professed to dislike the place and yet he knew all the details down to the menus served. Could he be covering something up? A small shiver snaked up her spine. *Don't be silly*, she reprimanded herself. "So you live near here." It was a statement, but an open invitation for him to share more.

He gestured vaguely southward. "Across the valley. Beyond Helmsley."

The snake wiggled again before Felicity could step on it. Near enough to slip out in the middle of the night for an assignation with a nubile young woman who then threatened to tell your bishop or the principal of your theological college? Felicity was so disgusted with herself for even thinking anything so outlandish she would have hit herself up the side of the head if she had been alone. Instead she merely said, "Let's join the others. Surely they'll be taking a break soon."

As she reemerged into the winter afternoon Felicity glanced at the sun already headed toward the western horizon. The day was passing too quickly. Antony would be taking the train to Blackpool this evening and they had had no time alone together since that early walk this morning which ended so disastrously. She almost ran down the path to where Antony stood by the film crew at the final station. Through the bare branches of the trees the abbey glowed golden in the westering sun in the valley below. The arched windows of the upper stories gave the effect of having a light turned on behind them. Joy was wrapping up, "Thank you, Stanton Alnderby, for sharing your family history with us."

Felicity spun back to Corin. "Family history? What does she mean? Wasn't this Duncombe land?"

Corin nodded. "Until they gave it to the National Trust."

"But your name isn't Duncombe..."

"My great grandmother was—Dad's mother's mother. Younger daughter of a younger son, so there's no title." He grinned. "And certainly no money. But lots of tales to tell for those who care about all that."

Now it made sense. No wonder Corin's father's was so set on his son following him onto the land rather than becoming a priest. Heritage was a fine thing, but it could be a burden.

Filming had stopped and Felicity reached Antony's side just as Harry was just dismissing his crew. "Right, that's a wrap. Excellent work, all of you. You get an early start on your Christmas break, so be good boys and girls. Not too much holiday cheer. We'll see you all back bright and shiny after Boxing Day at Ampleforth."

Felicity was surprised, shocked even, by his jocular manner. Only a few hours earlier they had found one of his crew members dead. She pulled Antony apart from the others. "How can Harry be so cheerful? I understand needing to carry on with the filming schedule, but he seemed almost elated."

Antony nodded. "I've been puzzling over that. At first I thought he was just putting a good face on it to keep everyone's minds off the earlier events—help them focus on the job at hand, but I'm not so sure—"

The rest of his thought was cut off by Harry Forslund himself. "Father Antony, you won't be rushing off just yet, will you? Someone here I want you to talk to. Melissa Egbert, meet Father Antony."

Felicity turned and blinked. She felt as if she were looking in a mirror. The woman Harry presented to Antony could easily have been Felicity's sister at least. She even wore her long blond hair in a single plait down her back, just as Felicity had done hers today. The only difference was that Melissa was at least five inches shorter and finer boned. *If I'd been built like her I'd be a ballerina today,* Felicity thought. But she merely acknowledged the introduction with a smile when Harry gave her name.

Felicity's attention sharpened when Harry continued, "Melissa's with *The Sun.* Doing a piece on our little project here. Told her you'd give her all the background, Father. But with recent, Er—events, I know she'll want to hear about your experience this morning."

He turned back to the journalist. "Great tie-in actually. Not that we'd claim any sainthood for our Tara—although she was a lovely girl." He shook his head dramatically. "Tragic, really. Still, it does make one think of the Lollards who died the same way."

The director turned back to Antony. "But don't let me steal your thunder. You're the storyteller, Father." Harry stepped back as if handing the baton to Antony. Felicity thought of the party game where someone started a story, then handed a stick to the person who had to continue the tale.

But Antony looked as uncomfortable as if a cudgel had been dropped in his lap. He cleared his throat. "Er—I believe the concept we're trying to convey here is that peace and holiness never come in this life without struggle. The gibbet could be seen as a symbol of that struggle. Richard Rolle, the first of the English Mystics—who entered the hermetical life just a few miles across the moors here at Pickering—"

Antony warmed to his subject, "came under undeserved suspicion of heresy because of his popularity among the Lollards. They admired and studied his works and interpolated insertions of their own into the text of some of his books. Many Lollards themselves were executed. Some hanged." He added the last sop to Harry's image almost under his breath, then came to an abrupt stop.

"And so what tie-in do you see in the tragic death of one of your crew member this morning, Father?" Melissa's pencil skimmed across her notebook even as she spoke.

Now Antony was free to express his true feelings. "None at all. As you say, it's tragic. Our prayers are with Tara's family, and also the police as they work to find answers."

"But this isn't the first attack on this project, is it, Father? Do you suspect demonic forces at work opposing you?"

Felicity caught her breath. She remembered all too vividly just a few months back when what should have been an idyllic walk through Wales turned into a life and death struggle against the forces of evil. She had learned the hard way that powers beyond the visible did exist in this universe.

But Antony regarded Melissa levelly. "What are you talking about?"

"I understand one of your cameramen had a serious accident last week. One that could have resulted in his death, even?"

"Well, thankfully it didn't," Antony snapped. "Besides, that was an accident. Pure and simple."

"Are you certain of that?" Melissa probed.

"I am certain there is no demonism at work here."

"And what about your own 'accident' a few days ago, Father?"

Now Antony gaped. "What! How did you hear about that?"

Melissa looked smug. "I have my sources." Her glance at Cynthia made Felicity groan inwardly. When could the reporter have talked to her mother?

Melissa forged ahead. "But really, now, it isn't so outlandish to think that the forces of darkness would be displeased with a documentary about the mystics' fiery passion for God, is it?"

Antony stared at her wordlessly.

Melissa's next attempt seemed even further afield. "The Duncombe family—still great landowners around here. Have you had any contact with them?"

Antony shook his head.

"But this is their land—historically, at least. It happened on their land. Is there any indication they are displeased with your project? Might any of them be involved in any way?"

Antony's face clearly said he had no idea what she was getting at. "The Terrace is National Trust property; the abbey is English Heritage." And that was an end to it.

Melissa attempted a couple of different approaches, trying to get Antony to speculate on Tara's death, but when it became clear Antony could be pushed no further she thanked him and walked off, her long braid swinging between her shoulders.

Felicity frowned. "Harry made that sound like the interview had been scheduled by the reporter, but do you think he called the press to capitalize on Tara's death?"

"I wouldn't put it past him. But then, the press was sure to get wind of it all anyway. I'm much more concerned about her questions about demons. 'The forces of darkness—' It makes it sound like Harry is trying to turn this into a zombie movie."

Felicity considered. "I suppose Harry could be playing up the sensational because he's afraid a straight series on the mystics won't draw the viewing audience they need."

Antony nodded. "Or not be attractive to a major network. He wants to sell this to the Beeb, after all. The other day he said something about having to take up an offer from Australia if this doesn't sell. I don't think he relished the idea."

But Felicity had a much darker idea. "Or he could be sabotaging his own film for the publicity." No, she argued with her own words, not even someone as headstrong as Harry Forslund would commit murder for a publicity stunt. Would he?

And even if he would, Sylvia would stop him. Wouldn't she?

No, in spite of all the unanswered questions Tara's death had to be suicide. That was the only rational answer.

# CHAPTER 12

## *Christmas Eve*

December mist obscured the green hillside beyond the window, the electric fire glowed on the hearth and Gregorian chant issued from the radio tuned to Classic FM. Tonight would be Christmas Eve. Felicity snuggled into a corner of the sofa with her long-abandoned volume of Richard Methley. It was hard to realize that by the time her essay on this fifteenth century Carthusian monk from Mount Grace Priory was due her life would have changed forever. She put a bookmark in the chapter on Methley's translations and took a sip of tea, smiling softly. Yes, just twelve more days and she would be Mrs. Antony Sherwood.

Her contented sigh ended with a frown. There was so much to be got through before that glorious day. And reading for an essay was the least of them. Christmas—alone here with her mother. Felicity was determined it would be good. She was honest enough to admit to herself that outcome would be mostly up to her. Cynthia brimmed with good cheer. That was the problem.

Then Boxing Day with a pageant rehearsal and two more after that—if all went well, more if not; and Antony would return for three more days of filming—Please, *Lord, let that get done without any more mishaps;* then family would begin arriving on New Year's Eve and there would be the wedding rehearsal and then the pageant and then... Delicious shivers of excitement overcame her worries as she gave in to imagining their wedding. *Let it be perfect,* she breathed.

Cynthia came in trailing ice pink ribbons. "Darling, I would have these poseys finished, but I ran out of ribbon. Do you think that quaint little shop up the street would have another spool?"

Felicity sat up with a jerk, her daydreams scattered. "Mother, what are you doing?"

Cynthia held out a ribbon-bedecked lace cone. "Making the base for the bridesmaids' nosegays. Then all I'll have to do is pop the fresh flowers in when they arrive from the florist on the morning of the wedding. Isn't that clever? I found the pattern in one of those bridal magazines under your bed."

When Felicity didn't respond Cynthia continued. "Don't look at me like that. I'm sure it's all right. It was an English magazine. I know you want everything to be proper."

Felicity remembered her earlier resolve to keep the peace and forced a smile. "No, it's fine. Very clever." She set her tea-cup aside. "I'm sure the yarn shop at the top of the road will have ribbon. I'll just pop out and get some. I was wanting some fresh air anyway." She hadn't been, but now she was.

She bundled into coat, scarf and her red bobble hat from the Dewsbury market and set out at her long-legged pace. Even so well swaddled she shivered as a blast of wind hit her. At least the snow had held off. She would normally hope for a white Christmas, but with all there was to do for the pageant things would go more smoothly without the complications of snow underfoot. At home her father would say it was too cold to snow, but she wasn't sure it worked the same way in England. Actually, accustomed as she was to judging temperatures in Fahrenheit and with Celsius being a foreign language, she never really knew what the temperature was.

In spite of the cold, though, the wet fields across the valley glowed emerald beyond the crooked, ancient stone houses running higgledy-piggledy up a meandering street with misty moors beyond. Two little old ladies walking their dogs went by, carrying shopping bags. Felicity slowed her step, filled her lungs with the invigorating moist air and looked around with that disoriented-yet-familiar feeling she often had. It was as if she'd been living in England all her life and as if she'd been dropped on another planet all at the same time. Then she had it—it was like living in a storybook. Certainly, if she were ever to write a children's book this is what she would want the illustrations to look like.

She was headed back to the cottage, her parcel of pink ribbon tucked under her arm, when she encountered a clutch of teenagers and recognized some who had helped with clearing out the quarry a few days ago. What a disaster that had been. She wondered if they had made any more progress on getting the theatre useable. She did hope the project wouldn't have to be canceled. "Hi. It's Tanya, isn't it?" She greeted the small, hollow-eyed girl, then looked around the circle. "Have you been at the centre?"

Tanya more ducked her head than nodded. "Yeah. Practice, like."

Syd, his hoodie pulled well forward over his face, broke out with a ragged, "Glo-o-o-o-o-o-o-ria, glo-o-o-o-o-o-o-ria," that seemed to shock his mates as much as it did Felicity. She was delighted with the idea that the sullen, self-appointed leader of the miscreants could have been won over by the Christmas spirit. Then she saw the glitter in the eyes behind the hood and was afraid it was more likely another kind of spirit. Or something worse?

One of the boys elbowed him sharply. "Get 'im. Thinks 'e's an angel."

Felicity tried not to show her dismay. "Great. I'm so glad Kendra has you working on the carols. How's it going?"

"Tanya's going to be narrator." The announcement of a smiling Afro-Caribbean boy behind Tanya made the girl's head droop even lower and her shoulders hunch forward.

Felicity's heart sank. Could she possibly coach this shrinking violet to project?

"And Balram," her informant added.

Felicity scanned the group. When her eyes met those of a good-looking Indian youth he all but bowed. Her heart rose. Ah, there was hope. "Wonderful! Are you busy now? Would you all like to go up to the theatre and give it a bit of a run-through?" She made the suggestion with considerable trepidation, wondering in what condition she would find the theatre.

Syd and a couple of the other boys slid away from the group but the others followed her along willingly enough. At the cottage she told them to go on to the theatre as she ducked in to give her mother the ribbon and pick up her script. She caught up with them just in time to open the gate to the community. On the way around to the back she fell into step beside the informative Joaquin from Jamaica who told her with considerable pride that he was to be Joseph and Flora to be Mary. Felicity looked at the bouncing brown curls of the chubby girl he indicated and nodded with approval.

They had just passed the Calvary beyond the monks' cemetery and picked up the path to the quarry when there was a rustling in the bushes ahead of them and the assistant groundsman emerged to block their way. "Oh, Alfred, you startled us," Felicity said. "We're on our way to the theatre for a bit of practice. There's no problem with that, is there?"

He looked over the group, then shook his head. "None at all, as long as you're with them. But see they don't leave any litter. Just been cleaning up again." He indicated the trash bag beside him on the ground.

More rubbish since the clean-out? Felicity was dismayed. How could it be worse than before? The grounds were locked to the public after dark. And the monks certainly wouldn't litter. "Don't worry, we'll be careful," she assured him.

Once into the theatre, though, she stopped and stared. She had left before the work finished Thursday, but she never imagined they had accomplished so much. "This is amazing! I had no idea it would look so great."

Habib and Aisha beamed. Habib said, "Our father brought men from the mosque. The Imam said it was community service. It would show good will for your winter festival."

"It is good to work together," his sister added.

"Absolutely!" Felicity couldn't wait to tell Antony. This went beyond the scope of even his ecumenical council. One tiny advance for good will. Perhaps there was hope after all. "Right. On the stage, all of you. I want you to get the feel of being up there."

They scampered across the newly scythed floor of the quarry and up the steps at the side of the structure dominating the far end of the arena. Two or three of the livelier ones began a cavorting dance while others, restrained by shyness or manners stood in a small huddle to the side. Felicity approached the quiet ones. "That's great, Tanya and Balram, just move downstage a little bit. That should be a perfect spot for the narrators. Joaquin, let's put Joseph and Mary here for the moment, of course, you'll enter from the back of the quarry." In her mind's eye she pictured them coming down the stone steps and making their way through the audience. She wondered if Nick and Corin had managed to procure a donkey.

It all began to take shape in her mind. She could see the torches flaring around the rim, hear the murmur of the audience, feel the excitement of the performers. She could even smell the smoke from one of the warming braziers. Then she realized what was wrong. She smelled actual smoke.

But none of the youth on stage had lit cigarettes. She spun toward the stairs and was down and behind the structure in moments. "All right, you lot. Come on out," she called into the stygian understage. She spotted a couple of pinpoint glows. If only she had a torch she would go in after them, but she realized her disadvantage. Their eyes would be accustomed to the dark.

She held her breath. What should she do? Send someone to fetch Alfred? She couldn't leave the youth here alone. To her relief the red dots disappeared and a scrabbling sound told her they were emerging. She held her breath, praying they wouldn't be hulks set on making trouble. What had she led her teens into?

"Sorry, Miss. It were just a bit o' fun." The first figure took shape in the light.

"Drue?" What was Flora's little brother doing here? Surely he wasn't old enough to be out alone.

Two more figures followed. They appeared to be only slightly older. "What is the meaning of this?"

Felicity summoned her most authoritative manner from her short-lived career as a school teacher. Drue hung his head. "We didn't mean no harm. I was just showin' me mates this place. It's wicked."

"And the cigarettes?" She hoped they hadn't been smoking anything worse.

Drue shrugged. "Found them there."

"But how did you get in?"

"Lock's rusted." He pointed in the direction of the bottom of the community grounds.

A memory flashed across Felicity's mind—A wet February day, running with Antony through the back of the monastery, uncertain whether they were fleeing the police or a murderer —or even whether or not Antony was the murderer. They had left by way of the same dilapidated gate on that fateful day.

She nodded. "I'll tell Alfred. He should have fixed that long ago." She turned to the two boys still standing just inside the doorway of the structure. "And you are—"

"Ralph 'n Eddy," Drue offered.

"Right. Ralph, Eddy, Drue—as long as you're here you might as well join us. On the stage with you." At least she could keep them in sight that way. But she would definitely be reporting this incident to the groundsman. Something was going on here that shouldn't be.

"Okay, let's just sing the first verse of 'O Come, All Ye Faithful' then, Balram, you begin the narration with 'and there went out a decree...' Remember, nice loud voice. You're speaking to the back wall of the quarry."

The rehearsal proceeded, in spite of the fact that the

singing was beyond ragged and the narrators inaudible. She tried to hide her consternation from the youth, most of them were overwhelmed enough at the idea of performing in public. And she suspected that those who were the most boisterous were the most intimidated.

"Tanya, 'when the days were accomplished that she should be delivered...' is your line. Joaquin, that's your cue. When she says it you pick up the doll that will be in the manger and hold it up."

They followed instructions—more or less. How could she possibly convey to them that they were portraying the greatest miracle in the history of the world? The birth of God incarnate. "That's right, Joseph, hold him out like you're so proud you could burst. Mary, smile. You're incredibly happy." She addressed Joaquin and Flora by their stage names.

She turned to the discordant chorus. "Fine. That's a good start. Just one verse of 'Silent Night' now, then I'll let you go."

At least some of them made enough of an effort that she could be reasonably sure they knew the words. Surely Kendra was planning to let them use songbooks. Assuming they could read.

"Great, great." She tried to sound enthusiastic. "This was just an impromptu, get-your-feet-wet thing. We'll have the angels next, then shepherds. The Wise Men will be the big finale because that's what Epiphany is all about.

"You can all go now, after all, it's Christmas Eve. Narrators, Mary and Joseph, try to read through the script a few times over the holiday to get familiar with it. We'll rehearse it all on Boxing Day. Thanks for your good work, everybody. Happy Christmas!"

A chorus of "Happy Christmas!" echoed around the quarry

as her charges raced across the floor and up the steps. Felicity followed more slowly. What had she taken on? Thank goodness Kendra had promised a sound system. And the singers weren't Felicity's problem. But she could only imagine the chaos when two dozen unruly youth took to the stage along with sheep, llamas and a camel, for goodness sake.

Camel. Who had Kendra cast as the wise men? What else should she be worrying about, Felicity wondered. For the moment her priority was to find Alfred and alert him to the faulty security. At least that explained the reappearance of trash in the newly-cleaned quarry.

Alfred, however, was no longer working in the area of the monks' cemetery, nor was he in the garden behind the monastery. He was sure to be at the service this evening, though. She could manage a quick word then. At one of the services at least. Felicity counted on her fingers—was it seven services they had ahead of them? Last year she had scampered back to London and spent the holiday going to shows and parties with friends from university and from her brief time living in London and teaching Latin in a C of E school. This year she was determined to soak in the complete 'Christmas in a Monastery' experience. She hadn't broken it to Cynthia yet. She wondered what her mother would say.

It wasn't long before she found out.

"*First* Evensong of Christmas? How many are there?"

"Two. One to start the festivities off and one to conclude them. Like bookends. That is, it will conclude the day—not the season, you understand. We still observe the twelve days of Christmas."

"Just like the song. How quaint." Cynthia continued with a

decided note of irony, "Festivities, you say. As in Gala, feast-ing, merrymaking?"

Felicity knew her mother would be skeptical. A year ago Felicity would have felt the same herself.

"Festivities as in one of the great Feast Days of the Church."

"Somehow I was afraid of that. Going to church, you mean."

Felicity admitted that was what she meant and made no attempt to explain that she was looking forward to it. She could never explain, even to herself, how the change had come about. The monks called it formation. And that seemed to be what had happened. A year and a half of just living the cycle of seasons by the Church calendar and now she couldn't imagine doing anything else.

Miraculously, Cynthia simply said, "I'll get my coat, then."

The community grounds were dark and deserted, but when they entered the church the light shone in the darkness. A bank of candles glowed in the austerity of the monastic church, reflecting on the pillars and marble altar against the backdrop of darkened apse beyond. Felicity had become accustomed to Solemn Evensong as celebrated in the commu-nity on all feast days so now she held her breath, waiting for the chink of the thurible before the procession began, the gleam of candlelight on gold vestments, the echo of the stately chant. And she was not disappointed. Father George, as presiding priest, wore a splendid white and gold cope and the monk serving as thurifer swung the thurible with vigor, sending clouds of incense heavenward during the Magnificat. The Gregorian Chant was hauntingly lovely as it reverberated among the Romanesque stone arches. Yet, for all the solemn splendor, the service followed its normal rhythm of psalms and canticles chanted antiphonally, a scripture lesson followed by silence and concluding with prayers and a hymn. It was soon over.

Too short, Felicity thought. The preceding week had been filled with alarms and fears. Sudden death, even. But here all was beauty and peace. She was safe. She got reluctantly to her feet and looked around for Alfred. Even here the unpleasant encroached. She needed to warn him about the intruders before they caused more trouble.

But Alfred didn't seem to be there. As soon as the monks filed from the choir she looked around. Most of the ordinands had gone home, but a few married students, for whom this was home, as well as some of the workers who supported the community in the office, kitchen, or gardens had filled the seats behind her. But not the under groundsman. Tony, the senior groundsman, had small children and would be at home with them. Oh, well, it could wait.

Felicity and Cynthia walked back, arm in arm, across the monastery grounds, the clouds bright with ambient light against the dark sky. Felicity wondered what her mother thought of the service, but she didn't want to break the companionable mood by asking.

It was Cynthia who spoke. "Do you have any idea how amazing that was?"

Felicity's mouth fell open, but she didn't say anything.

"Don't take all this for granted. Don't ever take it for granted."

"Um, what do you mean?"

"It's so civilized. So set apart. Such a unique experience. Do you realize what a minute fraction of the population get to experience such a life? Don't take it for granted for one minute."

"Yes, Mother." Felicity frequently had similar thoughts, but she had no idea her mother might feel that way, too. Did that mean her mother actually approved of her choice? She gave Cynthia's arm a squeeze in reply.

Felicity pressed the button to open the massive wrought iron gates in the stone wall surrounding the monastery and they crossed the road and slipped around the corner to the cottage. They shared a big bowl of pesto pasta, eating it in front of the Christmas tree with carols on the radio. It was as perfect as it could be without Antony there. She smiled. Next year would be their first Christmas together. The first of a whole lifetime.

The sound of Felicity's alarm clock broke through her reverie. She had set it so she wouldn't forget. "Antony and I agreed we'd pray Compline together at the same time every night we're apart. We, or I, can just do it here rather than going back up to the community." Felicity said it as a question. She didn't know how Cynthia would feel about that. And she was wondering what kind of reaction Antony would get on his end from his sometimes prickly sister Gwendolyn.

But Cynthia wasn't the least equivocal. "Of course. Tell me what to do."

"Would you like to light the candles in the Advent wreath?" Felicity held out the book of matches to her mother. This was the night when they could finally light the tall white Christ candle in the middle.

"'He comes in splendor, the King who is our peace; the whole world longs to see him.'" Felicity read the opening line, then passed the book to her mother for the response.

"'The eternal Word, born of the Father before time began, today emptied himself for our sake and became man...'"

"'Guide us waking, O Lord, and guard us sleeping; that awake we may watch with Christ, and asleep we may rest in peace.'" The service concluded.

They sat in the light of the advent wreath, listening to the music, "Silent Night, Holy Night." Peaceful, warm, companionable.

Why couldn't life always be like this? In this moment Felicity could easily believe the alarms and worries of the past days had all been phantoms.

# CHAPTER 13

## Christmas

The ringing phone broke the spell. Momentary apprehension seized Felicity. What had happened now? But when she heard Antony's voice at the other end of the line her contentment returned. Doubled even.

They exchanged news. Yes, of course they had both prayed Compline at 9:15 as agreed. Antony's surprise at his sister Gwena's consenting to join him and Aunt Beryl had been as great as Felicity's surprise at Cynthia's acquiescence. It was hard to beat the Christmas spirit.

"Have you seen anything of Derrick?" Felicity enquired after Gwendolyn's boyfriend that Antony and Felicity had both found less than satisfactory.

"No, thankfully. He no longer seems to be in the picture."

Felicity made a satisfied sound, then began telling Antony about the impromptu rehearsal earlier that day. Even after mentioning the smokers under the stage, the chaos of the acting, and the broken lock she was surprised at the change of tone from his end of the line. "Felicity, don't! Er—that is, be careful."

"What are you talking about?" He didn't reply. "Antony—

what is it? What's the matter?" She could tell he didn't want to say more. "Tell me," she insisted.

"Maybe it's nothing. I don't know what it means. It could be anything."

"Antony—" She sounded threatening.

"I found a note. In my coat pocket. It fell out when I pulled out my gloves. A warning."

Felicity frowned. "What? What did it say?"

"It just said 'This must stop. Or you'll be sorry.'"

"That's all? What did it mean?"

"That's the problem. I don't know. What do they want to stop—the film, the pageant, our questions about Tara's death..."

Felicity drew in a breath. "...our wedding?" Her voice was barely above a whisper.

"Surely not. Why would anyone want to stop that? You don't have a jealous old flame in the closet, do you?" His attempt at jocularity sounded strained.

"You know I don't." She thought for a minute. "When could it have been put in your pocket?"

"Just about any time in the last couple of days. I don't remember when I last wore those gloves. It could have been at the college or sometime while we were filming; at the B and B or even after I got here, I suppose."

"Could it be a joke? Surely if anyone meant real harm they would be more specific. One of your students, perhaps? Have you given any particularly onerous assignments they would want stopped?"

They were both heartened by the idea that it could be something as innocuous as an overburdened ordinand not wanting another reading assignment. Still, when they rang off a few minutes later Antony's last words to Felicity weren't "I love you," but rather a reiterated, "Be careful."

As a consequence, a short time later when she and her mother were once again walking up the hill to Midnight Mass Felicity couldn't help looking over her shoulder repeatedly. They were almost to the church when a crunching footstep on the gravel made her spin around. She gave a nervous laugh. "Oh, Alfred. I hoped I'd see you." She told him quickly about the broken gate.

He frowned, undoubtedly over more work to do at what should be vacation time, but merely said, "Aye."

Instead of following her on into the church Alfred started down the path to the back of the grounds. "Alfred, I didn't mean..." She began, but he didn't hear. She hadn't meant to keep him away from the Christmas Eve service. She took a step in his direction, then a rumble from the organ drew her to the lights and warmth of the church.

"Holy, Holy, Holy. This night the Word of God was made flesh and dwelt among us." The monks in their black cassocks and grey scapulars filled the choir. Cynthia leaned over and whispered in Felicity's ear, "I can't believe this is real, that I'm really spending Christmas Eve in a monastery."

Felicity smiled at her mother. Then the sound of an explosion and a blast of light beyond the rose window made her jump. What was that? Antony's warning rang in her ears louder than the distant boom. Were they under attack?

A second flash of light tore through the sky, followed by another. And another. The monks seemed unperturbed. Didn't they hear it? Then she smiled. Silly. This was England. Fireworks on Christmas Eve seemed to be a traditional part of the celebration.

She turned to survey the seats behind her. A good congregation filled the nave, people from the wider town, people who worked alongside the monks, several ordinands and their families. Felicity smiled at the wife of one of her fellow students, Kate, delicate and blond, beautiful with her baby asleep in her arms. A perfect picture for Christmas Eve. A picture of safety.

The choir sang the introit in Latin. The echoes ascended to the vaulted ceiling, accompanied by clouds of incense. Bells chimed high up in the tower; the high altar glowed. And beyond the rose window flashes of light continued to fill the sky like an intermittent Christmas star. One glorious bouquet of white flowers adorned the chancel, making Felicity think of her wedding flowers which would stand in the same place so soon.

After communion they sat in silence. And yet not silent. Clouds of witnesses surrounded them. The air was alive with angel wings. Holy, Holy, Holy.

Then, singing "O Come, All Ye Faithful," they processed to the Holy Family Chapel for the blessing of the Christmas crib, which Felicity still thought of as a crèche. And this a most unusual crib: Three banners proclaiming: Word, Word, Word, Word, Word and stacks of books surrounded the holy infant. The chapel altar frontal read, "And the Word was Made Flesh." All so appropriate for a community renown for their scholarship.

The crib was blessed with prayers, holy water and incense. Then everyone shook hands and exchanged "Happy Christmas" in hushed voices.

"I love being kissed by monks." Cynthia almost giggled as they left the church. Walking back home was like wandering into Alice's Wonderland garden as giant fireworks flowers suddenly burst into bloom over their heads. The glittering, erupting blossoms lighted their way home.

Felicity looked at the clock when they were back in the cottage. "Dawn mass is at 6:45, Mother. That's just over five hours from now. Shall I let you sleep?"

Cynthia paused in the act of kicking off her shoes, sensible, low-heeled shoes, Felicity noted with satisfaction. "Certainly not. What kind of a piker do you think I am?"

"Right." Felicity kissed her mother on the cheek. "Good night, then. And Happy Christmas."

Felicity went to bed, but not to sleep. Not yet. Just as they had arranged Antony rang at One-thirty. He reported that they had gone into Liverpool Cathedral for a Christmas Eve Mass glorious enough to impress even Gwena with two thousand worshippers, a full orchestra and chorus and lavish decor. Felicity wanted to hear all the details, but she could feel herself fading. Her final "Happy Christmas" was a mere mumble.

It seemed like minutes later when her alarm rang. She pulled on the warm clothes she had left on the chair next to her bed and went to Cynthia's room. Before she could knock on the door, though, Cynthia appeared, ready to go. Outside the cottage her first lungful of biting cold air brought Felicity fully awake.

"Dawn Mass, you said. So where's the dawn?" Cynthia asked.

Felicity started to answer, then stumbled on the uneven path. She held Cynthia's arm on the stone steps ascending the hill to the church.

The interior of the dimly lit church seemed cavernous.

Only two other ordinands joined the brethren at the side altar for a brief, silent meditation before the crib. Felicity hadn't realized this was to be a standing mass. As all masses had been in medieval times, Felicity reminded herself. She quickly found it concentrated the mind. There was no danger of a sleepy communicant dozing off.

And apparently Cynthia was concentrating, too, even if not on the spiritual. "What a gorgeous robe thingy," she whispered in Felicity's ear and pointed to the celebrant whose back was to them.

"Chasuble." Felicity supplied the word. And, indeed, it was beautiful—cloth of gold with rose embroidery like a French tapestry. Very old. Quite valuable, she guessed.

For just the briefest of moments Felicity wondered if there could be any way the misfortunes of the film company could be linked to the monastery and its treasures? It was only last Easter that the theft of their priceless icon had led to murder and mayhem. And Antony did provide a link between the two. The fireworks outside his study—could they be connected to the fire at Ampleforth?

She chided herself for fantasizing. Father Paulinus and Tara's deaths had nothing to do with the community. They were miles away and miles apart from each other..

Cynthia nudged her and they moved forward together to receive the Gift from the One whose birthday they celebrated.

They were back outdoors when the community bell rang the Angelus—three rings for each of three Ave Marias. And then the birds began. A glorious dawn chorus to welcome Christmas morning. Cynthia pointed eastward. "Ah, here's the dawn!" Red ribbons garlanded the sky.

Returning to the warmth of the cottage Felicity tumbled

back into bed, pulled the duvet up to her chin and was instantly asleep. She was in a large echoing hall—whether a church or a castle she was unsure. Tapestries adorned the walls. She reached out to touch the golden embroidery, but pulled back when she realized the figure was not a winter tree filled with birds, but a gibbet complete with a staring body. Felicity tried to run, but tripped over into a stack of books adorning an altar. The chasuble-clad priest frowned at her as the books crashed against the altar.

Finally the blows penetrated her consciousness and Felicity realized the knocks were on her door. "Yes?" Cynthia entered carrying a stocking Felicity had put in the laundry two days earlier. "What?" Felicity sat up.

"I read a blog about English Christmas customs." Cynthia sounded inordinately proud of herself. "Apparently tradition demands opening your stockings in bed." She placed the lumpy sock in Felicity's lap.

Felicity felt the thrill of being ten years old again, standing in front of the fireplace with her brothers, longing to grab her stocking, yet not wanting to spoil the delicious suspense. "Mother, you really are amazing." Slowly she drew out each object and placed it beside her on the bed as a beaming Cynthia looked on: a velvet ribbon bookmark, a pen, a small bag of licorice all-sorts... Felicity reached deeper into the foot.

"Oh, a snow globe." She turned the little glass ball upside down and watched it snow on the snowman standing in the woods. "I loved these as a child."

"I remember. I was so pleased when I found that in the market."

Felicity tried to reply, but her throat closed.

"Put your robe on, Darling. I have breakfast ready." Cynthia led the way to the little kitchen where bowls of porridge brightened with Christmas fruit mix, a platter of bacon on toast and a pot of tea awaited.

"This is delicious, Mother." Felicity was too amazed even to question the new Cynthia she was encountering. Had this person been there all along and Felicity not seen her? Or had this time the two of them were spending together brought out a completely new woman in her mother?

"Mmm, I'd love another cup of tea, but we can't dawdle." Felicity pushed her cup away.

"Don't tell me. Another service? Those monks do have stamina don't they?"

"Yes, they do, but this one isn't at the community, it's on up the road—parish mass at Saint Saviour's."

A brisk walk up the road past the community grounds took them to a grey stone Victorian church with bells chiming merrily from the tower under its spire. Inside, the sanctuary was heaving with children. Felicity looked around and was pleased to spot Drue and Flora with two women who were apparently their mother and grandmother. The warm, family communion service with lots of carols was much more like the ones Felicity remembered from her own childhood. She could still feel the flush of pleasure she had experienced on those rare occasions when her whole family attended church together.

After the service Father Douglas invited everyone to step next door for tea and sherry at the vicarage. While Cynthia sipped her sweet sherry and talked to the vicar—Felicity hoped she wasn't flirting—Felicity sought out Flora and her brother. "How nice to see you here this morning. Is this your mum?"

"And my gran," Flora introduced them.

Felicity told the women how pleased she was to have Flora and Drue in the pageant. They agreed it was a fine thing for the young people and assured Felicity they were looking forward to the event. Felicity commented that she had been pleased with the excellent job Father Douglas had done encouraging his congregation to attend the Epiphany pageant. She had good hopes that Saint Saviour's would be well represented.

As the women chatted, though, Felicity could feel Drue's growing anxiety. Under the excuse of getting a glass of sherry, Felicity took the boy aside. "What is it, Drue?"

"You ain't gonna snitch, are ya?"

"You mean tell your mother what you were doing under the stage yesterday? No, I hadn't intended to. Not as long as it doesn't happen again."

Drue seemed to relax a little, but his forehead still creased with anxiety. "I don't want Syd to think..." He bit his lip. "He said he'd do for us if we told."

"You didn't tell. I caught you. But what does Syd have to do with this?"

"Nothin'." Drue spoke too fast and darted away.

Felicity considered. Was Syd running some sort of gang? It was obvious he liked throwing his weight around, but was it something more sinister than that? Was Syd leading the younger boys at the centre astray? She would have a chat with Corin and Nick when they got back tomorrow.

In the meantime, she and Cynthia had the rest of Christmas Day. Back at the cottage they opened their gifts in front of the fireplace—only two parcels under the tree, since Felicity and Antony had agreed to exchange their gifts when they would be together again—that a gift in itself—and any other gifts from family and friends would show up in the form of wedding presents this year.

Felicity took a red and white candy-striped package from under the tree and handed it to her mother. Cynthia tore off the paper and exclaimed over the bright sapphire pashmina stole nestled in the tissue paper. She pulled it out and wound it around her neck before handing Felicity a shiny red package containing a soft, supple pair of fur-lined leather gloves. Felicity hugged Cynthia and kissed her. "Thank you, they're lovely." Then she laughed. "It seems we had similar ideas—to keep each other warm."

Cynthia shook her head. "I don't know how you put up with it—this climate. But since you seem determined to stay here you might as well be equipped."

Then they turned to preparing their Christmas Feast: Roast chicken with wine gravy, broiled, herbed tomatoes, grilled onions, Brussels sprouts, parsnips... Felicity set a folding table in the living room then ran outside to gather berry-laden branches from bushes along the path. By the time Cynthia had added the final touches to their dinner Felicity had the room decked and the candles lit.

When they were seated Felicity said, "We have to pull our crackers first."

"Oh, do we need crackers? There's some in the cupboard." Cynthia started to rise.

"No, Mother. Here." Felicity picked up one end of a gaily-wrapped tube she had placed on her plate.

"Oh, yes. That blog mentioned it." Cynthia grasped the other end. On the count of "three" they gave a sharp tug. The popper snapped, the ends came off and the contents flew out.

The ritual continued with the women pulling Cynthia's cracker, unfolding and donning the red and yellow paper crowns and playing with the miniature toys. "Okay, now the best part," Felicity said, unfolding a slip of paper from her cracker. "The jokes. What does Santa suffer from if he gets stuck in a chimney?"

Cynthia looked blank.

"Claustrophobia!" Cynthia's groan was louder than Felicity's crow of delight. "Your turn now."

Cynthia located the small piece of paper that had fallen on the floor. "Why does Santa have three gardens?"

Felicity shook her head. "No idea."

"So he can 'ho ho ho'!"

The meal continued in a similar jolly mood, timed just right to end with watching the Queen's speech on the television while they ate thick slabs of Christmas cake washed down with cups of steaming tea. After the brief, encouraging message they raised their teacups in salute while "God Save the Queen" played.

"Oh, that was lovely, but I can't believe I'm so full," Cynthia groaned. "I'll have to admit that cake wrapped in marzipan and fondant icing is nothing like the fruitcake I know."

Felicity smiled and refrained from saying *I told you so.* "There's about an hour of daylight left. Let's go for a walk."

Cynthia was on her feet. "Oh, yes. A nice country ramble in the fresh air is exactly what I need."

They bundled up, Cynthia wearing her new pashmina and Felicity her new gloves and set out walking down the hill away from the monastery, toward the Dewsbury Canal. The moist, cool air was almost like walking in a thin cloud and the moisture gave a dewy freshness to the green fields and bushes.

"So lovely to be only five minutes from open countryside." Cynthia drew in a deep breath.

They came to the old towpath, Felicity's feet picking up the firm footing of the way trodden by men and horses perhaps for centuries. Once the canal had been a major route for transportation of goods; now it was a useful recreation area. Her mind had just wandered to Mr. Toad's time on a barge, disguised as a washerwoman, when her mother's voice cut in on her reverie. "I know you hate my interfering, but, really, darling. Think how cold it is."

"Hmm?" Felicity's soft reply covered her apprehension. It had been days since her mother had meddled in her wedding plans. What would it be now?

"I know your bridesmaids' dresses are velvet with long sleeves but wouldn't you let me buy faux fur stoles to go with them? I saw them online yesterday and they were really lovely." Her voice was almost pleading.

Felicity gasped—more at the tone of Cynthia's voice than at the suggestion. Did it really mean that much to her mother?

"I do so want to help. And I haven't been able to do anything but tie a few bows."

Felicity still didn't answer.

Cynthia ducked her head "Sorry. Silly idea, I suppose. I just thought—"

"No, no, Mother. Actually you're quite right. They sound lovely. I'm sure Judy and Gwena will appreciate the warmth. And your thoughtfulness."

Felicity turned and hugged her mother. Now it was Cynthia's turn to be speechless. Especially when Felicity took her hand and they walked on side-by-side, Felicity thinking about the hidden depths she had seen in her mother lately. "Mother, have you ever considered becoming a Friend of the Community?"

Cynthia looked as stunned as Felicity felt at her own suggestion. Where had that thought come from? "Me? Become a nun?" Cynthia blinked.

"No, Mother, of course not. Friends aren't nuns, just people with strong ties to the Community." She wondered briefly if she should just let it pass, then continued, "Actually, I meant it. I know it sounds silly, but you seem strangely in tune to things here—in a different sort of way. I mean you'd get regular updates on events here and all that. It's just that... Never mind, daft, I know." She didn't want to say that if Andrew never came back her mother might need something new in her life.

Cynthia didn't reply, but she looked thoughtful.

The canal turned to the west, curving around the hill the monastery sat on, taking them beyond the back of the property. "Look." Cynthia pointed up the hill. "Isn't that where your quarry is?"

Felicity looked up the hill, across the road, beyond the stone wall bordering the property. Yes, indeed, halfway up the hill one could just make out the lip of the quarry. It seemed so secluded from the monastery side, she hadn't realize it was visible from the open countryside. And there, in the stone wall, almost hidden by bordering bushes, was the rusted metal gate. "Let's go up here, Mother. I want to see if Alfred got that gate fixed yet."

A few minutes climb up the hill told her that he hadn't. The lock looked solid enough, but with one twist it was in her hand and the gate creaked open. "We might as well go up this way. I hope there hasn't been more partying in the theatre."

Approaching from this side brought them to the lower edge of the quarry wall with the gently sloping path Felicity had suggested they might use to bring the animals in. Now she saw, though, that the way was not as disused as she had thought. Broken grass and a few footprints in the mud showed recent traffic.

And the floor of the quarry confirmed her worst fears. Spent skyrocket tubes, firework cones and Roman candles littered the stage. She had to admit it would have made an effective base for lighting fireworks and thought briefly of the slab of plywood her father had kept in the garage to bring out every Fourth of July as a launch pad for their backyard fireworks display with Jeff and Charlie squabbling over whose turn it was to light the next rocket.

Felicity bit her lip. Her brothers would be here for her wedding. But what of her father? Would he be here to walk her down the aisle as she had always dreamed of?

Felicity gave herself a little shake and returned to the business at hand. "Looks like it must have been a good show." She held up an empty packet that had contained sparklers— always her favorite as a girl. Again she was in her own backyard, a fizzing sparkler in each hand, demonstrating her latest ballet routine.

"More than a good show it looks like." Cynthia, on the quarry floor beyond the stage pointed to a pile of rubbish.

With a groan of frustration Felicity hurried to her side. Cynthia bent to pick up one of the discarded syringes. "Don't touch it!" Felicity stopped her. "That does it. Why hasn't Alfred done something about this?" Maybe she should call the police. But what would the brethren think of that? "I've got to find Father Anselm." She started up the hill.

Even with returning to the community at her best speed, however, by the time they arrived the Prior was already in the church preparing for the culmination of the celebrations in the Second Evensong of Christmas. There didn't seem anything to do but take their place in the nave.

Tonight Felicity found her concentration broken by more than the pops and bangs of fireworks beyond the monastery walls. Although, the skyrockets lighting the windows did seem oddly appropriate for the collect, "O God, who hast caused this holy night to shine with the illumination of the true Light: Grant... that as we have known the mystery of that Light upon earth..."

But what would the Superior say? Would Father Anselm withdraw his permission for use of the quarry for the pageant? What if the police closed it off? Would it be all her fault for blowing the whistle? Would Alfred lose his job? Perhaps she should give him one more chance.

She looked around, but he wasn't in the sparse congregation scattered behind her.

She could think of only one answer. She needed to talk to Antony. Even before the echoes of the organ voluntary faded she was on her feet, heading for the cottage.

When Antony answered her ring, the comfort of talking to him was vitiated by the concern in his voice. "Wait. Felicity, don't do anything. Whatever's going on, I don't want you involved."

She knew the very hint of trouble brought back to him the anxiety of dangers they had encountered in the past months —as it did for her. "Don't go near the quarry. Don't leave the cottage. Is the door locked?"

"Yes, silly. Of course it is." She frowned. It was, wasn't it?

Antony knew her habit of leaving the door on the latch to avoid having to carry a key.

"It's almost time for Compline. Then the community will be in the Greater Silence, so you can't bother Father Anselm tonight anyway. I'll catch the earliest train I can in the morning." Then he groaned. "No, wait. No trains on Boxing Day."

"Are you serious?"

"It's true. Let me think. Maybe I can talk Gwena into bringing me. Or I'll rent a car. Felicity, whatever it takes, I'll be there. You stay safe!"

# CHAPTER 14

## *Boxing Day*

Felicity was just combing her hair, still wet from the shower, when she heard the key in the latch. She flew to the hall, her arms already open to welcome Antony, when she stopped at the sight of the petite blond woman in a red coat. "Gwena! How lovely to see you." She proceeded to embrace her soon-to-be sister-in-law.

Gwen returned the hug then pulled back to regard her. "Good to see you, too. Even if Squib here did rout me out of bed before dawn. Not that I minded that so much, it was having to reassure him every mile of the way. He was expecting to be confronted with your bloody corpse."

"Gwen, don't!" Antony pushed past his sister and took Felicity in his arms. After a thoroughly heartfelt greeting for his betrothed he turned back. "It isn't a joking matter."

Before Gwen could answer Cynthia came out of the kitchen and ushered them all in for a cup of tea. "Gwendolyn Sherwood. How exciting to meet an actress. I Googled you. What fun roles you've played. I want to hear all about it."

Felicity was happy enough to let her mother and Gwen occupy the conversation as she feasted on looking at Antony and sipped her tea, holding her cup in her left hand as he hadn't let go of her right hand. Tightly as he was holding it, she wasn't sure he ever would. Not that she wanted him to.

"I did farce for years: 'Box and Cox,' 'Charley's Aunt,' 'No Sex Please, We're British'. I love the improbable plots and physical humor, but I've been trying to break into something a bit more serious. My agent wants me to audition for 'Comedy of Errors' next month. But then, of course, that's farce, too, so maybe I'm stuck."

Under cover of the conversation on the other side of the table Antony said quietly, "All right now, tell me."

Felicity poured it all out in something of a jumble: the illicit use of the quarry theatre, the broken lock, Alfred's unresponsiveness, the boys smoking, the needles, the chaotic rehearsal, her fears of spoiling everything by calling the police. Or spoiling everything by not calling the police. Or—her agitation rose with each enumeration.

As Antony had learned to do long ago, he cut off the flood with a kiss. "There now," he said, pulling back. "I think I've got the picture. It sounds like a good dose of youthful folly, but probably nothing worse."

"But you said—"

"I know. I'm afraid I spooked you with my own over-concern." He picked up a piece of toast from the plate Cynthia had put on the table. "Tell you what, let's have a bit more to eat, then we'll go take a look at it together. I know Gwena is bursting to see our stage."

"Oh," Felicity turned to their guest. "I hadn't thought. We've got a professional! There's a rehearsal this afternoon. Would you possibly be willing to help us? The youth would be so chuffed to have a real actress directing them. I'm sure you'll be able to get their attention better than I was. Half are too lively and half are too stiff. And I don't know which is worse."

As they walked down to the quarry, Antony was more than happy to have Felicity focus on the pageant as she began explaining the project to Gwena and telling her of the difficulty of getting the unruly cast to follow directions. He needed to decide how to proceed. Had he overreacted to Felicity's worries? Or had he under-reacted? Was this simply a spot of antisocial behavior or an indication of something far darker?

He didn't think there was any way these disturbances could be connected to Tara's death, but what if they led to a similar tragedy? No, surely not. He was exaggerating worse than he usually accused Felicity of doing.

Still, he was no clearer in his mind as to what should be done a short time later when the four of them descended the path to the theatre.

"What a fabulous space!" Gwena threw out her arms as if she would embrace the whole area. "Oh, I can definitely see it all. Torches you said?"

"Yes, all around the rim. And I thought the camel could enter from the side—" Felicity indicated the path over the far wall.

"Camel, yes! And llamas, you said? That's absolutely fabulous. Bells. We must have bells on all the llamas."

Antony hated to put a damper on Felicity's newly restored elation, but he wasn't here to put bells on llamas. He turned to Cynthia as the other women surged toward the stage talking and pointing. "So you were the one who found the needles?"

Cynthia turned to him with a quizzical look on her face. "Yes, I was. Right over here." She pointed.

"I don't see anything."

"It's so strange. I'm sure it was right here." She looked around. "Of course it was getting dark, so things looked a little different. Still, I'm quite sure..."

"And used fireworks, Felicity said?"

Cynthia shook her head. "I don't understand. It's all been cleared up."

Antony gave a sigh of relief. "Well, that's good, then." The responsibility of reporting to the Superior or calling the police was out of his hands. "Alfred probably got back to work this morning. I wouldn't be surprised if he has the gate repaired, too."

"So nothing to worry about?"

"Nothing to worry about." He smiled at his future mother-in-law, hoping he was right. A shout from the path behind him announced the arrival of Nick and Corin carrying several large boxes and accompanied by a short woman with dark, curly hair wearing jeans and an Aran sweater. "This is Kendra from the centre."

She extended her hand which Cynthia and Antony shook. "I direct the music. If I can get anything out of this lot, that is."

"My sister has offered to help." Antony led the way to the stage where he introduced the women then turned to help unpack the sound equipment from the boxes.

They were no sooner set up than the young people began

arriving. Antony, who had not been involved in the work with the St. James Centre and only met a few of the youth on the initial cleanup day, was amazed at the number and the diversity of their charges. And he could quickly see the challenges Felicity had mentioned to him. He smiled to himself. He had thought undertaking a television series was a venture, but this looked much more arduous.

He was impressed, though, at how quickly what seemed like an unruly mob settled down when Kendra introduced Gwendolyn Sherwood, "who has performed in the West End and agreed to help us, so listen up, all of you."

Gwen agreed with Felicity's earlier suggestion for the placement of the narrators, but this time sent Mary and Joseph to the back of the theatre so they could make their entrance from there once Corin assured her that, yes, a donkey could descend those steps. Ralph, Eddy and two other shepherds were sent outside the quarry stage left from where they would enter with the Alnderby sheep. And after a brief discussion about bells for the llamas, which Nick promised to see to, Gwen called for the Wise Men to take positions stage right.

Antony frowned when a tall youth with an unmistakably fractious attitude responded to the direction. Wasn't that Syd, the one Felicity had pointed out as a potential troublemaker? But surely Kendra knew what she was doing—co-opting the opposition, no doubt.

"Dylan, Shaun, You two with Syd also," Kendra directed and Antony's concern returned when Syd's companions in grey hoodies turned out to be the other two wise men.

That still left a goodly number on the stage. "Miss, where

do you want the angels?" A thin girl with straggly brown hair asked.

"Right where you are, Babs. All of you are angels."

That brought a chorus of giggles and snide remarks, including Syd's, "Yah, fallen angels, more like."

But Kendra was unfazed. She handed Cynthia a clipboard and asked her to write down names and estimated height so Nick and Corin could line up surplices or albs—anything white—needed for the angel choir, then handed the mic to Gwendolyn who explained about what they were to accomplish today with the first read-through and blocking.

To Antony, unaccustomed to youth work, it seemed like one long confusion of missed cues, garbled narration, and horseplay. Still, when Kendra put on the instrumental music CD and the ragtag angel choir began belting out, "Hark, the herald angels sing..." a tingle at the back of his neck gave him the feeling that it all could work. With lots of prayer and luck.

A little more than an hour later the wise men made their exit, 'returning home another way' and the angel chorus concluded the Epiphany story with a rocking version of "Joy to the World." Kendra turned to Antony. "I would have preferred something that tells the story better like 'As with Gladness Men of Old' or 'Brightest and Best of the Sons of the Morning,' but I thought it safest to stick with something familiar."

Antony smiled. "Yes, 'Why Impious Herod, Should'st Thou Fear' would only tell the story if your angel choir actually got the words out."

"Some hope of that. We'll stick to things the audience can sing along on, too."

Antony was about to congratulate her on her wisdom

when Nick approached carrying a sack of nails. "Borrowed these from maintenance. Now we can build the manger and get to work on all those pens we'll need for the beasts."

"What about lumber?" Antony asked.

"Corin brought a stack from the farm yesterday. And a set of great woodworking tools."

Antony forbore asking whether Stanton Alnderby had made his donation to the project knowingly. "Maybe we can get Alfred to help with the construction. He's pretty handy with a hammer."

Nick started for the stairs when a sheaf of papers slipped from under his arm. "Here, let me give you a hand with that." Antony picked them up and smiled at the detailed printout of instructions for building a manger.

"Thanks, and could you bring that bag of straw, too?" Antony complied and followed Nick around to the back of the understage.

Nick dropped his tools beside the pile of boards just inside the open doorway, but Antony suggested they move the lumber a little further in, away from the open windows in case it rained. Antony picked up a plank and stepped around Nick leading the way into the dimmer depths.

He had taken only two steps when his foot caught something on the ground, almost sending him sprawling.

"What—" He blinked, peering at what had nearly tripped him up.

Then he dropped his load. Alfred would not be helping to build any stage sets.

# CHAPTER 15

Detective Inspector Nosterfield glared at Antony. "You again. I should have known." He turned to Felicity, still scowling. "So you say this gardener fellow had been helping clear out the quarry for your pageant?" Antony and Felicity both nodded.

"And when did you last see him?"

Felicity thought for a moment. "Christmas Eve. Outside the church. We were going in to Evensong. He'd been complaining about the trash that kept appearing in the quarry. I'd just learned about the broken gate, so I told him."

"And it was his responsibility to keep things like that fixed?"

Antony answered. "Alfred was under groundsman. Tony is the head, but he was on Christmas leave."

Nosterfield scribbled in his notebook. "Right. And when were you last in the quarry? Before this?"

"Christmas afternoon. My mother and I were—"

A sharp gasp from behind Antony made them turn to Cynthia who had joined their group. "Oh, my goodness! You mean that poor man was lying there dead when we were here yesterday?" She shivered. "How gruesome."

"We haven't established a time of death yet. I'll send men to interview the monks, find out who saw him last. If we can get them away from their prayers long enough. The monks, that is, not my men."

Antony thought about the dark stain he had seen on the back of Alfred's head. What had happened here? Had he surprised an intruder using drugs and they lashed out at him? He couldn't have been meeting someone could he? Alfred, doing a drug deal that went wrong? Antony shook his head.

Or was it entirely more innocent? Alfred energetically, even impatiently picking up litter, maybe more joints and syringes, and straightening up too fast, hitting his head on the low, rough underside of the stage? Was it possible this was a ghastly accident?

Nosterfield had moved on, but Mark Silsden was nearby. "Sergeant, can you tell what's happened here? Could this have been an accident?"

"Anything's possible, Father. Early days yet." But he shook his head doubtfully.

Antony put his arm around Felicity as her face paled. He knew that she was thinking that she might have been the last person to see Alfred alive.

She trembled under his grip. "I just realized—I might have sent him to his death. If he went to the quarry to repair the gate when I told him—instead of coming in to church." She caught her breath on a sob. "If I hadn't bothered him he might still be alive..." She turned her face into Antony's shoulder and he led her to the back of the theatre where they could sit on a stone step.

Felicity didn't cry, but she clung to him as if to life. He held her firmly but his mind was in turmoil. There was so much at stake: The pageant, the film series, their wedding... He caught his breath and tightened his hold on Felicity. Their lives.

Everything seemed threatened. Could they go on in the midst of such turmoil? Could they succeed when they had no idea what was going on—or why? It all seemed so random, starting with that first explosion of fireworks under his window. Yet there had to be a pattern. If only he could see it.

Felicity gave a sniff and raised her head. "What will happen now? Do you think we'll be able to go ahead with the pageant?"

"I'll ask Nosterfield, but I expect we can use the quarry again when his men have finished searching for clues. You didn't have another rehearsal scheduled in here until Saturday, did you?"

She nodded. "Yeah, day after tomorrow. Will you be free to go ahead with your filming tomorrow?"

"I don't see why not."

Nosterfield's men finished getting statements from the teens and he dismissed them all with a wave of his hand and a barked order to be sure everyone gave their contact information to the sergeant. And let me now if you're planning to leave town." Antony wasn't sure a drive to Ampleforth constituted 'leaving town' but he gave the inspector his filming agenda for the following week. He didn't mention their honeymoon, though. Surely everything would be cleared up by then. Please, God. They couldn't have all this hanging over their wedding.

They walked back to his college rooms in silence, then he stopped. "Felicity, will you be all right to go on with your mother and Gwena? I need to go through my notes before I face those cameras again tomorrow. I'm afraid I rather put it all out of my mind over Christmas."

She smiled. "Don't sound so apologetic. Of course I'll be fine. And I'm sure a break was good for you. Come down for supper?"

He assured her he would and they kissed. He couldn't believe how hard parting was—even for such a short distance for a couple of hours. Ten days until their wedding... He took a deep breath and swiped his card to unlock the door on the deserted dormitory.

Inside his room he turned on the lights and shivered. He turned up the knob on the radiator and switched on his tiny electric heater. Still the space felt cold as a—he rejected the word that sprang to mind and substituted 'monk's cell'. That should help him get in the mood for swotting up a work written by a medieval Carthusian monk who lived as a hermit.

Without taking his coat off Antony settled at his desk and opened a drawer. He pulled out his file on *The Cloud of Unknowing* and flipped it open. Then stared. The file was empty. What could he have done with his notes? Surely he hadn't taken them out to study and forgotten? Oh, maybe he had misfiled them with one of the monasteries associated with the author. But they were in neither his Ampleforth nor Mount Grace files.

Nothing for it but to look in every file to see what he could have done. He found them at last in his Rievaulx file. But that made no sense. And he was certain they weren't there when he prepared his notes for filming that segment of the series.

He leaned back in his chair and took a closer look at his desk. The lid was secure on his carved wooden pencil box, his anglepoise lamp was exactly in the position he always liked it. His computer mouse just at the angle to fit his hand. Or was it? The question flitted through his mind to wonder if he should ring Inspector Nosterfield and ask him to dust it for fingerprints.

Surely that was the height of paranoia. After all, nothing was missing. And why would anything be? He kept nothing of value in his room. *Concentrate*, he told himself and turned to his notes. Still, he didn't touch his mouse. He preferred to work on paper anyway.

But his notes seemed such a jumble. Or was it his mind that was a jumble? He put his notes aside and took from his shelf a well-worn paperback edition of *The Cloud of Unknowing*. He let the volume fall open as it would and he began reading near the front where the author advises his reader on how to approach a God who is hidden under a cloud of darkness.

Antony gave a little half-smile. Darkness, indeed, he thought. Little surprise God seemed veiled from sight when human behavior was so shrouded. Antony began reading where the author sought first to define this cloud. "When I speak of darkness, I mean the absence of knowledge. It is a darkness of unknowing that lies between you and your God."

Antony closed the book with a sigh. Internal blindness. That was exactly what he was dealing with. Groping forward as one would grope one's way across a dark room. And stumbling over dead bodies in the process. He pushed the thought away. The police were handling that. The cloud he needed to find his way through at this moment was: how could he best introduce such an obscure work to a twenty-first century television audience in a way that would keep his viewers from switching over to the football?

How ironic, that this book which deals with the difficulty of knowing God was by a completely unknown author. Scholars were ninety-five percent certain the author was male; ninety-five percent agreed he was a Carthusian monk. From internal evidence in the manuscript, primarily the east Midlands dialect in which he wrote, it was often assumed he was from Nottinghamshire and very likely that he knew Walter Hilton.

Antony drew a line through that last phrase. They wouldn't be talking about Hilton for a week yet. Mentioning him now would just confuse his viewers. Yet, for all the difficulty Antony was having getting hold of his subject, the Cloud author was a practical mystic. He had produced a straightforward handbook of how to do what Americans called centering prayer, but was more widely known as contemplative prayer. In Carthusian monasteries across Europe the monks had practiced this wordless prayer for half an hour following their corporate worship every day, so this practical hands-on book became extremely popular in the fourteenth century.

And with that thought, Antony knew how to approach his audience. Not with a handbook on mystical prayer, but with today's newspaper. He would show current headlines to parallel the turmoil which had served as background for the writing of this ancient book: The Hundred Years War, schism in the church, the Black Death... Did times never change?

And yet the cloud writings show it is possible to possess peace in one's soul. Through it all it was possible to live above the turmoil.

# CHAPTER 16

## *Feast of St. John the Evangelist*

"Oh, how good to get away from that place. A change of scenery is exactly what we needed." Antony murmured agreement with Cynthia's words, but didn't release his grip on the arm rest as Cynthia swung the car around yet another curve in the narrow road bordered by hedgerows and tall grasses and swept on across the moor past Thirsk.

"I can't imagine why Felicity would prefer to go to that youth centre with your sister than come with us."

"I don't think she felt she had much choice. Sending Gwena off to deal with that lot on her own would be rather throwing Gwen to the wolves." He had been disappointed at Felicity's choice, too, but he understood her sense of responsibility. He wasn't sure, though, whether her protective instincts were for Gwena or for the teens. Felicity had said a few things that made him think she was developing quite a fondness for some of her young charges.

"So what's the topic today?" Cynthia asked.

"*The Cloud of Unknowing*, one of the masterpieces of English mysticism. Today we look at the book; Monday we do the man. Well, not the specific man because we don't know

170

who he was, but we'll go to a monastery very much like the one we believe he lived in."

"I thought we were going to a monastery today."

"We certainly are. Ampleforth is one of the largest, best-known monasteries in England. The community have been here since the early eighteen hundreds, but they claim descent from the pre-reformation community at Westminster. They are widely known for their scholarship and they run one of the top colleges in England."

"But you're just going there to look at books?"

"Yes, Ampleforth has the earliest manuscripts of *The Cloud*. I think Harry is hoping to attract scholars to his viewing audience and to make it all seem a little more concrete and—um, maybe even relevant by showing the books." Wondering what Harry's chances of success were, Antony sank into silence as Cynthia sped on across the north Yorkshire moors.

A few minutes later, though, she jerked him out of his reverie with a cry. "Duncombe Park. That sign said Duncombe Park. We must be going in circles. That's right by Rievaulx, isn't it?"

Antony agreed it was. He was rather surprised himself. He hadn't realized they were this close. But he returned to his earlier worry as his statement about making the mini-series concrete and relevant spun in his mind. He was all-too aware that much of the burden was on him. If his narrative was boring even stellar camera work and cutting wouldn't carry the day.

When they turned off High Bank Road to Ampleforth Abbey and the impressive breadth of the golden stone buildings set on the edge of sweeping green fields spread out

before him he at least had no worries about picturesque subject matter. Nor did he when Sylvia lead them from the
reception area to the church. "Midday prayers first," she said.
"I got permission to film—as long as we're unobtrusive.
Should provide great atmosphere."

And a few minutes later Antony mentally applauded the
visual wisdom of the producer's choice. Two long rows of
black-robed monks processed in before them, the lines
curving around each side of the gray stone altar, chanting the
introit for the day, the feast of St. John, apostle and evangelist.
*"In medio ecclesiae aperuit os eius."* *In the midst of the Church
he opened his mouth.* The Gregorian chant rose to the tall,
gothic vaulting overhead and swirled around the nearly
empty sanctuary which would have been full to bursting with
students during term time.

Antony joined in the antiphonally chanted psalms, but it
was the midday prayer that most spoke to his own concerns:
"All-powerful and ever-living God, with you there is no
darkness, from you nothing is hid. Fill us with the radiance of
your light: may we understand the law you have given us and
live it with generosity and faith..."

Back out in the narthex Harry approached with a gaunt,
bespeckled monk in tow. "All right now Father Antony,
Father Theobald here will take you on down to the archives so
you can get organized for explaining the manuscripts to our
viewers. We'll be outside, getting some footage of the
grounds. Great place you've got here, Father."

Theobald ducked his head in assent, but Antony caught a
gleam of amusement behind the spectacles. The monk led the
way through a long corridor of the monastery, then around
back to the monastery library which he unlocked with a key

from a large ring he pulled from his cassock pocket. "I hope you will be comfortable here, Father Antony. This is the room we make available to what we call externs—people who come from outside to read our holdings."

He ushered Antony into a white-walled room filled with a long table scattered with a variety of periodicals and artifacts. Antony thanked him, then asked, somewhat diffidently, "So then, this isn't the room where... Er—I'm so sorry about Father Paulinus."

Theobald removed his wire-rimmed spectacles and pinched the bridge of his thin nose. "Mmm, yes. Thank you. Terrible shock, it was. The fire inspectors still haven't figured out how it happened. Terrible." He shook his head. "But, yes, you're quite right. Paulinus had a study retreat at the back of the community grounds. Rather in emulation of the hermits he admired. The accident occurred there."

"So he didn't have the manuscripts with him?" Antony was afraid it would sound callous to say that, at least, was a blessing when a life had been lost.

"No, we must be thankful for small mercies. Although I'm afraid his notes are irreplaceable. He was a fine scholar and had covered some quite new territory for his book. Still, we must be thankful for what is spared to us." He indicated a chair for Antony to take at the end of the table.

"We actually have two early manuscripts." He pointed to the volumes in sturdy white archival boxes on the table. "I imagine you'll be most interested in this one, as it's the oldest. And I've also pulled some other things you might like to take a look at. I know Father Paulinus spent some time with them." He opened a box containing four slim volumes. Antony reached for the top one labeled: *"SECRETUM SIVE MYSTI-*

*CUM,* containing an Exposition of the Book called the Cloud:"
It was dated 1678.

Expositions. Not the manuscripts themselves, Antony
noted. If only Father Paulinus had left a sheet of his notes
tucked neatly inside. Antony opened the book hopefully, but
no revelatory sheet fell out. Apparently he would have to do
his own spadework.

"I'll leave you to get on with it then." Father Theobald
moved toward the door. "Toilets just there." He indicated a
door at the back of the room. "If the place catches fire leave
by that door." He pointed in the opposite direction.

Antony winced. He supposed that was the standard health
and safety notice, but in the light of what had happened to his
predecessor he didn't find it comforting. The fire that destroyed Paulinus and his papers, though, had taken place in a
remote part of the monastery, not in this secure inner
sanctum to which one must have a pass and a guiding monk
with a sturdy ring of keys for access. If the conflagration had
been anything other than the accident it was assumed to be,
however, its isolated location would have certainly made it
more accessible to intruders.

If that were the case the fire inspectors would find the
answer. Or would they only find more questions?

He turned to the boxes in front of him and opened the
first volume. It was approximately nine inches by seven
inches and an inch thick, bound in a rich, golden calfskin.
Seventeenth century. One of the earliest—perhaps the earliest
extant copy. Antony felt a small tingle of excitement to be
holding such a treasure. It was inscribed "Be ye humbled
under ye mighty hand of God. 1 Pet.15 A Brief Treatife called

The Cloud in which are contained many high points of Divine Contemplation, gathered by the Author thereof..."

Ampleforth's ornate library stamp of a medieval monk bearing an oversize quill pen filled the rest of the page. Antony turned a few of the carefully preserved parchment pages. A note in the front had told him that the scribe of this manuscript was Dom Wilfrid Reeve who made the copy in 1677 and died in 1693. Dom Wilfrid had written in a tidy flowing hand that was still easily read today. But time was getting on.

Antony took the other volume from the box, this a dark brown calfskin stamped with a gold chrysanthemum design. Inside, the cover revealed colorful end papers swirled in red, gold, white and blue and a bookplate stating the name of the donor of the volume to Ampleforth Abbey. But the thing Antony found far more interesting, were the copious doodles that filled every corner of the pages. Random letters and figures danced across formerly blank pages at the beginning and the end of the volume, as well as several copies of the alphabet. Here, A to p, leaving out the letter j and on another page A to q, omitting I. And yet another page of alphabet practices, this with many A's and then the letters A to r, again, omitting the j.

Antony briefly pondered whether or not this could be some kind of a code. He knew, however, that the letter j was one of the last to be added to the English alphabet. So the only clue this held was to when the owner of the book lived.

Only one scrawl seemed to give any indication that the owner understood anything of the contents of the volume he apparently found most valuable for its blank pages. "If you expect to conquer this vaine airs your working mind must largely surrender" he had written.

Although shocked by such treatment of a priceless treasure, Antony couldn't help but be drawn to the exuberance of the scrawls. And then he discovered the perpetrator of the graffiti. "John Ward Book" it said, and on the next page John Ward had written his name three times as if practicing his penmanship. But most of John Ward's energies had gone into creating animal figures. On one page a rambunctious fire-breathing dragon stood on his hind legs and clawed the air.

But by far John Ward's favorite subject was peacocks. One fine male cock seemed in danger of having his speckled tail feathers set alight by the fire-breather while five peacocks looked on from across the page.

Antony considered. Had Master Ward simply been taken with the beauty of these strange birds? Or perhaps been attempting sketches of pets on his family property? Or was there a larger meaning here? In heraldry the peacock was a symbol of resurrection and immortality and was also used to represent beauty, power and knowledge. An association with John Ward's own family crest?

But that was idle speculation and the film crew would be upon him soon. Antony started to close the book, then a scramble of letters caught his attention He turned the tome around in an attempt to decipher it and the book slipped form his grip. Horrified that he might have damaged the ancient volume, Antony picked it up and turned it over carefully. Then breathed a sigh of relief. No damage done. He put it back in the box.

That was when he noticed the sheet of paper that had fallen from between the pages. It was on modern paper and in a much more modern handwriting than the pages it had dropped from. Several columns, each one a list of names. And, interestingly a small doodle that looked like one of John Ward's peacocks by the last and shortest list.

Could Father Paulinus—surely it was his work—have been on the track of identifying the Cloud author? What an academic coup that would have been. Or was he tracing the lineage of the scribe who made this copy? Or of the scribbulous John Ward? Whatever it was Father Theobald might have an idea—or at the very least, be interested to see it. Antony returned the paper to the box. He must remember to tell the Archivist when he returned.

Antony turned to one of the treatises on the Cloud from the other box, this one by Maurice Chauncey, a monk of the Charter House in London who fled to Flanders under Henry VIII, but before he could tuck into the reading Father Theobald entered again, this time followed by a most unmonastic entourage.

"Right now, camera in that corner." Harry pointed to Fred, unaccompanied by Ginger. He was obliged to use a handheld camera in these tight spaces. "Lenny, we need lights. Sylvie, our good father here is looking peaky. See what you can do with him." It seemed that under the pressure of a shooting schedule Harry was capable of forgetting that his wife was the producer of this series, which technically made her his boss.

In a few minutes all was ready and Antony faced the camera holding the small rectangle of golden calfskin. "I hold here a book of mysteries. Who wrote it? When? Where?

"We don't know. The best we can guess is a monk. Sometime in the fourteenth century. But it's all guesswork really. And yet this slim volume, written with great force and originality in singularly vigorous and eloquent English, about which we know so little, has influenced some five centuries of those seeking to deepen their devotion and understand more of the ways of God. Or, as our unknown author puts it—to pierce the Cloud of Unknowing."

Harry shouted "Cut" in a voice geared to a room several times the size of the one they were working in and led his crew out to a more spacious, more picturesque area where they finished their filming beneath a Gothic arch with a statue in the background. Joy Wilkins took her place beside Antony wearing a silky blue dress that emphasized the color of her eyes.

He was ready for her first question as to why readers still choose to engage with a work written half a millennium ago. Antony held up the papers he had selected from a newsstand that very morning, telling of war, disease and conflict. "Because people are still looking for answers for the same problems. People are looking for God."

"And how does the Cloud Author suggest people find him —or her?"

"'The most godly knowing of God is that the which is known by unknowing,' our unknown author says. Finding God can never be a merely intellectual pursuit. The nature of God can't be understood by our rational minds alone, so we must apprehend him another way—through love because God is love. As our author says, 'love may reach to God in this life, but not knowing.'"

"So love can break through the Cloud of Unknowing?" Joy prompted.

"Our author recommends short prayers, which he calls darts which 'pierceth heaven', he says. But feelings are more important than words. We can pierce the cloud with 'a sharp dart of longing love.'

"And he tells us that seeing God this way is a 'blind beholding,'" Antony added. He hoped his words made more sense to his listeners than they did to him. Recent events had done nothing but emphasize to him the blindness—the un-knowing—of so much of this life. But he didn't dare examine it too closely. This was no time to encounter a crisis of faith.

Yet, what if he didn't find answers to the questions piling up in his daily life? Could he in good conscience continue without a 'beholding'? At least a blind one—whatever that was?

# CHAPTER 17

A short time later Antony held a single, golden thought to himself, allowing it to draw him forward across the darkness of the moors, even causing him to be thankful for Cynthia's high speed driving as the headlights sliced through the black that descended like a pall. At home there would be, if not an answer, at least light, warmth, comfort, love—all that Felicity had come to represent in his life. At the end of the day, at the conclusion of the journey across the stygian moors, Felicity would be there.

Father Paulinus, Tara, Alfred... Not to mention the list of alarms and accidents that had plagued recent days... It was too much. The darkness from the moors seeped into the car. Into Antony's mind. Even the golden talisman of coming home to Felicity dimmed under the onslaught of darkness.

And then Cynthia turned off the Leeds Road onto Stocksbank. The familiar towers of the Community of the Transfiguration loomed silhouetted through the bare tree branches on his right. A turn to the left and a rectangle of golden light poured onto the lane from their cottage window.

Hardly waiting for Cynthia to turn off the engine, Antony

jumped out of the car and was through the front door. "Felicity!"

"In here, Squib." His sister's voice called him into the front room. Gwena sat in the middle of the floor, surrounded by a pile of pink bows.

"Felicity. Where is she? Is she all right?" Antony was surprised at the urgent harshness in his own voice.

"Of course she is. Why shouldn't she be?" Gwen held up a bow. "For the tables at the reception. Pretty, huh?"

"But where is she?"

His sister shrugged. "She went down to the quarry with some reporter woman. Melissa somebody. Promo for the pageant, I suppose." Gwen looked vaguely at the darkened window. "Been gone a long time."

Cynthia breezed in and tossed her coat on the sofa. "How did your rehearsal go today, Gwen?"

"Just went over the music at the centre. Too dark to work at the theatre by the time the police were done at the quarry."

Cynthia dropped to the floor and began twisting a length of satin ribbon into a pink puff. Antony couldn't wait around to hear more. He couldn't explain why, but he was seized with a sense that something wasn't right.

He charged back out into the night. Felicity had gone to the quarry with Melissa Egbert. Little chance the *Sun* reporter was any more interested in the pageant than she had been in a mini-series on the mystics. She would have sniffed out Alfred's death as she had Tara's and would be set on sensationalizing it. Serial murderer—or something even more demonic—stalking Yorkshire Moors. Antony shivered.

Inside the community grounds Antony lost his footing on the slick path and fell to one knee. He pushed himself upright, berating himself for his failure to bring a torch. There was nothing for it but to call in at in his room.

Torch tucked under his arm, he took an extra moment to try ringing Felicity's mobile, realizing how foolish he would feel if she and Melissa were having a cozy coffee in the common room. The incessant, hollow, unanswered ring at the other end of the line, however, only served to increase his urgency.

Antony wouldn't have thought it possible, but the tarry darkness was even thicker on the back side of the community. His torch barely made a pinpoint of light on the stone steps descending into the quarry. "Felicity!" He shouted. Surely the women wouldn't still be here. What could they possibly accomplish in this blackness? And cold. He shivered. "Felicity!" His voice echoed off the walls of the quarry.

At the foot of the stairs Antony stopped and played the thin light of his torch as far as it would reach over the floor of the quarry. Empty. He started to turn back when his beam struck something. Something red in the grass.

Two strides took Antony to Felicity's red knit cap. He held it at arms' length, considering. What did this mean? What was it doing here? Why would she have taken it off?

He played his flashlight over the ground. The newly cut grass was too short to tell him if there had been a struggle. But were those red splotches? He dropped to his knees and examined the rough quarry floor in the dim light of his torch. Blood? Could it be blood?

The picture of Alfred so recently sprawled only a few yards from here with similar rusty brown smears seeping from his broken head made Antony's stomach clench. What had happened here?

Every possible answer his mind could pull up chilled him

more. All that had happened since his involvement in the film began—it was far too much for normal human error. Or even malicious pranks. Someone was trying to stop the project. Stop him. And there was one thing in this world that would stop him dead in his tracks. Felicity.

If any harm had come to her—

No. Harm to Felicity was not what would stop him. It was what would spur him to action. He had held back far too long —denying any need for his own involvement—when the evidence was swirling all around him—beginning that first night with the fireworks explosion interrupting his study. The fire that destroyed Father Paulinus' notes and killed him, the accident with the camera, Tara's death—they were obviously connected. It was harder to see how Alfred's death and drugs in the quarry could be related—but they must be.

And now—Felicity. It was fine to say the police would deal with it, they were the professionals. But Felicity was his.

All the fine determination in the world, however, was of little use. Felicity was still missing.

His mind slowed with dread, and yet his feet stumbling with urgency, Antony circled the quarry, calling her name repeatedly. Always answered only by the empty echo.

Even in the dark it was obvious that there was little hiding place here now that the weeds and scrub had been cleared out. Even the smallest gum wrapper or fag end would have been bagged by the police squad so recently looking for evidence to explain Alfred's death.

All that was left was the stage itself with its cavernous black underbelly. Getting a firm grip on himself, Antony forced his stiff legs to carry him forward.

He had to steel himself against the fear of seeing again

Alfred's bloodied head in the stream of torch light, even though he knew it had long been removed by the police. And, indeed, a few minutes later he could confirm that the under-stage was as pristine as the entire quarry.

Clutching Felicity's hat as if it could lead him to her whereabouts, he blundered his way back to the cottage. This time the golden light falling from the windows seemed a garish warning of danger rather than the welcoming beacon it had been earlier.

And then his heart filled with gladness. Through the window he glimpsed a head of long, golden hair. "Felicity!" He punctuated his joyous cry with a slam of the door.

But the radiant blond woman who met him in the hall was not Felicity.

"Oh, isn't she with you?" Melissa Egbert asked, flipping her hair back over her shoulders.

And now he could see that, indeed, it was the shorter, slighter woman he had seen through the window.

"Yes, we were together earlier this afternoon," Melissa replied to Antony's urgent grilling. "She was anxious to tell me about the pageant, even if I can't manage to get a line on this second unexplained death. The police don't seem to have much, either. Or if they do, they aren't sharing with the press, that's for sure. It's all just too, too coincidental, though, after that make-up girl hanging herself, don't you agree?"

Antony felt he would like to shake her. "Where did you leave Felicity?"

"At the quarry. About four-thirty I suppose. It was starting to get dark, but she wanted to walk through some business she was thinking of for the pageant. Something to do with llamas, I think she said. I had an appointment with Father

Sylvester at the St. James Centre. Quietest man I've ever met. How on earth he puts up with those noisy youth I'll never know. Anyway, I came back to tell Felicity..."

But Antony had long quit listening as he pulled his mobile from his pocket and scrolled down to his entry for the West Yorkshire Police. It was a depressing fact that he even had the police in his phone. A pleasant female voice answered on the second ring. Antony forced himself to sound calm and explain the situation as clearly as he could.

"And how long has this person been missing?" The efficient voice enquired, the speaker obviously filling out a form.

Antony explained. "Yes, only a few hours," he had to admit. But he was certain something was wrong. "Definitely out of character. Yes. Absolutely." Well, there was her inclination to impetuous behavior. Still... "Capable of taking care of herself?" He sighed at the next question. "Yes. Yes, she is." At least she would think she is. He prayed God that she was.

The last of his description entered on the form, Constable Jones gave him her set speech: "In cases like this we advise families to contact 'Missing People' who will be able to provide support, advice and practical help at this difficult time." She gave him a number which he didn't bother to write down.

"I can assure you sir, that the majority of persons reported missing return soon after their disappearance without suffering any harm."

Antony rang off. Afterwards, he couldn't remember whether he had thanked the constable or not. Thank her for what? Filling in a form? It was obvious that was the extent of the help he would get from that quarter. Felicity was not a 'majority of persons reported missing' she was the dearest person in the universe. And she was missing. On a cold, dark night. With three unexplained deaths in a few days.

Antony pulled on his recently discarded coat and checked that his torch was still in his pocket. "I'm going out. Search the grounds—" His thoughts were incoherent, but he knew he couldn't stay here and do nothing.

"Just a minute, I'll go with you," Cynthia said. "Did you look in the church? Maybe she's checking something for the wedding."

Antony's heart soared. Was it possible? He picked up Felicity's red hat. She would need it. Without waiting for Cynthia he lunged toward the hall.

The front door slammed so hard it almost knocked him back into the living room. "Oh, I am sooo mad!" A stomping of feet punctuated the angry voice. The lovely, beloved angry voice. "Can you believe they stole my notes!" A wild-eyed, wild-haired Felicity stormed into the room. "And I've got a blinding headache."

She looked at Antony, standing there speechless. "You've got my hat!" She flung herself into his arms, and broke into sobs.

# CHAPTER 18

"Darling! You're bleeding!" Cynthia was the first to spring into action. She tore her daughter from Antony's arms and led her to the kitchen where she pushed her into a chair and began bathing the cut beneath the red-streaked golden hair with warm water.

"Well, don't just stand there," she glared at Antony. "Isn't there a first aid kit around here somewhere?"

That jarred him into action. Yes. Somewhere. Bathroom, maybe? He stumbled down the hall. By the time he had finished tumbling the bathroom cupboard to no avail, Gwena had produced the small white box marked with a red cross from the shelf beside the cooker and Cynthia had parted Felicity's matted hair to reveal the oozing goose egg lump on the back of her head.

Melissa looked up from the notes she was scribbling. "Shouldn't we take her to accident and emergency?"

"No!" Felicity was adamant. "The last thing I want to do is spend the rest of the night in a dingy emergency room. I'm fine. At least I will be."

Felicity flinched as Cynthia dabbed at her head with a fresh cloth. "Sorry, darling, I am being careful."

"Here." Gwena held Felicity's hand and shook two paracetamol into it, followed by a steaming mug of sweet tea. "Get that inside you."

Antony drew breath to argue about going to the doctors. Surely she should be seen to. What if she had concussion? A fracture? What if...

"Where's that torch you had?" Gwena demanded. Antony drew it from his pocket. Gwena took the half-drunk tea from Felicity's hands, tilted her head back and shone the light into her eyes. Felicity blinked. "Pupils constricted. Good. Do you feel dizzy?"

"No."

"Nauseous?"

"No."

"Did you black out?"

"It *was* black," Felicity answered with considerable asperity.

"She's all right."

"How should I bandage this? I don't see any ointment." Cynthia was rifling through the contents of the first aid kit.

Melissa looked up from her mobile where she had been scrolling down the screen. "NHS says, 'Do not use antiseptic because it may damage the tissue and slow down healing. Pat the area dry with a clean towel. Apply a sterile adhesive dressing, such as a plaster.' There you have it."

"No adhesive," Felicity ordered.

"Clean gauze, then an ice pack," Gwena prescribed.

The first aid seemed interminable to Antony who could only watch helplessly from the sideline. He was grateful for the ministrations of Felicity's mother and her efficient female assistants but he wanted Felicity to himself. He wanted to know more about what had happened. He wanted to tell her how much he loved her.

As it was, the activity in the kitchen was followed with a hot bath for the patient, during which Antony, abandoned in the front room, notified Constable Jones that, indeed, the missing person had shown up. But not as unscathed as the constable had so blithely predicted.

Melissa kept him company on the sofa. "So, how did your work at Ampleforth go today?"

Antony had no desire to be distracted by idle chatter, but courtesy demanded that he answer, so he told her about examining the early manuscripts of *The Cloud*. Then he remembered, "Oh, I forgot to tell Father Theobald."

At Melissa's probing he told her about the sheet of notes he found tucked in the ancient volume. "I suppose I should ring Theobald."

"Don't worry," Melissa said. "I'll be in that area tomorrow. I'll pass on your message. Which box was it in?"

Antony told her, then they both lapsed into silence until the gurgling drain in the bath gave Antony hope that he could have some time alone with Felicity. But Cynthia tucked her daughter up in bed and shooed Antony on his way. "She'll be much better in the morning."

"But shouldn't someone sit up with her? What if she needs—"

"We'll take it in turns. Melissa is staying over, too. Sharing the sofa bed with Gwena. You go get some sleep." She ushered him to the door. "Or pray." The door clicked behind him and he was alone in the night.

# CHAPTER 19

## *Feast of the Holy Innocents*

Cynthia's advice was good, Antony supposed, but neither her directive to rest nor to pray seemed within his reach as he tossed, turned and fretted through the dark hours of the night. At least the cold, moist air was halfway reviving as he hurried, almost blindly, down the hill to the cottage at first light the next morning.

He raised his hand to deliver an insistent knock on the door. In just over a week he wouldn't have to knock. He would be at home here. Cynthia flung the door open. "You look worse than she does." She stepped back for him to rush past her into the narrow hallway.

Felicity was sitting up in bed, propped against a pile of white pillows, a tray with tea and toast on her lap. Antony just shook his head and gazed at her, his heart too full to speak. She held out her hand to him, drawing him into the room. He leaned over and kissed her gingerly, afraid of doing anything to increase her discomfort.

Felicity, however, put her other hand on the back of his head and pulled him forward. When they broke for air she giggled. "Silly, I won't break."

Antony moved the tea tray from the bed and pulled up a chair. "I was so worried." He swallowed. "How's your head?"

"Not bad. Tender. Not as bad as the whack I got at Fairacres." She grimaced. "Goodness, if I'm going to make a habit of this I should take to wearing protective head gear. That bobble cap wasn't much protection."

Antony gripped her arm. "Felicity, it isn't a joking matter."

"Oh, I know. But truly, I'm all right. I just wish I could wash my hair."

"Keep it dry, NHS orders." Gwena stood in the doorway with a cup of tea for Antony. "I'll give it a dry shampoo when I get back from rehearsal."

"Oh, rehearsal. I forgot." Felicity started to push her duvet aside.

"Stay right where you are." Gwena tugged the duvet back into place.

"But—" Felicity protested.

"I can handle it."

"Are you sure?"

Gwena gave her a look that made even Antony wince.

"Oh. Right," Felicity agreed. "You are the professional." She started to lean back against her pillows. "Still—" She sat up again.

Gwena pushed her back.

"I'll stop at Boots on the way home and get some dry shampoo." She turned to Antony. "You, Squib—keep her in bed." The order was followed with a wink that held more than a hint of suggestiveness.

"I just wish I had my notes to give her. Why on earth would anyone steal them?" Felicity's voice still held a trace of the anger she had expressed the night before.

"What notes were they?"

Felicity shrugged. "It was a prompt book: script with blocking. Cast list. Notes for the characters. Lights and sound cues. Reminders for the house crew... Usual stuff."

"Tell me what happened."

"After Melissa left I walked through the entrances I had in mind for all the animals. I wanted to be sure the paths were clear from where Nick and Corin plan to put the pens. I was at the bottom of the stairway, making notes for Mary and Joseph. It was getting pretty dark, but I could see enough to scrawl a bit..."

Antony nodded. "Yes, that's where I found your hat."

"I heard footsteps. I thought it was Nick and Corin. I called out to them and then my head exploded. Literally. Everything went dark and I saw stars. Just like they say. Well, fireworks more than stars."

"Did you lose consciousness?"

"I don't think so. I fell forward onto my hands and knees. Dropped the prompt book. They put something over my head. Pillowcase, maybe, and pulled me to my feet."

"They?"

Felicity blinked and bit her lip in thought. "I'm not sure. I had the impression there were two of them. But maybe that was just because I was expecting Nick and Corin."

"Did you have an appointment?"

"No, nothing like that. I just thought..."

"Could it have been them?"

"But why? What possible reason? I'd have given them my prompt book. Besides, we're friends."

Antony sighed. "I know, nothing makes any sense. But you're sure they were male?"

"I'm not sure of anything." She thought. "One man definitely. I just had the impression that there was someone else, too." Felicity raised her cup to her mouth, then set it down. "Ugh. It's cold."

"Where did they take you?"

"Out of the quarry. I started screaming but it was mostly muffled by that bag on my head. I tried to kick, but I think I was pretty feeble." She pulled up the sleeve of her pajama top. "He had big hands."

Anger surged through Antony when he saw the purple bruises on Felicity's arm. "This will give that useless Constable Jones something to put in her report." This time he got through to Sergeant Silsden and filled him in with a few emphatic phrases and a demand for action.

"How did you get away?" He turned back to Felicity.

"I think they—he—I'm not sure—were taking me to a car or something. I had the feeling we were heading toward the road that runs behind the community. Definitely going downhill. It was steep."

"Did you hear traffic?"

Felicity considered. "Maybe. That bag on my head muddled me. And all my energy was on trying to get away. I think I scratched him." She held out a broken fingernail. "Then I'm not sure what happened. I was struggling—kicking—and I lost my balance. I rolled. And that bag thing fell off my head —or maybe I pulled it off. It's all a bit of a blur. Anyway, he started to pull me to my feet and—yes, we must have been by the road because there was a light. A car must have come along. Or maybe he turned a torch on. Anyway, I guess he saw me because he gave this really angry grunt like he was disgusted and shoved me away.

"I landed face down in some bushes and I think maybe I did black out then. Anyway, next thing I knew I was back on the path coming home. And I got here and you met me with my hat." She looked like she could cry again.

Antony gathered her into his arms and knew it was beyond his strength to keep from crying himself.

There was no knowing how long they might have remained clinging to one another if Cynthia hadn't entered then with a fresh pot of tea and rack of toast.

Antony pulled himself together. "But you never did get a look at him? Them?"

"I should have tried, I suppose, but I was just concentrating on getting away."

"And good job you did." Antony's heartfelt reply was accompanied with a fervent squeeze of her hand.

"I'm not sure I did, really. It sort of felt more like he threw me away."

Antony was quiet for a minute, considering all she had told him. At last he turned to her desk and drew out a pen and sheet of paper. "Let's make a list. Anyone who could possibly have anything to cover up or want to destroy for any reason. No matter how absurd it sounds." He sat with the pen poised.

"Um, well, anyone doing drugs in the quarry," Felicity suggested.

"Right." Antony wrote. "Or worse—doing a drug deal. Who do we know that that could be?"

Felicity grimaced. "What's the population of Kirkthorpe? Of Yorkshire?"

"Yes, I know, it could be anyone. But think. This sounds more personal. I mean, if you're right that he/they 'threw you away' when he got a good look at you, that indicates it was someone who knew you."

"Or didn't know me."

"Huh?"

"Maybe they thought they had somebody else. Then saw they didn't."

"Ah, like Melissa, you mean?"

"It was pretty dark and our hairstyles are a lot alike."

Yes, Antony himself had momentarily confused them when he glimpsed Melissa through the window. Surely, if he could mistake another woman for Felicity... "We'll have to ask her who might want to abduct her."

"We could call her or something if anyone has her number. She's gone back to work this morning." Felicity paused. "But you know, if that's the case, they might have thrown my prompt book away too. Maybe they thought it was some story Melissa was working on."

"But wasn't she just doing a promo piece about the pageant?"

"I thought so, but she was awfully interested in Alfred's death. She asked if I thought it was connected with Tara's."

"I wondered about that, too." Antony wrote Tara's death and Alfred's on his list. Then added Father Paulinus. And his fireworks explosion and Fred's accident with Ginger, which now seemed very far away.

Felicity looked at the list. "Your hit-and-run accident." He wrote. "And that threatening note in your pocket."

Antony sighed. "No shortage of suspicious events, but who could possibly be connected to any of them?"

"Well, I hate to say anything. I mean, I could be completely wrong..."

"No matter how wild, we just need ideas here, then maybe we can see a connection. Fantasize. Who's the least likely person connected in any way to any of this?"

Felicity giggled. "Father Anselm."

"All right. I asked for that." But it did make Antony think. "Do we know anything about Father Sylvester?"

"What? You're kidding!"

"Only a little. I mean, someone is selling drugs. Father Sylvester certainly has access to young people. He knows everyone who comes to the centre."

"He would be well-placed, I guess. And I suppose he would use the money for the centre. But can you imagine that mouse killing Alfred?"

An image of the mousy lay brother who had abducted Felicity months earlier flitted across Antony's mind. He wrote down Sylvester's name, then changed tack. "The police seem to think Alfred's death could have been an accident. And if someone involved in the drugs business thought you had found something—something you were writing in your notebook..."

Felicity chewed thoughtfully on a piece of toast, then held up her hand. "Wait. Stop. This isn't getting us anywhere. Take it in order. What were the first things to happen?"

"Father Paulinus. Then the fireworks explosion—if that was even part of all this. Then the camera thing—if it really was sabotaged. Then the hit-and-run, then Tara."

"Hm, all that seems focused on the mini-series. Could someone be trying to stop the film?"

Antony frowned. "Who would want to do that?"

Felicity took another bite of toast. "Well, a competing film company? Someone with a grudge against Harry? Or Sylvia?

Someone with a grudge against the mystics?" She grimaced. "Sorry. Not a laughing matter."

Antony considered her words. Competing film company? What about that Australian company that wanted Harry to work for them? But that wasn't competition, was it? Felicity continued probing. "Think about it—Rievaulx, Ampleforth—did you see anyone hanging around the set? Anyone not part of the crew? Were you aware of Harry or Sylvia getting any threatening phone calls?"

Antony shook his head. "No, nothing."

"Okay, what about someone in the company? Someone Harry owes money to, for example?"

"If that were the case it seems like stopping the film would be counterproductive. Harry doesn't give the impression of being short of a quid or two. Still..." Money could be a strong motivator. Maybe he could find out if Studio Six was behind on salaries or anything. He had seen a worried look in Harry's eyes whenever the topic of selling the series to the BBC came up. It was likely he would be in trouble if he couldn't sell it.

"The company must be insured. Is it possible they could collect more from a ruined project that from selling the series?"

The question hung in the air. Antony determined to find out all he could about the management of Studio Six. Perhaps he could ask some pertinent questions when they resumed filming on Monday. But first, he would look closer to home. The more recent happenings had been right here on the community grounds. That implied a culprit close at hand.

"Felicity, you stay in bed. Don't even go out in the garden without your mother." He spoke more sharply than he meant to, but if he let himself he could easily become overwhelmed with concern for Felicity. "I have to go to noon mass—I told Father Anselm I'd give the homily. I can't imagine what I was thinking. Anyway, I'll look in on the pageant rehearsal afterwards."

"Oh, would you please? I'm sure you could give Gwen some good support. She knows all about productions, but I don't think dealing with stroppy youth is really her thing."

Antony kissed her and let her think his motive was purely to help with the pageant. He didn't want her worrying with more thoughts of evil deeds. "Remember, you've got a wedding to get ready for."

"And don't you be forgetting that, either." She waved him away.

Antony walked slowly up the hill, forcing his mind from Felicity, from the unexplained deaths and mayhem around him. He had to focus on a more ancient slaughter, one that people still struggled to make sense of. Today was the Feast of the Holy Innocents. What could he say in recalling the long-ago deaths of those blameless children in Bethlehem that could be of help to people in this day? How did one make sense of any of the evil in the world?

Today not even the peace and beauty of the community church served to order Antony's thoughts as his feet carried him automatically to the vestry, his mind struggling to recall what he knew of the story. Estimates of the number killed varied wildly from 144,000 to fewer than twenty. Given the population of Bethlehem in the first century, a lower number was more believable. The historicity of the event itself was sometimes questioned by scholars. But there was no doubt of Herod's use of violence to protect his power. Including murdering his own sons.

As he tied the cincture on his white alb Antony's mind leapt ahead. Killing to protect power. A strong motive for murder. Could that be behind the present deaths? No, he jerked his mind back with a physical shake of his head. He must stay with the subject at hand.

Whatever the historical facts, the traditional account held together, especially as a spur for the Flight into Egypt and as a fulfillment of Old Testament prophecy and paralleling Pharaoh's slaughter of the Hebrew children in Egypt. But most of all it was consistent with human nature. Antony sighed. Throughout the history of humankind there had been those who were willing to kill for their own purposes—those who would put their personal gain above the right of others to life itself.

*"Hymnum canentes martyrum*
*dicamus Innocentium,..."*
*Sing praise to the martyrs,*
*let us say of the innocents...*

The chant began and Antony automatically followed along in the procession up the aisle. In the period of quiet meditation that followed his homily Antony wasn't sure what he had said, but he knew he could do no better than the words of the collect which he repeated again in his own mind: *Heavenly Father, whose children suffered at the hands of Herod, though they had done no wrong; by the suffering of your Son and by the innocence of our lives frustrate all evil designs and establish your reign of justice and peace...*

That was it. For all who suffer innocently, frustrate all evil and establish justice and peace. Amen and amen.

He was still holding that thought uppermost in his mind a short time later as the sound of a ragged, but enthusiastically sung "We Three Kings" made Antony hurry toward the quarry. If they were already at the coming of the Magi rehearsal must be nearly completed as the visit of the Wise Men to the manger was the grand conclusion.

And Gwendolyn's directing was geared to ensure that that fact would be lost on no one. "...Westward leading, still proceeding/ Guide us to Thy perfect light." The carol came to an end and Gwena strode to the middle of the stage. Even in these rustic surroundings Antony was impressed with how his sister's stage presence commanded the attention of everyone in the theatre. She barely had to raise her voice to be heard clearly throughout the quarry. "Excellent. Wonderful! You're all stars!" She flung out her arms to incorporate all her youthful troupe. "This will be really, really good on the night. You have all the energy and enthusiasm it will take to put this thing over.

"I want you all to picture it with me. Everyone in costumes, torches flaring all around the rim of the quarry. Live animals around the stage. The theatre full of your admiring audience—family, friends—"

"Enemies," Syd murmured just loudly enough to draw guffaws from those nearest him.

Gwena undoubtedly heard, but she ignored it as she turned to her lead Wise Man. "Melchior, you were wonderful. A natural. You have real stage presence." Some of Syd's assumed insouciance fell away as he puffed out his chest. "Now, we don't want any of this to be lost on our audience. Especially when they bring in the animals. You know, we say in the business that's the hardest thing to do—work with animals. They are terrific scene stealers and we don't want that to happen to you.

"Caspar, Baltasar, all three of you, come with me. We shall have a deportment lesson. You are doing very, very well, but you must walk like kings." She demonstrated. "Head up—so. Shoulders back. There now—stride like you own the earth."

Antony was amazed as Syd and Dylan and Shaun, who normally mimicked Syd's slouching swagger, were transformed before his eyes. "That's it. You've got it. Now. Your gifts. Remember, you are carrying gold and costly spices, the perfume of Arabia. Hold them out. Higher. That's right. Proudly. Kings presenting to a King. The King of Kings.

"Now, when you turn, feel the weight of your robes. It'll be easier when you're in costume, but try imagining it now. Heavy fur, velvet, tapestry hanging from your shoulders. Stand tall and turn so your capes swirl out." Antony wasn't sure whether they actually followed her instructions or Gwen just drew such vivid word pictures that he could see it in his mind, but he was amazed at the transformation in the scene before him.

"Now, everybody," she turned back to the full cast assembled on the stage, "Rehearsal Monday. In the meantime, I want you to practice staying in character until then. Mary." She pointed to Flora, peeking shyly around her mass of brown curls. "I want everyone who sees you the rest of the weekend to ask why you're so happy. I want you to practice radiating joy. You're the Mother of God. Think about that. All the time.

"Joseph," Joaquin all but saluted her. "Protective. Caregiver. Strong. Everyone who comes near you feels safe. You're the man to have around in a crisis. You can handle it. You've been chosen by God almighty to be the earthly protector of His Son. Got that?"

Antony could have sworn Joaquin grew four inches before his eyes.

And back to Syd and his scruffy henchmen. "Kings. Stately rulers. Wisdom. Men of knowledge and determination. Walk proud."

She went on, inspiring the shepherds to faithfulness, obedience, courage. When Gwen finished with the angels Antony all but expected to see them fly away in their beauty and grace rather than walking the earth. He wanted to tell her how brilliant she was. Just a short time with these young people and his sister had given them a vision of whole new self-concepts. But she was busy working with Tanya, inspiring the narrator to more powerful projection, more precise elocution, so instead he approached Syd.

What could he ask him to get any idea of his possible involvement in the recent string of misdeeds? How realistic was it to suspect Syd of attacking Felicity because he feared she had spotted some involvement of his in the drug use that had gone on in the Quarry? And if Felicity had been correct in sensing a second presence could it have been Dylan or Shaun? They certainly seemed to follow every lead from the older youth. "Um, sorry I got here late. Sounds like it went well, though." He supposed that was as good an opener as any.

"Yeah, brilliant," Dylan said.

"Is she really your sister?" Shaun looked at Gwena in open-mouthed wonder. The implication was clear. How could anyone so stellar possibly be related to such a weedy priest?

Antony assured them she really was. "Did you have a good Christmas?" Their colorless answers told him that ploy was a washout. "Enjoying your holiday?" He didn't wait for a reply. "What did you do last night?"

Syd frowned. "What are you—my mum?" His slouch returned, then he remembered Gwen's instructions and squared his shoulders. "Same as any night—kicked around with me mates. Right?" He looked at Shaun and Dylan for confirmation. They agreed.

How could he get them to be more specific? What else could he ask, Antony wondered.

Then Syd continued. "Why? Somebody been slashing tires again? It weren't us. You aren't gonna get me on any more ASB charges. You can ask that old priest if you don't believe us."

"Old priest?" Antony frowned.

"Yeah, Father S. S for silly." Dylan and Shaun guffawed. "He were at the centre all evening, weren't he?"

Antony certainly would check that out. Did it clear Syd or implicate Father Sylvester?

He opened his mouth to ask another question, but was interrupted by a red-faced Corin. The frequently on-edge ordinand looked ready to boil over. Syd and the others made their escape. "Corin, what is it?"

"My dad." He swiped the blond hair out of his eyes with an angry gesture that exaggerated the size of his hand. "Same old, same old—I suppose I should be used to it by now, but this time it's the pageant."

"What?"

"The sheep. He's decided we can't use them. Says he doesn't want to stir up the beasts. As if those dumb creatures could be stirred up. It's not the sheep. It's just an excuse. He'll do anything to block my work here. I'll bet he agreed to let us use them just so he could leave us in the lurch at the last moment. I wouldn't put it past him." It seemed that once he'd started Corin was determined to pour out his turmoil over the long-standing conflict with his father.

"He thinks by pulling stunts like this he can discourage me from becoming a priest—get me back to that godforsaken sheep farm. I'd see him in Hades first. It comes to the same thing."

"Have you tried to talk to him?"

"Talk? I talk myself blue in the face trying to explain about my sense of calling, my passion to be a priest. He thinks I should be able to just switch all that to a piece of land because it's been in our family since the flood. Why can't he see my doing that is just as likely as his taking holy orders? I'll grow out of it he says. Grow out of it—I'm twenty-seven years old!"

Antony had been aware of the conflict between Corin and his father, but hadn't realized the emotional power behind it. He tried to say something conciliatory to him, but the best he could think of was to suggest Kendra might know a nearby farmer who would be willing to loan his sheep. This was York-shire, after all.

Feeling a considerable failure for his lack of concrete counsel for Corin and wondering what helpful advice he could possibly have given the young man, Antony walked on into town to Saint James. The tall, yellow brick tower pro-claimed the High Street presence of the former church now turned over to Churches Together to run as a community centre. A red-lettered banner hung over the door announcing their main focus which was the active youth program, but posters lining the porch outlined a variety of other programs:

women's aerobic morning every Tuesday and Thursday, mothers and toddlers group three mornings a week, and weekly tea afternoons for old age pensioners.

Father Sylvester, looking shrunken in his grey clerical shirt, his pale eyes hidden behind thick lenses, came suddenly alive when Antony asked him about activities at the centre the evening before.

"Yes, yes indeed. How kind of you to take an interest, Father. Yes, come. Let me show you. He led the way toward the former church hall which now served as a multipurpose room and gymnasium. He stopped just inside the door and swept the room with his arm. "Well, what do you think? It took forever to get committee approval. Of course, it isn't a listed building or anything, but we had to be sure there wouldn't be anything to offend the OAP's or be inappropriate for the kiddies. They all use the space, too, you know. But I think they're doing a rather fine job. What do you say?

Antony stared, amazed. The formerly dingy, off-white walls were coming alive with scenes of the Yorkshire country-side. At least, he assumed that was what they intended to depict. Yes, that bit was definitely Emley Moor with its tall transmitting station.

"So many of our young people had been given anti-social behavior warnings—or worse—many for graffiti. We wanted a way to harness their—Er, creative powers. I had suggested perhaps Biblical scenes, honoring the fact that this was once a church. I'm afraid that idea didn't fly, but I think the children —Er, youth—did come up with something quite apropos."

"Yes." Antony blinked. "Yes, indeed. Very colorful." Once one got past the rather acid shade of green the budding artists had chosen. "It certainly takes the eye." He couldn't help wondering how long it had been since a sky that blue had canopied Yorkshire.

"Who were the artists?" Antony reminded himself that he was here to check on alibis, not to serve as an art critic.

"Oh, we had a lively group yesterday. Far more than I had expected, but you know, so many of them really have nothing for them at home, even on Boxing Day. So we gave them a good tea after Kendra's choir rehearsal—I understand your pageant up at the community is going to be quite a treat."

Antony nodded. "And after tea they set about painting?"

"A good number of them, yes. We barely had enough brushes. Thank goodness someone had the foresight to put down drop cloths. I'm afraid some of them spilled as much paint as they got on the wall. Still, a good time was had by all, as they say."

"And they stayed until what time?"

"They painted until half seven. Then we cleared everything out for a basketball game. Fortunately the paint was quick-drying, although we did get a few smears. Some stayed on for that."

Half seven. About the time Felicity burst through the door of the cottage. Antony was so flooded with the remembered relief his knees almost went weak. "Yes. That's grand. Do you have a list of who was here?"

"Oh, certainly. Sign in, sign out. One of the rules. And no ducking in and out between times. They know. Only get up to no good if you allow that." Father Sylvester produced a clipboard and Antony perused the list of scrawled signatures. To the best he could decipher them it read like a program for the cast of the Epiphany pageant. He ran over the list twice.

At last he pointed. "S. Worsley. Is that the young man they call Syd?"

Father Sylvester peered at it through his glasses. "Yes, Syd, that's right. The tall one. Very useful. He only needed a step stool to paint the top of the transmitting station." Father Sylvester pointed to the silver spike on the top of the tower that rather made it look like a skinny rocket taking off into space. "Kept saying how awkward the brush was. Those street artists, as they call themselves, work with spray cans, you know."

"And he was definitely here the whole time?"

Father Sylvester pointed to the recorded sign out time. Antony thanked him and turned to leave. At the door he paused and turned back. "Nick and Corin. Were they here all evening, too?"

"Oh, the young ordinands from your college? Excellent young men. I don't know what we'd do without them. Yes, yes, they were here. Such dedication. And excellent role models for our young hoodlums."

Antony nodded and turned again.

"At least, wait. I tell a lie. Nicholas was here all evening. Quite an artistic flair he has. I was so grateful because I'm afraid I'm quite color blind." Antony smiled. Ah, perhaps that explained the battery acid moor. Apparently they were lucky it wasn't bright red. "Corin was here for the rehearsal. He left with Kendra. I believe they were going to check into some sound equipment for the pageant or some such."

Antony started back up the hill, the stimulating cold air invigorating his thoughts. So, in giving Syd and his sidekicks an alibi, Father Sylvester gave himself an alibi as well. Did that mean the whole theory of drug dealing from the youth centre was a nonstarter, or was the emaciated priest far wilier than he appeared?

So if not Syd or Sylvester, where to look next? Nick had been here at the time of Felicity's abduction, but apparently Corin had not. The sight of the vicious bruises on Felicity's arms and Corin's big hands melded in Antony's mind. Could a young man who claimed to be so passionate about ministry possibly be guilty of such brutality? Or was it all a cover of lies? What could he believe?

At least tomorrow was Sunday. No scheduled rehearsal. No filming. If Felicity would stay safely tucked in bed he could forget this sordid business and concentrate on preparing for Monday's filming. Mount Grace was a favorite of his. He hoped he would be able to convey at least some of its serenity and beauty to his potential viewing audience. Then Thurgarton and Walter Hilton after New Years' Day and he would be finished with this blankety filming and could concentrate on the main event—their wedding.

Please God it would all be settled by then. No worries about appearing before a camera. No worries about Felicity's safety. No worries about lurking murderers.

# CHAPTER 20

## *First Sunday of Christmas*

Antony awoke to the sound of the community bells with the sense that he had been dreaming about the wedding. He closed his eyes and let the images float before him: The congregation and choir singing; candles, flowers and incense swirling like Van Gogh's Starry Night; And Felicity, tall and stately, draped in white, walking toward him up the aisle. Walking, walking, walking, but as so often in a dream, never arriving. The church aisle stretched endlessly. He reached out to her to help draw her forward.

Then he remembered: Felicity coming to him; never reaching him. Felicity struggling. He calling out to her. Then the shadow. From behind the back pillar. Jumping out at Felicity, a heavy object raised in his hand. It had been Felicity's scream that had wakened him, not the bells.

No, not Felicity's scream, but his own—when he saw the bright red blood staining her cloud of white veil.

Antony wiped his hands roughly over his eyes to clear the image. No. That would not happen. He would not let it. He had one week. He must solve this before then.

Please, Lord that all would be cleared up. He couldn't imagine spending their honeymoon looking over his shoulder, fearing for Felicity—for his bride's—safety. He wanted their wedding to be a thing of beauty, peace and holiness. Not shadowed by a lurking killer.

Antony didn't know whether to be relieved or disappointed that no one from the cottage appeared at church that morning. As much as he would have been delighted—and astounded—to see Gwena there, he was glad that it must mean that his sister and Cynthia were attending to Felicity. If it only didn't mean that Felicity was feeling worse. What was he thinking not to insist that she have an x-ray? What if there was a fracture? What if she had taken ill in the night? What if her attacker had come back to finish his job? No, he reminded himself, they had decided it had all been a mistake. Felicity wasn't even the intended victim.

Antony tasted blood before he moved to the communion rail. In his worry he had bitten the inside of his mouth so hard it was bleeding.

He was half way down the hill to the cottage before the echoes of the recessional hymn had faded. "Felicity, how is she?" He demanded before Cynthia had the door fully open.

"She's fine. Come in." But he was already in.

He found Felicity and Gwen sitting on the sofa their heads bent together over a black ring binder. "Oh, Antony, I'm so sorry we missed church. We were all ready, but the police came. Look." She held up the book. "They found my prompt book. Isn't that great!"

"It'll be a real help," Gwena seconded. "She has a great eye for detail, does your Felicity."

But Antony wasn't interested in pageant directions. "The police were here? On a Sunday?"

"It must mean they're taking all this very seriously. I don't

think they believe that gardener's death was an accident."
Cynthia, who had followed him into the room, sat in the chair
still hidden by the Christmas tree which would remain up
until Epiphany.

"They found this Friday," Felicity was still concentrating
on her returned notebook. "They said they couldn't return it
until they had checked it for fingerprints. All they learned,
though was that my would-be kidnapper wore gloves. I think
the fact he threw it away proves he had the wrong person—
just as we suspected."

"Did you tell the police that? What did they say?"

"I mentioned Melissa. I think they'll check up on what
stories she's working on in case there's a tie-in, but they aren't
giving much away."

"Do you think they believe the deaths are connected?"
Antony asked.

"If they are, Melissa could be a link because she definitely
was asking questions about them both."

"Yes, and if the murderer knew that he might want to
know what she had in her notebook."

Gwena stood, still holding the prompt book. "Mind if I
take this to the kitchen to study the lighting cues?" She didn't
wait for an answer.

Just then a timer dinged in the kitchen. Cynthia emerged
from behind the tree. "Lasagna done. You'll stay for lunch,
won't you, Antony? I just have to toss a salad." Like Gwena,
she didn't wait for a reply.

Antony took the place his sister had vacated on the sofa.
"Are you sure you should be up? No headache? No dizziness?"
It was such a relief that his gloomy prognostications hadn't

come true that Antony had trouble accepting the evidence of his own eyes.

"Truly, I'm all right. I slept really well with only one paracetamol." And to prove her well-being she gave him a hearty kiss. "Now, back to business. Do you know anything about any other stories Melissa might have been working on?"

Antony considered, trying to remember. "It did seem like she mentioned something when she interviewed me at Rievaulx Terrace, but then we were all so sidetracked by Tara's death. I had the feeling she was using Harry's desire for publicity as an excuse for her own purposes, but there wasn't anything too specific, other than probing for sensationalism." Still, something tickled the back of his mind. Had the reporter introduced a topic that seemed tangential? Could that have been her real purpose?

Antony went on to tell Felicity of the dead ends his gentle sleuthing had reached yesterday. "Seems that Syd and Co. and Father Sylvester have pretty solid alibis. As does Nick. Corin is still in the frame, as I think they say. He and Kendra left the centre not too long before you were attacked."

Felicity frowned. "I hate to think of Corin mixed up in anything shady. He comes across as—I suppose this sounds odd, but I think of him as a simple soul. Straight forward might be a better term. Awkward, a bit of a bull in a china shop, but good-hearted."

Antony nodded. "Yes, I would agree with that. At least I would have, but the anger he displayed yesterday was rather alarming."

"And he does have access to the young people—if someone is pushing drugs. But that's just conjecture. We found those joints under the stage, and then some needles, but anyone could have walked up there through that broken gate."

Antony wrestled with himself. He didn't want to think badly of Corin—or of any of his students. Kirkthorpe's ordinands had a stellar reputation for being of the highest calibre. But then he looked at Felicity. Gwena's dry shampoo hadn't entirely removed all the rusty brown stains from around her wound. And he remembered the bruises on her arms. Someone had been capable of brutality. He needed to be more rigorous in his search. "You said there might have been a second person, possibly a woman. Think. What gave you that impression?

Felicity closed her eyes and dropped her head in concentration. "I'm not sure. There might have been a scent."

"Perfume?"

"No, subtler than that." She took a deep breath to aid her memory. "Something fruity. Could have been a shampoo, maybe." She thought more. "And the footsteps. On the stone stairs. I think there might have been a lighter one." She shook her head. "Useless, I know. I'm sorry to be so vague."

"No, not at all. You're doing great. So it could have been Kendra?"

"Theoretically. But..."

Cynthia stuck her head through the doorway to tell them that dinner was ready.

"So we're off to another location tomorrow?" Cynthia asked as she served large rectangles of lasagna onto each plate.

"Oh, yes." Antony had forgotten that Cynthia would once again be his chauffeur. "It's north of Rievaulx. Should take us about an hour. Are you sure you're all right to drive me? Shouldn't you stay with Felicity?"

Felicity wasn't having any of that. "I don't need a minder. And if I did Gwena is more than capable."

Was she? Were any of them? Antony wondered. He wanted to insist that Felicity come with him, but then, how did he know that the film set would be any safer? After all, Tara had died at Rievaulx. "You will be careful. You won't go off by yourself. Or be alone with—anyone suspicious." He worded them like questions, but they were commands.

As a reply Felicity leaned over and brushed his cheek with a kiss. "Worry wart."

It was later when he had his coat on and was ready to return to his room to prepare for tomorrow's filming that it flashed into his mind. "I remember. It seemed so out of the blue—disconnected to anything else—that Melissa asked me about the Duncombe family in connection with her probing about Tara's death and her pressing an occult theory."

"So you think there could be something there? She's doing some sort of exposé or something and someone wants to know what she has on them?" Felicity thought for a moment. "You realize, if it's something like that, the perp could be anyone in Yorkshire."

Her words rang in his ears all the way back to his room, *anyone in Yorkshire.* It could be. And in that case, there was absolutely no use his looking for a solution. It was hopeless.

# CHAPTER 21

"Antony, darling, this can't be right. We're supposed to be on an A road—isn't that one of those little green lines on the map? This is a footpath."

Antony smiled at his future mother-in-law. "Nope, this is absolutely right. You're doing fine, Cynthia."

"But what if I meet someone?"

"One of you gives way." Antony had a sneaking suspicion that 'someone' would not be Cynthia. But as they continued on northward with the bare branches of trees interlocking overhead and heavy clouds looming beyond, Antony did appreciate Cynthia's steady driving. The last half mile down a country lane which was, indeed, barely more than a footpath, brought them to a carpark below terraced gardens which in the summer would have been dripping with colorful flowers and beyond that a fine golden stone house with a red tile roof.

Antony was barely out of the car when he was given an enthusiastic welcome by a handsome Golden Retriever, her freshly-brushed amber coat glowing as if the sun were shining on it. "Hullo, Zoe." He hardly needed to stoop to pet her silky head. "Good girl. Everything ready to go today, is it?" Zoe led the way to the front of the house where her mistress had the crew assembled for today's shooting.

Still filling in for Tara, who had not been replaced, Sylvia saw to Antony's make-up, then turned him over to Harry. "I'll catch you later, love," Sylvia told her husband. "I'm going to take Zoe walkies." Antony noted Cynthia joined the other woman as they set off toward the woods.

Antony started forward as Fred, with Ginger dancing on her dolly, followed smoothly behind him. Antony walked along the wide graveled path and stopped in front of the seventeenth century manor house. "Today we're at Mount Grace Priory, a Carthusian monastery on the edge of the North Yorkshire Moors, the last monastery established in Yorkshire before the Reformation. This is very much like the monastery the author of *The Cloud of Unknowing* would have lived and worked in. Beautiful in its peace and simplicity, it was built at a time when piety and strict living were valued. A perfect setting to give rise to the mysticism of the Cloud author."

Feeling more like a tour guide than the priestly scholar of his job description, Antony supplied their future viewing audience with historical background. "Like so many similar establishments, this was bought after the Dissolution for farm land and the priory was left to decay. The owner rebuilt the former guesthouse using stones from the abandoned priory. At the end of the nineteenth century a London barrister inherited the property and encouraged excavation on his land.

"Sir William St. John Hope, the leading monastic scholar of the day, was brought in to head the excavation and he uncovered the most complete Carthusian priory in England. This was a find of international importance." Antony turned from facing the camera and walked to the end of the house where a Gatehouse led through the precinct wall to a vast green sweep of lawn. "Typical of Carthusian monasteries Mount Grace is divided into two large spaces inside the precinct wall. On this side we have the Inner Court where the workday services of the priory—granary, kiln, stables—went on, mostly conducted by lay brothers." He pointed to the jigsaw puzzle of broken foundations of these buildings as he crossed the grass to the remains of the simple church which stood in the center of the property, dividing the two spaces.

"Like most Carthusian churches, this one, built during the fourteenth and fifteenth centuries, is small and quite plain. This reflects the size of the community and the little time the monks spent here. Of the twelve periods of prayer Carthusians observed each day between eleven o'clock at night and six o'clock the next evening, only three of the offices would occur in church. The others were said privately in their cells, punctuated with periods of study, writing and work in their gardens." Antony walked on into the Great Cloister, knowing that further shots of the bell tower and interior of the church would be edited in according to Harry's instruction.

Ginger's bright eye swept the perfect lawn before them. "This cloister is far larger than you will find in most monasteries because they needed room for each of the monk's individual cells to be built around it. Carthusians were hermit monks who lived primarily in their cells."

Antony started to cross the grass when Harry barked, "Cut. We'll do that later, Father. Need to see to our special guest. Busy man, can't be left to cool his heels."

The way Harry spoke Antony was half expecting a member of the royal family. He turned to Sylvia, who had returned from walking Zoe. "Sylvia achieved quite a coup—landed Dr. Samuel Dedinder, our Sylvie did."

Sylvia gave an appropriately self-deprecating smile. "It happened that he was staying with a friend in Yorkshire, so he agreed. I think he has a new book coming out, so his agent thought it would be good publicity." She added in something of an aside to Antony, "Harry was so pleased not to have to take a crew to London for the interview. Budgets, you know."

Samuel Dedinder, Antony was impressed. Sylvia had snagged a coup indeed. Yet Antony was puzzled. Dedinder was a well-known psychiatrist who had built much of his notoriety on writing about emotion and religious experience of all stripes. And deriding it. What would he make of the mystics? Why would Harry want a naysayer for his series?

Antony followed along to the back of the church through the Gothic arch under the bell tower. Here the lawn ran up to the broken wall beneath the green wooded hillside which sheltered the priory and provided much of the sense of serenity. And standing in the center was one of the most remarkable pieces of sculpture Antony had ever seen. He wished Felicity were here now to enjoy it with him. He would definitely bring her another time. Maybe in March when the hillside would be covered with delicate white snowdrops.

He turned now to the Madonna of the Cross. In the act of dedicating her child to the purpose of the Creator, a tall, slim Mary, her head thrown back, held her swaddled infant at chest level, arms raised, elbows bent, forming a perfect cross. Harry placed his star interviewee in front of the statue and Joy Wilkins, swathed in a Marian blue scarf, asked their celebrity to define mysticism.

Looking dapper in his tweed overcoat with a leather

collar, his blond hair waving across his forehead, the psychiatrist wrinkled his long, aristocratic nose. "I can do no better than William James says in his classic work *The Varieties of Religious Experience*. First, a mystical experience is ineffable—it defies expression in words. It must be directly experienced. James says one must have musical ears to know the value of a symphony; one must have been in love one's self to understand a lover's state of mind. Lacking the heart or ear, we cannot interpret the musician or the lover justly, and are even likely to consider him weak-minded or absurd." Here he gave a smile that conveyed sympathy to his viewers who might share that opinion.

"Secondly, James points to the nonetic aspect of a mystical experience. The mystic sees his or her experience as revealing states of knowledge—insight into depths of truth unplumbed by the discursive intellect. They are illuminations, revelations, full of significance and importance, all inarticulate though they remain."

"So, Doctor Dedinder," Joy turned to her subject, "if mystical experiences are inexpressible, what is their value?"

"James, as have I, studied mysticism in many religions: Buddhism, Islam, Hinduism, as well as Christianity. He also looked at experiences beyond those of the writers we normally label mystics, such as Luther, Newman and Tennyson." Dedinder turned to his interviewer. "I am certain you will be struck, as I was, by his conclusion that, and I quote, 'The Anaesthetic Revelation is the Initiation of Man into the Immemorial Mystery of the Open Secret of Being, revealed as the Inevitable Vortex of Continuity. End, beginning, or purpose, it knows not of.'"

Joy looked as stunned as Antony felt. He had the

impression it was all she could do to keep from shaking her head. "Um, yes. I wonder, would you care to put that into simpler words?"

"Yes, indeed, Joy. I believe that what James is saying is that the mystical experience is its own event. It affords no particular of the multiplicity and variety of things; but it fills appreciation of the historical and the sacred with a secular and intimately personal illumination of the nature and motive of existence, which then seems reminiscent as if it should have appeared, or shall yet appear, to every participant thereof."

Antony despaired. After all his effort to make mysticism accessible and understandable to the casual viewer. People didn't need complicated theology. They needed a simple invitation to peace, to quiet, to God. Come and see. That was enough.

Antony turned to look at Harry. His ashen face made his black beard stand out sharply and Antony sensed he would like to be pulling his hair. Surely, Sylvia couldn't have known what she was doing when she lined Dedinder up to interview. Harry made a frantic circling motion at Joy which meant wind it up.

"And what conclusions have you reached after your study of mysticism, Doctor?"

Dedinder smoothed the lapels of his coat. "Again, I must agree with James. To the medical mind these ecstasies signify nothing but suggested and imitated hypnoid states, on an intellectual basis of superstition, and a corporeal one of degeneration and hysteria." Perhaps Dedinder read in Joy's appalled look the fact that he had gone too far, so he continued quickly. "The great thing mysticism has to offer is optimism.

"And I would hasten to add, an approach to the Divine. This overcoming of all the usual barriers between the individual and the Absolute is the great mystic achievement. In mystic states we both become one with the Absolute and we become aware of our oneness. This is the everlasting and triumphant mystical tradition."

Now Joy showed she had done her homework. "And didn't James say of the mystics that, 'Perpetually telling of the unity of man with God, their speech antedates languages, and they do not grow old.'" Antony felt like he could have hugged her.

Dedinder drew himself to full height. "James, rather grudgingly, one feels, concludes that 'The mystic is, in short, invulnerable, and must be left, whether we relish it or not, in undisturbed enjoyment of his creed.' He then emphasizes that 'mystics have no right to claim that we ought to accept the deliverance of their peculiar experiences.'"

"So the value of mysticism, you would say, lies in its optimism and in bringing the individual closer to God." Joy, who was obviously struggling to rescue the interview, did not wait for an answer. "Worthy goals, one might say, which could serve as beacons for other seekers to follow. Thank you, Dr. Dedinder."

He gave a gleaming smile for the camera and graciously accepted her thanks.

Harry rushed up to shake his guest's hand. "Fine. Fine job. Thank you so much. Will add some real gravitas to our little project. So appreciate your taking time to come by."

Antony was puzzled. Did Harry Forslund really think those indecipherable speeches would help him sell the series to a major distributor? He must be banking heavily on the celebrity value of the Dedinder name.

"Ah, I see your host has returned for you. Good timing, that." Harry waved with vigor to a Barbour-clad figure striding across the courtyard.

Antony started to turn away, then blinked. He recognized that man. Stanton Alnderby was Samuel Dedinder's host? An old friend, Harry had said. That could explain much. If Corin's father was perhaps overawed by the supercilious esteemed psychiatrist it was little wonder he had withdrawn his support of his son's work in a monastery. Perhaps Corin himself had told his father's guest of his studies. It was likely the ordinand's enthusiasm for the pageant bubbled over. Undoubtedly Dedinder would have belittled the calling of which Corin's father already disapproved.

As Alnderby and Dedinder strode toward the gatehouse Joy turned to the director. "Harry, I'm sorry. What a fiasco. I did try."

Far from being upset, Harry threw back his head and gave a shout of his bracing laughter. "It was fine. Absolutely fine. No worries. Sylvia is a genius in the editing room. His own mother won't recognize that interview when Sylvie's through with it. Name and face recognition. That's the celebrity game. No one expects toffs to make sense."

He turned to his crew. "Right, boys and girls. Break. You've earned it. Our lovely Gill," he waved vaguely in the direction of the Outer Court where the catering van was parked, "is sure to have a tasty treat ready for you all."

Antony could only admire Harry's buoyancy. To Antony's mind the morning had been a disaster and the director's earlier expression had indicated he felt the same. But it seemed that nothing got Harry down. Antony thought again of Felicity's questioning whether the Studio Six company might be in financial difficulties—so deep in trouble that Harry could be tempted to an insurance scam of some sort to rescue the company? Seeing Harry's dauntless optimism just now made it seem more impossible than ever to imagine.

Or was Harry as good an actor as some of the thespians he directed?

Antony joined Cynthia, who was already enjoying her lamb curry, at the catering van. "Nice walk this morning?" He asked, letting the steam rise from his beef and mushroom risotto.

"Mmm," she nodded, then swallowed. "Lovely overview of the monastery grounds from the hillside above the wall. Sylvia had to get back for the filming, but Zoe and I wandered all around. I think I quite wore the poor creature out."

Antony barely had time to finish the crusty bread that accompanied his risotto when he was called to a conference with Harry and Fred to discuss camera angles for the interior of the reconstructed cell they would be filming next.

A short time later Antony, at Harry's direction, paused halfway across the Great Cloister to point out what would have been the site of the water tower. "One of the most out-standing aspects of a Carthusian monastery, universal to all Charterhouses, was the provision of good drains and clean drinking water. Mount Grace had a very advanced plumbing system. Three spring houses on the hillside above the priory kept the water tower filled. From here drinking water was piped to each cell by lead pipes. Each cell also had a latrine set over a channel flushed by running water." Antony pointed out the remains of the elaborate plumbing system for the benefit of the camera then moved on across the green.

"This reconstructed cell is like the one the Cloud author

would have occupied." He opened the door, but did not yet enter as he turned back to the camera. "A Carthusian schedule would have allowed our author an hour between nine and ten in the morning for meditation and work—following after five periods of worship and prayer which began at eleven o'clock the night before. Then again, after the office of *None* at noon he would have had until two-thirty at his disposal for writing or gardening.

"That's less than three hours a day for personal contemplation and writing to produce one of the spiritual classics of the western world. It's easy to imagine our scholarly hermit suffering a certain level of frustration when the bell sounded at half two every day, requiring him to say the office of Colloquium privately in his cell before going to the church to sing Vespers. At four o'clock he would return to his cell where a lay brother would bring him the second—and final—meal of the day."

Antony pointed to the small square opening beside the cell door. "Meals were delivered through a hatch so as not to disturb the monk's solitude. At six o'clock he would recite Compline privately in his cell and retire to bed. Before beginning it all over again five hours later. This was an extremely economical schedule, requiring the use of almost no candles even in the dead of winter. It was an ascetic, austere way of life. The Carthusians alone among monastic groups of Western Europe returned to the rigors of the early ideals of the Church Fathers.

"And yet the monk who lived this demanding life is never harsh with his readers, never requires drastic self-denial from those who would pierce the Cloud of Unknowing. He had chosen this stringent lifestyle for himself, but it was not the only way to know God."

Antony opened the arched wooden door and ascended the stairs to the first floor work room, pointing out the spinning wheel and loom, the use of which would have cut further into our hermitic author's daily schedule.

"As would gardening." Antony stepped away from the leaded window for Lenny to capture an overview of the walled garden below, charming even in its winter dormancy. Leading back down the wooden stairs, he continued, "The whole cell is small. There is almost a dolls' house feeling. And it is sparsely furnished, and yet it has a remarkably cozy atmosphere—a very domestic feeling with a study, bedroom, oratory and living room."

The camera panned the tidy bedroom and lingered on the finely carved chest. "The harshness of the monks' required poverty was not necessarily reflected in their buildings and contents. We need to see this in relationship to other religious orders of the time, many of which amassed great wealth, and also in comparison to the higher levels of society, remembering that most of the monks came from the upper classes and would have been accustomed to great luxury at home.

"Still, they enjoyed such amenities as this sturdy fireplace in the living room where a fire would be most welcome on a winter's afternoon when the mists rolled in over the moors." As he spoke Antony turned toward the hearth where a fire had been kindled for the sake of the film.

Antony stopped at the unexpected sight of Zoe snoozing by the fireplace. His mental script fled from his mind. Should he mention the fact that the monks would not have kept pets? The director saved him from having to decide.

"Get that almighty nuisance out of here!" Harry roared.

That should have been enough to dislodge the animal from her snooze, but she didn't so much as flick an ear. "Sylvia, get that blasted dog off my film set!" Harry's ferocity seemed out of proportion to the inconvenience of needing to redo the take.

"Here, girl, come on." Sylvia pushed forward, stooped and ruffled a long, golden ear.

Zoe was unresponsive.

Sylvia drew back with a cry. "She's not breathing! Zoe!" Sylvia threw her arms around her dog and buried her face in the silky amber hair.

Harry charged forward and put a rough hand on his wife's shoulder. "Don't be daft. Come on."

Sylvia jumped to her feet with such force it made every-one else in the small room step back a pace. "She's dead! You killed Zoe! Murderer!" She pounded Harry's chest with both her fists. "I knew you were desperate, but I didn't think even you would stoop this low!"

Sylvia jerked her hands up. Antony thought for a moment she was going to scratch Harry's face with her long nails but instead she covered her own face with her hands to stifle her sobs.

Harry stood there helplessly. Antony was wondering if he should do something. The blessing of animals was a fairly common practice, although he had never conducted such a service. Was there such a thing as last rites for pets? Certainly a prayer for the bereaved owner would be in order.

He was saved from action, however, by Cynthia entering from the hall. "What happened?" Her voice was shrill with anxiety over the dog she had so recently been walking.

Without waiting for an answer she knelt by the prone Golden Retriever and put her head to the soft chest. "There's a heartbeat." She struggled to get her arms under the animal. "Help me. We need to get her to a vet."

Sylvia fell to her knees beside Cynthia with a cry and the two women struggled to lift the dead weight of the animal. "Here," Antony pulled the pewter candlestick and mug from the trestle table and lifted the top. "Use this."

Harry turned to help Sylvia place Zoe's limp form on the stretcher, but Sylvia spat at him, "Don't you dare touch her! I can't believe even you could stoop so low."

Antony and Fred helped the women with their burden, but after a few steps Antony halted. "Wait. Lenny, take Sylvia's corner. Sylvia, is your car in the park?" She nodded. "Good. Drive it up to the door of the manor house." Sylvia gave a jerk of a nod and set off running across the Great Cloister.

Cynthia took her place in the back seat with Zoe's comatose head nestled on her lap, then looked up at Antony standing by helplessly. "You may as well come with us. You can't drive the hire car and I may be hours."

His door was barely closed when Sylvia drove off, her tires spinning gravel behind her.

# CHAPTER 22

## *New Year's Eve*

The next morning Felicity, sitting up in bed sipping the morning tea her mother had brought her, listened, wide-eyed, as Cynthia recounted her adventure of the night before. Antony had rung late in the evening to tell Felicity of the startling scene and to let her know not to wait up for her mother.

"Is Zoe all right?" Felicity asked, indicating that Cynthia should make herself comfortable beside her on the bed.

"Yes, thank goodness. That gorgeous creature. Who on earth would want to harm her?"

"Did the vet think it was done on purpose?" Felicity set her half-drunk tea aside.

Cynthia spread her hands. "How do you prove a thing like that? The drug was most likely Acepromazine—I think that's what the vet called it. It's apparently a widely used calmative for animals, but can be dangerous. Especially in high doses. The vet thought Zoe might have eaten double the safe limit."

"So she could have died?"

"Probably would have if we hadn't got her to the vet."

"Mom, you saved Zoe's life. You're a heroine!" Felicity leaned over and hugged her mother, then flung herself back on her pillows. "Oh, how frustrating that I wasn't there! I might have seen something, heard something..."

"Antony was just trying to protect you, darling."

"Oh, I know. He wants to wrap me in cotton wool. It's very sweet, of course, but it won't work. I'll go cross-eyed if I can't be up and doing."

Felicity started to fling her duvet off but Cynthia smoothed the covers back over her. "There's nothing to do at the moment. You can get up when Charlie and Judy arrive. Here," she put the china mug back in her daughter's hands, "finish this."

Felicity took an obedient sip. "But who would do such a thing to a dog? This is England, they idolize their pets."

Cynthia nodded. "Yes, I couldn't help noticing that Sylvia became hysterical over her dog, but seemed to take Tara's death in her stride."

"Does anyone have any idea how it happened? Zoe, I mean."

Cynthia sighed. "Not really, but something worries me. Sylvia said to let her run in the gardens after our walk. She didn't eat anything in the woods, so it must have happened after that. I did see someone walking there when I was on the hillside, but there was no reason to think they were up to no good."

"Do you have any idea who it was?"

Cynthia shook her head. "I wouldn't think it was any of the film crew."

Felicity nodded. "Besides, why would any of them want to harm Zoe? Everyone adores her, she's the company mascot." Felicity thought for a moment, then answered her own question. "Someone with a grudge against Harry, maybe?

Someone who wants to stop the film? Someone who blames him for Tara's death? Antony said Lenny seemed really fond of her."

"The one built like a wrestler? I'm pretty sure he was out behind the church with all the others. It looked like everyone wanted to observe that bit of the filming."

Felicity nodded. "Yes, Antony told me about Dr. Dedinder's interview. He was still fuming about it." She smiled. "I suppose it could have been someone from the catering van, Antony mentioned they were out front."

"They were, but the person I saw seemed taller than Gill. And I think it was a man."

"That would leave Savannah out, too. I think the grips sometimes help out with catering. Did you see Mike anywhere?"

Cynthia laughed. "Goodness, I don't know those people. Sylvia called the police, so if someone was sowing the garden with poisoned food, they might find something. I suppose it could have been put there long before we arrived, even."

"Yes, I remember reading the news when someone put marshmallows filled with rat poison in the park in Leeds. Horrible." Felicity shivered. "But what did Sylvia say about Harry? Antony said she was hysterical. Do you think Harry killed Tara? Did you learn anything about the company? Could Harry be pulling an insurance scam?"

"Darling, do you still have that insurance scam bee in your bonnet? Surely you're reaching—"

"What insurance scam? Can I get in on it?" A rich male voice asked from the doorway.

"Charlie!" Felicity just missed flinging her tea at her mother in her excitement to get to the newcomer. She bolted over the end of her bed and launched herself into the arms of the brother she hadn't seen for three years. "When did you get here? Why didn't we hear you knock? Did Gwen let you in? Where's Judy?"

"I'm right here," a voice from the hall was followed by the entrance of Felicity's sister-in-law.

Felicity squealed and hugged her, "You're gorgeous!" She ran her hand down Judy's long, redgold hair as Charlie moved on into the room to greet his mom.

"And enormous." Judy patted her rounded belly. "I wasn't sure they'd let me on the plane—or that I'd fit once they did. I think I had the seat belt out as far as it would go."

Felicity grinned. "Yeah, you really are blooming. Don't worry, though, we can let the bridesmaid's dress out if we need to."

Gwena appeared in the hall. "I've got tea in the living room when you want it."

"Yes, shoo—everyone out and let me get dressed. Go get acquainted with your future sister-in-law. She's great. I'll join you in a minute." Felicity ushered everyone out of her crowded room.

A few minutes later, feeling the best she had since her encounter in the quarry and with her hair still damp from its first real shampoo, Felicity joined her family to hear the details of their flight from San Francisco and all the latest news from Silicone Valley where Charlie worked as a high-level computer engineer.

Judy, who had done some acting in college, hit it off immediately with Gwena. "Farce? Oh, how fun! What have you done?" Gwena launched into an animated account of her role as the sexy psychiatrist's wife in an upcoming production of "What the Butler Saw" and Judy burst into gales of laughter.

Felicity sipped her tea and looked around the snug little room. It seemed as though this family thing might work out all right after all. She knew Antony had been especially worried, wanting everyone to get on well and knowing his own clashes with his sister—not to mention Felicity's with her mother.

As if her thoughts had conjured him up, a knock at the door announced Antony's arrival. He entered the already crowded room followed by a slightly shorter, darker, more serious-looking version of Charlie. "Found this fellow on the pavement. Claims he's part of the family." Antony grinned.

For the second time that day Felicity squealed and flung herself into the arms of a brother she hadn't seen for years. "Jeff, why didn't you let us know? We didn't know when you'd get here. It's so good to see you! How do you like London?" She pulled him into the room and introduced him to Gwena.

Jeff seemed very pleased to meet this striking English-woman who would soon be his sister-in-law. After giving his mother a warm hug he squeezed in beside her on the sofa and Antony brought in a chair from the kitchen table. Before Jeff sat, though Judy scrambled up from the depths of her chair to give him a hug, then laughed when her bump got in the way.

"Right. Meet your almost nephew. He's definitely making his presence known. I'm afraid it's a warning."

When everyone was settled Cynthia and her sons dominated the conversation, catching up on family news.

Except for the piece of news Felicity most wanted to hear. She noted that Jeff and Charlie avoided the topic of their father, just as she had been doing for days, while asking their mother about her legal practice instead. Andrew was definitely becoming the elephant in the room. The wedding rehearsal was in three days. Would her father be here to walk her down the aisle or should she ask Jeff? She needed to know.

"Now, what's this about an insurance scam?" Charlie's question broke in on Felicity's reverie.

"Insurance scam?" Jeff asked.

"Long story," Felicity replied. "Do you want the details, or are you too jet lagged?"

"No, no. I slept on the plane," Charlie replied, then turned to his wife. "Poor Judy, though. I don't think she ever got comfortable." He gave her a consoling pat.

But Jeff wasn't to be distracted. "Tell us what's going on."

"Yes, with your business acumen, and Charlie's computer skills you may be just what we need. You see, Antony's helping this film company with a mini-series—"

"For my sins," Antony muttered as he reached for a teacup, then found the pot empty.

"Time for another round." Cynthia and Gwena were on their feet together. The morning moved on to another round of tea, this one with bacon and eggs for everyone except Judy who turned slightly green at the suggestion and stayed with nibbling dry toast. "They gave us breakfast Paninis on the airplane." Judy shuddered. "They had some sort of yellow glue they called cheese."

"Let me know when you're ready for a lie-down and I'll take you up to the house where you'll be staying," Antony said. "A married ordinand—an American, actually—has taken his family home to Texas for the holiday and offered their home for our wedding guests."

"Oh, how lovely. How about now?"

It was mid afternoon before Jeff, Charlie and Antony returned to the cottage from settling Judy and their luggage in their borrowed accommodations, leaving Cynthia in attendance on the mother of her first grandchild. Gwena had gone off to confer with Kendra about final details for the dress rehearsal, accompanied with appropriate reminders from Felicity to be careful—they still didn't know who was lurking about out there hitting people over the head. Or why.

That left Felicity, Antony and her brothers alone to tell Jeff and Charlie about the mysteries, mishaps and possible murders surrounding the film-making and the pageant. "You mentioned insurance?" Charlie asked.

Felicity explained. "We can't make any sense out of any of it. But we did wonder if Studio Six might be in dire need of funds." She grinned at her brothers. "Maybe if you two combined your talents you might be able to find something out for us."

Jeff, two years older than Charlie, more somber and with none of Felicity's full steam ahead impetuosity, frowned. "And you think that might have something to do with someone running Antony off the road and assaulting you and maybe even killing people? Look, this is serious business. You shouldn't be mixed up in it. Aren't the police on the case?"

"Of course they are," Felicity replied. "If we learn anything we'll tell them."

"I don't think—" Jeff began.

But Charlie, his eyes sparkling, cut him off. "What do you want to know? Exactly?"

Felicity sighed. "If we knew that we probably wouldn't need to ask. But it would be useful to know if Studio Six is solvent. Or might their director Harry Forslund be desperate for money—desperate enough to run an insurance scam, for instance."

"Ah, so there's the insurance angle," Charlie said.

"That's something else we need to know. Can you even get insurance on a dog?"

Now it was Charlie's turn to frown. "For enough to bail a company out of bankruptcy? Who is this dog—Lassie?"

Felicity made a face at her brother. "Just see what you can find out. Okay? Maybe you can come up with a better theory."

"Why someone might want to hit you over the head? I can't imagine." Charlie ducked as she threw a sofa pillow at him.

Jeff gave his slow grin with an air of submission. "All right. Where's your computer?"

Felicity gave a hoot of triumph and led them to her room. She settled on the bed across from her desk, where she would have a clear view of the computer screen. "Out." Jeff pointed at the door.

"But I could help. You might not recognize the leads..."

Jeff gave her a strong-eyed stare. The same one he had used long ago to control a pesky ten-year-old sister. She scrambled off her bed and closed the door behind her.

Antony, waiting in the hall, laughed. "Ah, I'll have to get Jeff to teach me that technique."

But in the end Felicity and Antony spent the time more pleasantly snuggled on the sofa. It was getting dark outside the windows when the brothers emerged. Felicity jumped up. "What did you learn? Did you find anything? Is Harry broke? Should we tell the police?" She cut off her own flow at the sight of the smug smirks on their faces. "You didn't do anything illegal did you?"

"Little sister, we love you but there are limits to even our devotion." Jeff took the chair by the Christmas tree.

"Actually, it wasn't necessary to do any hacking. Jeff knew where to look." Charlie sounded just the least bit disappointed.

"So?" Felicity sat on the edge of the sofa.

"Pet insurance is readily available everywhere in England —even at the super market. But only liability and health. If Zoe is insured, her owner will be able to recover the vet fees," Charlie said.

"Or if she had bitten someone and they sued, the policy holder would be covered," Jeff added.

"But not if she died?"

Jeff shook his head. "Nothing I could find for a normal household pet. Maybe, like Charlie suggested, if she were Lassie."

Felicity sighed and slumped back on the sofa. "No, just a lovely, beloved pet. So much for that theory."

"And did you find anything on Studio Six?" Antony asked Jeff.

"From what I could find out the company is solvent. Just. Looking at the figures I could turn up I'd say they could be on the brink, but haven't fallen over yet."

"So not bad enough for Harry to be running a scam?" Felicity asked.

Jeff considered. "I would think it's more likely to make him very, very anxious that his project succeed. Rather than putting everything at risk by trying something illegal."

"So not likely to be sabotaging his own enterprise," Antony said.

"Did you learn anything about his recent projects? Did they pay?" Felicity asked.

Jeff nodded. "A little. Assuming the figures they've made public are legit. It would take a full audit to be absolutely certain."

Then Felicity jerked forward. "Or maybe it means he *has* been running a scam and has been successful so far."

Jeff grinned. "Remember Occam's razor? The simplest explanation is usually the correct one."

"Meaning?" She challenged.

"Meaning maybe it's what it looks like—that he's just marginally successful with his documentaries and historical mini-series. It is possible."

"Yes, but if he isn't." Felicity wasn't letting go. Not yet. She had heard a passing reference to a director's job in Australia. Could Harry be looking for an excuse to emigrate? "Could he be trying to make the series fail on purpose?"

Jeff shook his head. "Not unless he has some ulterior motive we haven't thought of. Not for insurance, at least."

"You can't get insurance on a film?" Felicity's voice was heavy with incredulity.

"Of course you can. The coverage for media projects is endless." Jeff counted them off on his fingers. "Negative and videotapes, nonappearance of cast, producers indemnity, filming equipment, props, sets and wardrobe, employer's liability, public liability, errors and omissions, fire, flood..."

Felicity held up her hand. "Okay. I get it. In short, disaster and liability insurance, but no insurance against the film flopping."

"You got it."

"So there would be absolutely no reason for Harry to sabotage his own film." Felicity threw up her hands. She had been so certain they had solved the puzzle. At least that part of the conundrum. Where could they look now? She was convinced something was going on. There had been far too many calamities around that project to write it off to simple human error or bad luck.

"You're certain there isn't anything?" She looked from one brother to the other. There it was again, that look passed between Jeff and Charlie that could best be described only as a leer. "What? You did find something, didn't you? Tell us!"

Charlie's cat-with-the-cream look turned to a genuine smile, but before he could speak Cynthia, Judy and Gwena came in, full of plans for the evening.

"It's almost New Year's Eve!" Cynthia breezed down the hall and pulled an apron from the cupboard even before Judy, followed by Gwena had the front door closed. "I'll make my traditional spaghetti." Cynthia grinned at her three grown-up children. "You always loved it when you were little. Do you remember?"

Felicity boggled. Certainly she remembered. Vividly. She remembered her father in an oversized chef's apron wafting a wooden spoon. *Come here, Muffin. Tell me if I've got enough oregano in this.* She did recall, however, that her mother usually marked the holiday by coming out of her office long enough to eat Andrew's spaghetti with them. Sometimes she even stayed with them to watch the Times Square celebrations on the television.

Felicity gave her brothers a meaningful look. Jeff was first on his feet. "It sounds great, Mom. I'll give you a hand."

Felicity swallowed, remembering her father's scratchy beard on her cheek when he kissed her happy New Year but stuffed it away as she got to her feet to follow them into the kitchen.

Antony, with a worried look on his face, came into the kitchen to ask what time Cynthia was planning to have dinner. "Oh, the sauce should simmer for at least an hour. Are you going to be too hungry to wait?"

"No, that's perfect. I, uh—well, it's the first evensong for the Naming and Circumcision of Jesus." He pointed in the direction of the monastery.

Cynthia looked up from the onion she was slicing. "You what?"

Gwena came into the room behind him. "Sheesh. You priests are never off duty, are you? What a way to spend New Year's Eve."

Antony held up his hands. "Sorry. I don't want to put a damper on anyone's celebrating."

His sister laughed. "No worries. Actually, Squib, I think I'll go with you."

Antony stared. "Are you serious?"

"Of course I am. Everyone knows high church liturgy is the best theatre in town. You'll have to give me absolution for coveting your costumes, though."

"They're vestments." Antony said it almost under his breath but he gave his sister a wide smile. "Great, fifteen minutes, then? Anyone else want to go?" He made the invitation general. "No pressure."

In the end everyone but Cynthia, who stayed home to oversee the simmering of her sauce, chose to bundle into their coats and trek to the community church. Felicity slipped her arm through Antony's and smiled all the way up the hill. So soon she would be holding the same arm walking back down the church aisle as Mrs. Antony Sherwood.

If the monks had realized that at least one of their

congregation would be coming purely for the spectacle they couldn't have done a better job of being sure not to disappoint her, beginning with the prelude from Bach's Christmas Oratorio. Then the procession as the congregation sang "At the Name of Jesus." It seemed that the thurifer produced an entire cumulus of incense and the white and gold vestments, especially Father Anselm's sumptuously embroidered cope, were especially luminous in the candlelight. Or maybe it was just Felicity's state of euphoria as wedding visions morphed with the service before her.

The acclamations and responses followed on cue. "Unto thy name give praise, O Lord," then Scripture readings, canticles and prayers proceeded through their stately pace: "Almighty God, whose blessed Son was circumcised in obedience to the law for our sake and given the Name that is above every name: give us grace faithfully to bear his Name..." Father Anselm led them in the Collect of the Day followed by the Collect for Aid against all Perils, "Lighten our darkness, we beseech thee, O Lord; and by thy great mercy defend us from all perils and dangers of this night..."

Felicity was still smiling as they stood and sang the recessional, "All Hail the Power of Jesus' Name." Perils and Dangers were behind them. Surely they were. She breathed an additional prayer that it would be so, then hurried out to catch up with their departing guests.

Her smile widened as she heard Gwena say, "That gold cape thingy alone was almost enough to make a convert of me."

They were at the top of the stairs leading down the hill to the community gate when it began. Felicity shouldn't have been surprised, the amazing fireworks display of Christmas

Eve was still fresh in her mind, but still it was startling and thrilling when seemingly the entire hillside on the other side of the river came alive with a wall of orange and red flame. Popping and fizzing, skyrockets sailed into the sky, the entire scene multiplied in its effect by the misty cloud cover that amplified and reflected every spark and flare like a series of mirrors, turning the night to daylight.

Gwena gave the first joyous shout and flung out her arms, connecting with Jeff who stood beside her and ending in a hug that must have come close to knocking him off his feet. Felicity turned to Antony and copied Gwen's example. A moment later the whole group was running down the hill, except for the very pregnant Judy who was being escorted by her attentive husband with great care.

It seemed that the fireworks not only lit the night, but warmed it as well. And brought all the neighbors out of their homes to run up and down the street shouting "Happy New Year!" Felicity had never before experienced such a sense of camaraderie with people she didn't know in all her time in England. It was like one of those block parties one saw in news accounts of the Queen's Jubilee or something.

They crossed the main road and were about to turn into Nab Lane when a particularly bright rocket bursting just over their head illumined a dark passage behind the corner shop and Felicity recognized a familiar silhouette. "Syd! Happy New Year!" She called and waved.

But the shape did not return her greeting. Perhaps he hadn't heard her. If he had merely continued walking away she would have thought no more of it. It was the furtive manner with which he slipped behind the building that aroused her suspicions. "Antony!" She pulled him aside. "That was Syd. I'm sure of it. And up to no good, I'll wager."

"No, Felicity, wait."

But it was too late, she was already concealing herself behind the hedge that bordered the walk. She put a finger to her lips and mimed for Antony to be quiet, but with the fireworks exploding all around them it was hardly necessary. She peered over the top of the bushes in time to see another form step from the shadows to meet Syd. She ducked down again. "It's Harry," she hissed. "What's he doing here? Why is Syd meeting him?"

Felicity risked one more look over the protecting vegetation, then dropped to her knees with a gasp. They were coming her way. It was too late to run or to hide. She grabbed Antony, pulled him to the ground on top of her and planted an enormous kiss on his face. She was aiming for his lips, but somewhat missed her target. Antony didn't seem to object, however, as he folded his arms around her.

She waited until the footsteps on the pavement were well past them before sitting up.

But she didn't get up. She leaned against the solid, if scratchy, hedge as she played the scene again in her mind. "We were wrong, Antony. Not an insurance fiddle. Drugs. I'm sure I just witnessed a drugs deal."

"Harry?" The glow of the fiery sky made Antony's normally pale face look flushed.

She nodded. "We must have been right about Studio Six needing money. And that's how Harry was getting it." She jumped to her feet, pulling Antony after her. "Come on. We need to call Inspector Nosterfield or somebody."

They were nearly back to the cottage when a dark figure

standing on the sidewalk outside the garden made Felicity stop so abruptly Antony almost tripped over her. Had Harry spotted them? Was he waiting to silence them before they could ring the police?

Felicity looked around frantically for a place to hide, but there was nothing. The dormant bushes bordering the narrow front garden offered no shelter. Nothing to do but face him. Surely even a truly desperate man wouldn't attack her ten feet from her own front door.

A trio of gold and silver rockets exploded over their heads just as a clutch of youth from the centre ran by, calling New Year's greetings to everyone and to no one.

The man on the pavement turned. Felicity gasped. "Dad!" She hurled herself at him with a joyous cry.

"Oh, Dad, I didn't think you'd come! I was so afraid...! Oh, I'm so glad you're here!" She muffled her face in his shoulder as another missile went off with an enormous bang.

"What nonsense. Of course I wouldn't miss my chance to walk you down the aisle, Muffin." Then he held out the hand that wasn't gripping Felicity. "You must be Antony. I'm Andrew."

"Come in. Everyone's here. You won't believe it. Mom's made spaghetti." Felicity pulled both men toward the cottage, its wide front window reflecting the fireworks.

Felicity's happy New Year had begun.

# CHAPTER 23

Felicity woke late the next morning with a hammer pounding her head. That was unfair. She had toasted in the New Year with Martinelli's—or rather, what the English called Schloer—which she couldn't say without laughing because it made one sound drunk even when only consuming sparkling grape juice.

Then on the stroke of midnight, as Big Ben chimed on the television, Gwena, who was stage-managing everything, ran to open the back door. "Got to let the old year out!" she cried, then stuck a broom in Antony's hands. "Here, Squib, your honors—you've the darkest hair. Even if I wouldn't call you tall and handsome. At least you're strange enough."

"Thanks," he said and took the broom obediently.

And they had all followed Antony as he vigorously swung the broom, backing from the open front door through the cottage to the back, sweeping the New Year in and the old year out. Felicity put her hand to her throbbing head. It would have been all right if Gwen had merely concluded with their rather raucous singing of "Auld Lang Syne" but then she pulled all the pots and pans from Felicity's cupboard and insisted they march through the house—and around the garden—repeatedly—banging pots and lids. Felicity was certain her cooking utensils would never be the same again.

"Why are we doing this?" Antony had demanded on the second loop through the cottage. "We didn't do this as kids."

Gwena laughed above the ruckus. "Can you imagine Aunt Beryl allowing such a thing? I learned it when we had a long run in Stoke—it's to scare the devil out the back door."

Felicity saw Antony's grimace at that. He was undoubtedly thinking their annual house blessing at Epiphany was more to the point. But the clatter had continued.

As it did now in Felicity's head. She had to admit, though, it had been a New Year's Eve she would never forget. Especially when the pot-banging procession marched down the hall past the living room and she had glanced in to discover her parents sitting very close to one another on the couch in the glow of the now-drooping Christmas tree with the light of distant fireworks illuminating their shared smiles.

A pounding head was a small price to pay for that sight.

Felicity was wondering whether to make the attempt to get out of bed when Gwena came in with a tea tray. "Ready for a cuppa?"

Felicity reached for a mug. "Just what my head needs. I've never welcomed in a new year like that."

Gwen sipped and leaned back in her hair. "Fun, huh? Only thing we missed was having a tall, handsome stranger carry a lump of coal over the doorstep." She was quiet for a moment. "That brother of yours would qualify."

"Jeff? He's all right, isn't he?" Felicity hadn't thought of either of her brothers in those terms.

"More than all right, I'd say. What about the women in his life?"

Felicity raised an eyebrow. So that's what Gwen was getting at. "I don't have any idea about anything current. He's always been such a workaholic. I suppose he got that from our mother. Shall I enquire?"

"No, don't bother. I like a bit of mystery. And competition." Gwen gave her a saucy grin.

A knock at the door announced the arrival of Felicity's family which necessitated bringing out the slightly battered frying pan. "Scrambled all right for everyone?" Cynthia pulled a bowl of lovely brown eggs out of the refrigerator as Felicity dug in the back for a package of bacon and Gwen filled the electric kettle. Felicity took secret pleasure in watching Cynthia serve Andrew. Then she smiled as Gwena seemed to take delight in making a special pot of coffee for Jeff who requested that rather than tea. All that reminded Felicity to put a few slices of bacon aside for Antony who would be joining them after mass.

Antony's arrival was later than she had anticipated, however, and the bacon had long gone cold. "No worries, I'll just have a butty," he said.

Felicity put the bacon between two slices of buttered bread and handed it to him. "I thought you'd be here ages ago. Is everything all right?"

"I hope so. I've been swatting up Walter Hilton for tomorrow. Haven't taught him for donkey's years. Think I've got it down now, though."

Jeff and Charlie drifted back into the kitchen from where they had been visiting with everyone in the living room. Their entrance reminded Felicity of their unfinished conversation from the day before. "All right, you two. I still want to know the meaning of those supercilious looks you were exchanging yesterday." Felicity started a fresh pot of coffee for her brothers.

"Well, it might be nothing," Jeff began.

"You didn't look like nothing yesterday," Felicity insisted.

"Thing is, I was typing fast—" Charlie began.

"Stop making excuses, we all know it was Freudian," Jeff interrupted with a smirk.

Charlie grinned in return. "Okay, so I somehow searched for Studio Sex rather than Studio Six."

"And something turned up?" Felicity asked.

"Your firewall warned me I might not want to go there. Then I knew I did." His brother started to jeer. "To the website, I mean."

"So what is it, a massage parlor?"

"No, it's a film studio." Now Charlie's lighthearted leers turned to a grimace.

"Porn, you mean?" Felicity prodded.

Jeff nodded. "Afraid so."

"But that doesn't mean..."

"No, but there's more. Thing is, Jeff checked the company's registration. It's in the name of H. F. Lund. Awfully close to be a coincidence, don't you think?"

"Harry Forslund?" Felicity frowned. It sounded plausible. She turned to Antony. "What do you think? Would Harry drug Sylvia's dog to get her out of the way so he could shoot porn?"

"I suppose it's possible. Certainly as good as any other theory we've come up with." Antony paused, then shook his head. "Does that mean Harry killed Tara?"

"Because she found out what he was up to? Maybe tried a bit of blackmail? Threatened to tell Sylvia, for example?"

"Interesting speculation. But that's all it is," Jeff reminded them.

Antony nodded. "We're still missing something. It doesn't seem like all the pieces fit."

"It still seems worth a call to Nosterfield," Felicity said.

But before Antony could ring the police his mobile rang. He looked at the name on the screen. "Melissa Egbert. I wonder what she wants." He stepped into the hall before taking the call.

He was back in the kitchen a few minutes later. "You'll never guess. She thinks she might have found Father Paulinus' notes."

"You mean they weren't destroyed by the fire? Where did she find them? What do they say?"

Antony explained briefly to Felicity's brothers about the fire that killed the monk whose role as guide to the miniseries Antony had then been drafted in to fill. Then back to Melissa, "When she was here before she mentioned she would be going to Ampleforth—research on some article she was working on. I mentioned the doodles I found in an early copy of *The Cloud of Unknowing*."

Antony smiled. "It seems they must have been a clue. As least she said she found what appears to be Paulinus's notebook shelved with a book by J. Peacock. I think it was Paulinus's joke. She was very clever to figure it out. I certainly didn't."

Felicity tried to recall what she knew about Melissa's work. "She told me she was intrigued to learn how one family had hung onto the Rievaulx lands for so long. Could there have been something in Father Paulinus's notes about that?"

"She said she's not sure how to interpret them, but if she's right it could be important. That was all she'd say on the telephone. That's why she wants to meet."

"You mean she has the notes? She took them out of the library? Stole them?" Felicity was shocked.

Antony spread his hands. "Or copied them. Or photographed, or something. I didn't quiz her. I just agreed to meet and look them over."

"She's coming here?"

"No, she had some family do on this afternoon. I suggested we meet tomorrow after my filming at Thurgarton."

"I wonder what she can have found?"

"I don't know, but she sounded excited. Whatever it is, she's convinced it's important."

"Great, I'm going with you. I can't wait to see what she found." Felicity's mind was racing. "Do you realize this could be the key to the whole thing? You just said we were missing a piece of the puzzle. The cost of keeping up an estate like that must be phenomenal today. I saw a program about that on the BBC not too long ago—all the things they have to do. Creating tourist attractions and selling farm produce and all that. Maybe Harry is working for the Duncombe family. There can be a lot of money in drugs and porn, can't there?"

Jeff was practically convulsed with laughter by the time his sister stopped for a breath. "You're wasted in ministry, Sis. You should be writing fiction. Do you realize you just took bits from unrelated sources and spun all of that out of thin air?"

Felicity tossed her head. "I don't care what you say. I want to read those notes."

Antony didn't protest, but it wouldn't have mattered if he had. It was settled in Felicity's mind. If Father Paulinus had found out about Harry's extracurricular work and now Melissa was going to share that information with Antony—practically under Harry's nose—there was no way Felicity was going to let Antony go alone onto the film set of a man who had already killed three times.

# CHAPTER 24

Antony took a deep breath and looked into the camera. "Today we are at Thurgarton Priory where Walter Hilton wrote his spiritual masterpiece. Hilton is a most unusual man: a monk who was also a lawyer; a lawyer who was also a mystic." Antony paused to smile.

"Hilton is often cited as the most practical and accessible of the mystics. The very title many editors have applied to his major work *The Ladder of Perfection* implies concreteness, an orderly ascent in easy steps to progress in the spiritual life." The pale midmorning sun hadn't yet melted the tiny jewels of frost that sparkled on the ragged winter grass where Antony stood on the lawn beside Thurgarton church.

Their journey that morning had taken over an hour and a half, the longest they had traveled for a filming, but much of it had been on the M1 and Antony never failed to admire Cynthia's efficient, if fast, driving. It was with a sense of enormous relief that he delivered his prepared speech on Walter Hilton, the last of the English mystics they would be covering for the series. If all went well this would be his final day of filming. Antony couldn't believe the sense of relief that thought gave him. He was determined to stay on track and get his part finished as efficiently as possible.

Antony turned to view the church. "Only a fraction of the ancient Priory Church remains today. The old priory was taken down in the mid-eighteenth century and the owner erected the present mansion on its site, the cellars of which are the only portions of the religious sanctuary that now remain." Antony waited while Fred turned Ginger's eye on the fine red brick stately home which abutted the church.

When Ginger pointed again at the tower of the church Antony continued. "What you see here is the Priory Church of St. Peter, the southwest tower of what was originally a pair of such structures, built in the thirteenth century. Even though it's only a fraction of the original, there is still much that Walter Hilton would recognize from the busy days he spent here. And it's still a magnificent structure, rising six stories from the green lawn." Antony pointed, inviting the camera to pan the height. "Each level is pierced by a series of Gothic arches in what students of church architecture would identify as the Perpendicular style.

"To the south, where they would have caught the warmth on sunny days, would have been the cloisters, dormitory for the sixty members of the community, the prior's lodging, kitchen and chapter house where the canons would have gathered daily to hear a chapter read to them from the Augustinian Rule they followed and to conduct business."

Out of the corner of his eye Antony caught a gesture from Harry that he interpreted to mean "get on with it." Well, he was giving them the facts. Sylvia could always edit it. But he obediently shifted his focus, "Just four years after Wycliffe began pronouncing against religious orders, which he called 'sects,' and agitating for their abolition, Walter Hilton, at the age of 43, joined the order of Augustinian Canons here at Thurgarton Priory."

Antony began walking slowly toward the church. "They followed the Rule of St. Augustine, which, while requiring a life of poverty, celibacy, and obedience, allowed sufficient flexibility that canons could follow either active or contemplative vocations. Unlike fully professed monks who were strictly confined within a monastery, canons could, and very frequently did, undertake outside work.

"This must have been exactly right for Walter who was trained for an active life in the law courts and yet was drawn to the contemplative life, and even as a contemplative, spent so much of his time busily engaged in writing and giving spiritual direction. He may even have continued with his legal practice.

"During the time Walter was here the Prior of Thurgarton was appointed to examine those suspected of Lollardry, so it is possible Walter himself took part in these enquiries as a lawyer.

"It takes very little imagination to envision the vigorous figure Hilton must have been, striding forward, brisk, erect, assured, in a black robe—they were known as the 'Black Canons.' One can almost see him now with light hair, a long, straight nose, firm mouth and luminous eyes moving swiftly along the sandstone cloister of the priory, perhaps coming from Mass or the Divine Office which held central place in the life of the Community, or maybe coming from giving spiritual direction to a seeker, or even legal advice to his Prior.

"But whatever was behind him, Walter's active mind

would be looking forward to reaching the solitude of the undercroft of the Priory where he could get back to his writing.

"Is he on his way to answer a letter requesting spiritual guidance, such as his Latin *Letter to Someone Wanting to Renounce the World* addressed to a lawyer who, like himself, had experienced a religious awakening? Or perhaps today he will work on the English version of one of the many works he is translating, such as the *Eight Chapters on Perfection*? Or one of his Biblical commentaries, especially on the Psalms? Or is he thinking of the spiritual advice he would write to the anchoress to whom he was addressing his great work that was to become *The Ladder of Perfection*?

"Whatever might have been in his thoughts at any one time, we can be sure his mind was never idle, because his output was enormous, especially for one who had chosen an active order that embraced work in the world alongside a life of prayer, contemplation and writing."

Antony crossed the grass to the heavy, wooden door under the tower of the church. He pointed out the intricate zigzag design in the Gothic arch surrounding the door, then produced an ancient heavy, black iron key and unlocked the door. But before Antony could enter the cool, dark interior Harry called a break for lunch. Antony was more than happy for a respite. His throat felt parched and breakfast seemed like it had been hours ago. Probably because it had been. He walked toward the catering van where he hoped he'd find Cynthia and Felicity.

Before he reached the van, however, he was greeted by a beautiful blond that wasn't Felicity. Zoe bounded around the end of the high brick wall that shielded the private lands from the public and raced toward him, her golden hair gleaming in the sun. "Hello, girl," he stroked her glossy head. "Am I glad to see you!"

Cynthia followed, slightly out of breath. "I promised Sylvia I wouldn't let her out of my sight, but I can't keep up with her. I was afraid Sylvia wouldn't trust me to take her walkies again."

"She looks fully recovered."

"She's full of energy. We have to be careful that she drinks plenty of fresh water, though. It's probably time to give her another drink now." Cynthia led to the back of the caravan where she found Zoe's bowl, emptied it and refilled it with fresh water from a hosepipe there.

That made Antony even thirstier, so he got two bottles of water from Gill and gave one to Cynthia. "I thought Felicity would be with you."

"She was, but she went off with that reporter before Zoe and I went on our walk."

"Melissa?" He looked around, but didn't see either of the young women. "She must have gotten here earlier than I expected. But that's fine. Felicity may be more help with Paulinus's notes than I can be. Do you know where they went?"

"Felicity said she'd be back for lunch. She and Melissa went to the Red Lion on the Southwell Road. Melissa said there was someone she needed to see who was driving down from the north for a meeting." She paused and frowned. "Some kind of association. No, that's not right. Cooperative, maybe?" She shrugged. "Something like that."

"Another interview for her article?"

"I suppose. She seems to think her series could be something rather big. I thought it was just some historical piece, but she sounds more like an investigative reporter. Do the English have something like the Pulitzer Prize for newspaper articles?" Cynthia asked.

"A Press Association award, maybe? Not the prestige of a Pulitzer, but nice. No wonder she's so intense, though. Sounds like she's aiming for the big time."

Just then a pair of arms encircled him from the back, engulfing him in a big squeeze. "Ha, gotcha," Felicity crowed.

He turned in her arms and returned a proper hug. "Just in time for lunch. Or did you eat with Melissa?"

"No, I just walked her to the pub. She had an appointment. Said she'd just have a drink, then meet me back here for lunch. So I picked up this great footpath map and came back by way of Robin Hood's barn."

"Given that we're in Nottinghamshire, that could be literal." Antony guided them back to the catering van where Gill was handing out mouthwatering kebabs.

"All right, back to work." Savannah, the best boy, called them to order. Observing her saucy manner, a new thought struck Antony. If Harry was making porn films, how many of his crew were involved? Was it possible that the nubile best boy took her clothes off in front of the camera after hours? Antony shook his head to clear the thought. That was the trouble once one started down the path of suspicion—one could suspect almost anyone of almost anything. *Whatsoever things are true, whatsoever things are pure, whatsoever things are of good report, think on these things,* he admonished himself.

Sylvia scrutinized Antony, then apparently decided he was camera-worthy. "Right, go ahead and set the scene inside the church, then you can finish up with a summary of Walter's philosophy. There's a memorial plaque to Hilton on one of the pillars. I want you standing by that when you talk about the Ladder. It's a rather fetching engraving of him, should have viewer appeal. Then Joy will interview the parish priest about what their ties to Hilton mean to the parish today."

Antony obediently took his place just inside the door he had opened earlier and turned to face Ginger. The lights Lenny and his crew had arranged that morning came on and Antony opened his mouth. "Wait, I'm getting a shadow across your face," Fred called. "Take one step back and two to your right."

Antony did so and felt the light fall across his face. Fred was good. And pleasant to work with. But did he moonlight filming porn? Again, Antony pushed the thought away. *Focus*, he ordered himself. "The church was restored in the nineteenth century and a useable parish church was created from the medieval fragments of what had once been a magnificent structure ringing to the sound of Gregorian Chant."

He moved down what had formerly been merely a side aisle of the now much-reduced church. "Three of these pillars were part of the original twelfth century nave. In Hilton's day pairs of pillars would have proceeded in stately procession beyond the present chancel up a great aisle, past a transept, to the quire where the sixty resident canons would have chanted the Divine Office eight times a day. There would have then been a chapel extending to the east beyond that." Antony gestured and turned to the pillar with the memorial plaque where he was to conclude his lecture.

It was all he could do to make himself walk in a seemly way as he realized that in a few minutes he would be finished. He could go back to Kirkthorpe free of the weight this project had been. "Of all his enormous literary output, Hilton's masterpiece is *The Ladder of Perfection*. It is still in print more than six hundred years after he wrote it. Hilton's is a common sense path which makes it a surprisingly fresh and vigorous approach even for a modern reader seeking a more meaningful—"

"Wait! Sorry." Fred stepped out from behind Ginger. "Sorry to interrupt," Fred repeated, looking at a fuming Harry. "Camera's picking up something back there. Need to clear it out."

He started toward a dark shape no one had noticed on the floor beyond the pillar. Apparently Lenny or someone had left a pile of drop cloths or something where they would catch a camera angle.

Fred reached for the pile then drew back with an oath. Antony stepped over for a closer look. Then groaned and crossed himself. Not a pile of discarded tarps, but the body of Melissa Egbert.

# CHAPTER 25

"Please, can we just get this over? We have a wedding rehearsal in a few hours. *Our* wedding rehearsal." Felicity shifted an inch closer to Antony on the sofa. The living room of her cottage seemed much too small and stuffy this morning and she felt like she'd said it all before. "I told the officer yesterday. Didn't he write it down?"

Besides, they had their man, didn't they? Felicity shook her head as she recalled the chaos yesterday when, in the middle of the questioning by Nottinghamshire police, Inspector Nosterfield had arrived from the West Yorkshire division to arrest Harry Forslund on charges of drug dealing and suspicion of murder and pornography.

But she had no impulse to smile when she saw Sylvia's shocked face. "Harry, no!" The director's wife had been wordless.

Harry had blustered. "Murder? Nonsense! You can't arrest me. There's no law against filming racy movies. We didn't use kids! Consenting adults. Never hurt anyone."

"Harry, why?" Sylvia persisted.

"For the studio, of course. We're doing good work here. No one else makes films like this. But it doesn't pay. Cheap thrills, that's all anyone wants today. Entertainment. So we give it to them. You do the books. You know. How do you think I meet the payroll?"

Sylvia buried her head in her hands and they led a still protesting Harry away in cuffs.

The officer sitting across from Felicity cleared his throat to bring her back to attention. "I'm sorry, miss, but we do need to hear it again." Sergeant Scott Simenson of the Southwell and villages division of the Nottinghamshire police had short, dark hair and round, dark eyes in a round face and seemed, to the impatient Felicity, to move considerably slower than the proverbial molasses in January. Of course, in England that would be treacle, she reminded herself.

Police Constable Perry Crawford, as angular as the sergeant was round, and fortunately, somewhat quicker-motioned, looked back through his notes. "If you could just tell us again about your last conversation with the victim." He held his pen poised.

Felicity sighed. It was a good thing she had managed to get everything for the wedding so well organized before Christmas because there hadn't been a minute to do anything since. At least Cynthia had happily promised to see to the adjustment on Judy's bridesmaid's dress, but helping the police with yet another murder investigation was the absolutely last thing Felicity had planned to be doing two days before her wedding. At least they had the murderer. That was a relief. "As I said, we walked to the pub. Melissa rambled on and on about this article she was writing, but I didn't take in the details."

Felicity closed her eyes as she thought. "Let me see. Rievaulx and all the lands were granted to somebody after the abbey was suppressed. The Earl of Rutland, maybe. Would that be right? Then somebody named Buckingham—like the Palace, I remember that—owned it, but Cromwell confiscated it all and gave it to his general after the civil war. But Buckingham got it back by marrying the general's daughter. I'm sure I got that right because I thought it rather clever, although I think she said Buckingham was dissolute.

"But it turned out to be all for nothing because Buckingham died childless so the estate was sold to the present family in the seventeenth century. I asked her if it wasn't unusual for an estate to stay in one family for—what? more than three hundred years—and she said it was almost unique. That that was her slant for the article—how they've managed it.

"I started to ask about that, but then we were at the Red Lion where she was meeting someone for a drink. She was excited to interview him."

"Him? You're certain she was meeting a man?"

Felicity considered. "He—she—it—whatever. They had come down from the north for some meeting. I'm sure you can check what was on in the area that afternoon. I think she said he."

"But she definitely didn't mention any names?"

"No. And I didn't see anyone. I just stepped into the pub to get a map, then walked back to the church through the fields."

"And how did she seem?" PC Crawford asked.

"Excited. She had just found some new information..." Felicity paused and thought. "Keyed up might be better. Like she was ready to confront someone. Or maybe spring a surprise on them. An unpleasant surprise."

"But you don't have any idea what it was?"

"No, I don't." Felicity controlled her breathing to keep her voice from rising.

The officers now turned their interrogation to Antony, sitting beside her, but he could add little to what he had already told them. All he knew was the topic of Melissa's series, nothing about what she might have uncovered.

"And now I'll never know what she wanted to talk to me about." No one could doubt the sincerity of Antony's regret.

Felicity certainly wasn't going to prolong the interview with speculation, but when the police left she let her breath out in a long sigh and turned to Antony, "It must have been something about those notes Melissa found."

"Yes, that's very possible. I wonder what happened to them. I don't suppose we'll ever know." Antony's voice was heavy with regret. "Her killer probably has the notes now."

"Ah!" Felicity jumped to her feet. "Wait here." She rushed to her room and returned in a moment, brandishing a handful of papers. "Surprise! I suppose I should have given these to the police, although I couldn't see anything in them." She held them out. "Maybe you can spot something."

Antony's mouth fell open. "You mean you have them? Father Paulinus's notes? What a sly thing you are. Why didn't you tell me sooner?"

"Because you would have insisted on handing them over to the police. She gave them to me and I wanted a chance to look at them first. Not that it did me any good. Maybe you can see something in them."

Antony examined the papers. "Photocopies."

"Oh yes, Melissa had the original, but she intended to return them to Ampleforth. I suppose her killer has them now.

Doesn't that prove there has to be something in them? But I can't spot what it is."

Antony read the first few pages slowly, Felicity peeking over his shoulder at Father Paulinus's precise, old-fashioned handwriting. Antony lowered the pages and nodded. "I can see why Melissa was so excited. It looks like Paulinus was doing research along the lines of her articles."

"I thought these were supposed to be his notes for the film?" Felicity frowned.

"They are. I think. The Richard Rolle material is pretty straightforward."

"You told it better." Felicity's fierce loyalty was rewarded with a grin. She pulled a sheet from the stack Antony hadn't read yet and held it up. "But this about the Rievaulx lands, I just don't see how it fits in at all."

Antony scrutinized that page and the following sheets. "This is interesting. A family tree. And then all this detail about the Duncombe family. Looks like Paulinus got sidetracked. It doesn't seem like anything he would have used as narrative for the film."

Felicity studied the family tree carefully. "Look, there's Corin's family."

"Corin Alnderby? Our Corin? What's he doing there?"

"His great, great grandmother was a Duncombe. He told me that day at Rievaulx Terrace when Joy was interviewing his dad." She ran her finger over the branch Father Paulinus had drawn in beside the chart printed in the Rievaulx Terrace guide book. "It looks like all the men for four generations of that line have been named Stanton. I didn't realize that was Corin's middle name." She pointed. "But the thing is, that must be why Stanton Alnderby is so avid about Corin carrying on with the land."

Antony scrutinized the chart, frowning. "That can't be right."

"What?"

"Look. There." He pointed. "The first Stanton was born in 1900."

Felicity nodded. "Corin's great, great grandfather. So?"

Antony pointed to the line above. "Anabella Duncombe, wife of George Alnderby, died in 1899."

"Oh," Felicity felt her eyes widen. "That's why Father Paulinus had those photocopies from the General Register Office. I think that's about the point where I fell asleep last night." She took the papers from Antony and pulled two from the stack. "Death certificates for Anabella Alnderby, age twenty-five, and George Alnderby, age two years, both from poliomyelitis on the last day of December, 1899."

She pulled out the birth certificate below it. "Stanton Alnderby born 1 January 1900. Is that possible? Could a baby have been delivered post-mortem? On New Year's Eve?"

Antony shook his head. "Look again. I think that number looks more like a 7 than a 1. What do you think?"

Felicity took the document from his hand and scrutinized it, then went to her desk and pulled a magnifying glass from the top drawer. "You're right." She handed it to Antony for another look.

"So Stanton was born a week after his mother supposedly died?" Then Felicity looked over Antony's shoulder at the scrawl of the mother's signature. "The first name could be Ana, short for Anabella, but the last doesn't look like Alnderby. And the father is listed as unknown."

The room almost hummed with the intensity of their thoughts. Felicity was the first to speak. "So George Alnderby's wife and heir die..."

"And the wife is the Duncombe—the one with a share of the estate. And if she was pregnant at the time of her death—almost ready to deliver..."

"George could take an infant of close to the right age—"

"Most likely one he fathered on a servant girl," Antony added.

"And keep the land for himself in the name of Anabella Duncombe's supposedly second son." They finished together.

"Which has passed on in the line to this day," Felicity added. Then she paused. "But why would Father Paulinus have cared?"

"He cared about the truth. He probably just stumbled across the confusion in dates when mugging up background for the film. It must have piqued his interest, so he followed up."

"Do you think it's important?" Felicity asked.

"It could be. I definitely think you should ring the good Sergeant Simenson and make a full confession about 'forgetting' to tell him about the notes. And you can tell him what we suspect."

Felicity gulped. The sergeant wouldn't be happy with her. But delaying wouldn't make him any happier. She picked up the card he had left with them with his telephone number on it.

When she finished her call Antony glanced at the clock on the mantelpiece. "Time to get back up the hill. Sylvia's determined to finish the series, Harry or no Harry. Thank goodness, she offered to come here."

"Might as well. They wouldn't be able to get back into the Thurgarton church until the police are done there."

Antony shook his head. "I can't tell you how glad I'll be to have this over with. It's been a disaster from day one."

Felicity shivered, thinking of the trail of bodies the miniseries seemed to have produced. And on such an innocent topic. It didn't seem possible.

Antony moved toward the front door and Felicity pulled her coat off the peg. "I'll come along and then we can go over to the church together." She was as anxious as Antony to have the film project behind them so they could concentrate on nothing but their wedding. After the pageant, of course, she amended. They had set their wedding rehearsal a day early because of the pageant tomorrow.

"You know, I've been thinking," Antony mused as they approached the community gate, "We had pretty much settled on Harry as our prime suspect for those murders and the police obviously agree. But he couldn't be responsible for Melissa's death. He was in full sight of the whole crew all morning. I don't think he even took a loo break. We were all pushing to get it wrapped up.

"Besides, it has to have happened while we were all standing around the catering caravan because I had just unlocked the church door. The unlocking was staged, of course, because everyone was in there earlier setting up the sound and lights: Lenny, Simon, Pete..." He shrugged. "I don't know who all, but Melissa was alive then because she was with you."

"And you left the door unlocked when you broke for lunch?"

Antony nodded "Yes. We didn't take more than half an hour off."

Felicity was still thinking about it all, struggling, without success, to make sense of it, as she took a seat in the corner of the library to observe Antony's final time on camera.

Sylvia pointed to Fred, and Ginger's red eye blinked.

Antony pulled a popular edition of *The Ladder of Perfection* off the shelf beside him and held it out to the camera. "As Hilton sees it, scaling the ladder can never be a quick process, but rather, a 'gradual, cumulative process of receiving and responding to God's grace' one rung at a time. Hilton's great subject is to consider how the soul, once formed in the image of God but now both defaced and debased by sin, can be re-formed to God's image."

Antony smiled. "Perhaps a beanstalk would have been a better image for Hilton than a ladder, because he sees progress in the spiritual life as organic—a matter of growth. The soul grows into an ever-deepening union of love with God so that its entire will is surrendered and united to the Holy will and desires nothing outside Him who is its Life and Joy."

Here Antony stole a quick sideways glance toward Felicity. "Rather like a perfect marriage."

Joy Wilkins came on camera, standing beside Antony. "A lovely analogy, Father, but you said earlier Hilton was considered practical and concrete, can you make that a little clearer for us?"

Antony smiled. "Well, we're talking about being concrete for a mystic, you understand. Essentially Hilton's practicality rests in the fact that he stresses doing rather than feeling, in contrast to Richard Rolle who was all feeling.

"There are just three rungs to Hilton's ladder and scaling

them is, he says, 'the practical business of cooperating with grace.' There is a simple-sounding three-step progression: first, *reforming in faith* where one becomes disciplined and dutiful with a love for God as Brother and Father; second is *reforming in feeling*, whereby the emotions are illuminated so that one can truly worship; and then we are ready for the third stage—*contemplative union with Christ*, truly being at one with Him in our meditations."

Antony walked over to a small table where he had arranged a simple prop for his conclusion. He pulled a fat white candle toward him, struck a match and the wick flared. "Perhaps we could see faith, the first step on the ladder, as lighting the flame. Hilton says the second rung could be called 'love on fire with devotion.' the third 'love on fire with contemplation'."

The camera zoomed in on the flame as Joy picked up Antony's cue, "Which brings us full circle back to Richard Rolle, whose central image was the fire of love."

"Cut! That's a wrap." The words were met by unanimous cheers and applause from everyone in the room.

"Oh!" Felicity interrupted her clapping with a cry. She was among the first to realize that the decree had been issued, not by Sylvia, but by Harry.

The director was instantly surrounded by a cacophony of questions and greetings. Harry waved them all away and reached out to put an arm around his wife. "I told you not to worry."

Sylvia pulled away only fractionally from his grasp, but the questions persisted. "All right, all right." He held up a hand. "I told you there was nothing illegal about my little sideline—you'd better all be glad of it. It pays your salaries."

Sylvia's frown said she was more worried about the morality of her husband's actions than about the letter of the law.

"And they have no evidence at all involving me in the murders." Harry all but puffed out his chest. "Naturally, because I didn't do it."

Felicity noticed he didn't say anything about the drugs charges. And surely that meant he was responsible for at least Alfred's death. His lawyer might have got him out on bail, but she felt certain the police weren't through with Harry Forslund.

*Never mind. All that could wait*, Felicity determined, as Antony, finished with his farewells to the film crew, came to her with open arms and engulfed her in a hug. "Let's go practice getting married."

# CHAPTER 26

Felicity came to with a gasp and bounded out of bed the next morning. Life was so unfair. This was the day before her wedding and she didn't even have time to think about it. Why in the world had she ever agreed to help with that pestilential pageant? It had seemed like such a good idea at the time. And she supposed it had been good for the youth. And Gwena had certainly flourished as she took over Felicity's directing responsibilities, subtly enrolling Jeff to help her the last couple of days, Felicity had noticed. But Felicity was in no mood for distractions from what she considered the main event.

At least the wedding rehearsal had gone more or less all right yesterday evening. Father Anselm, as Master of Ceremonies, told everyone where to stand. And Bishop John, who had ordained Antony and would be marrying them, went through the highlights of the ceremony. Sweet and simple. Just like she wanted their wedding to be. Straight from the prayer book. Their only extravagance had been hiring a small choir to sing Palestrina's *Missa Brevis* for the mass.

Thank goodness weddings in the Church of England were considered worship services, not the production that some of her friends' at home had been. Certainly this one, in a monastery, would keep to the essentials. The community had been so charming about making their church available to "one of their own." After all, it wasn't every day that someone as nearly a member of a monastic community as Antony was got married.

She smiled again thinking about the fact that when they met he was planning to become a monk. And then there had been her brief, but enthusiastic period of considering joining a convent. She shook her head at the memory. A special touch of irony because the dinner after the rehearsal last night had been at a pub called The Three Nuns.

Gwena had been astonished when she first heard the plans. "What? No hen party?"

"Absolutely not." Felicity was adamant.

"What's a hen party?" Judy's innocent question had touched off a major discussion that just avoided becoming a row.

"Something like a bachelorette party," Felicity explained. "The bride and her friends dress up and make the round of local pubs the night before their wedding. Lovely for the bride to have a splitting head on her wedding day." She grimace. "I think a male stripper is part of the tradition, too."

"It can be good fun," Gwena insisted. "And the men have a stag do at the same time."

Of course, Cynthia had joined in, "Darling, I realize that wouldn't quite suit, but couldn't we do something? A tea party! Wouldn't that be sweet?"

Judy patted her pregnant tummy and smiled. "I remember my bridesmaids' party. It was lovely. We made strawberry daiquiris and watched 'Pride and Prejudice'."

Felicity smiled. "Yes, that was fun, Judy—Colin Firth in a wet shirt. But absolutely not. We rehearse for the wedding, then dinner. Then everyone goes home to bed." And that was what they had done.

But she couldn't avoid the complication of the pageant so easily. It had to be gotten through.

Felicity and Gwendolyn spent most of the day at the quarry, making sure costumes and props were in the right places and that the stage was marked with masking tape so their young thespians would know where to stand without getting the scene hopelessly out of balance. Kendra set up her borrowed sound system and checked it repeatedly, making sure the narrative and music would reverberate from the quarry walls.

And Nick and Corin seemed to be everywhere at once seeing to the animals. "The camel and his handler will be here at three o'clock. I just put another bale of hay in his pen," Nick said, on his way to fill the animal troughs with buckets of water which had to be carried from a hosepipe in the community garden. "I read camels eat three and a half kilos of hay a day and he'll share his pen with the llamas." He looked around. They haven't arrived yet, have they? They should be here soon."

Felicity observed the sheer drop at the far end of the quarry behind the stage. "Be sure you keep the gates secure, Nick. We don't want any of our animals going over that precipice."

"No worries," Corin said, coming up behind Nick with more water. "The sheep are secure." At that moment there was a lull in the activity and Felicity could hear the soft baa of the band of ewes Corin had secured from a local farmer. "And I brought Shep."

"Shep?" Felicity asked.

"Our sheep dog from home." Felicity saw the black and white collie at Corin's heels. "Sheep won't be led, they have to be herded. Shep can take care of that for us."

Felicity wished she had his confidence. And what if Mary's donkey balked, she wondered? She had visions of Shep nipping the donkey's heels and their chubby, gentle Flora, as Mary, being dumped on the ground. Why had they ever undertaken this? It was guaranteed to be a disaster. Maybe no one would come. That seemed to be the most comforting thought she could come up with.

Antony, Jeff and two of the youth who had been installing the tiki torches around the rim of the quarry joined them. "I think I saw the llama trailer pulling off the road, Corin. You might want to go show them where to put the beasts."

Felicity just shook her head. Antony continued his directions, "Drue and Joaquin, if you want to help us fill those braziers with charcoal I think we can take a break and go get something to eat then."

Gwen and Kendra said they would stay there to help any early arrivals get into costume, but Felicity was more than happy to take an extended tea break.

It was starting to get dark when Felicity and Antony returned to the quarry, having sent the others on ahead to get into costume. Some of the youth were in place to direct visitors across the community grounds and Father Sylvester sat at a small table at the top of the quarry steps, selling tickets to guests who had already begun to arrive. When Felicity saw everyone's enthusiasm and the enormous effort that had gone into organizing every detail she felt ashamed of her earlier desire for it all just to go away.

And when, halfway down the stairs, she emerged from under the bare, but still thick, tree branches, she stopped with a gasp of delight. "Antony, it's amazing!" Torches flared, turning the rim of the quarry into a circle of fire, braziers glowed among the seats, and the ebullience of the audience supplied warmth and energy as members of the well-bundled assembly set up their folding chairs, then pulled flasks of steaming tea, coffee or mulled wine from picnic baskets, sharing leftover mince pies or slabs of Christmas cake with their neighbors. The sense of community and feeling of good will was far beyond what any of them could have imagined.

And then the disparate band began its opening number "Tomorrow Will Be My Dancing Day." Little matter that the drums and trumpet nearly drowned out the keyboard and guitar, Felicity could have danced the rest of the way down the stairs. "Let's put our chairs there." Felicity pointed to an empty space halfway down the quarry slope. Before they had their chairs set up they were joined by Cynthia, Andrew, Jeff, Charlie and Judy, as Felicity had expected, but to her surprise Cynthia instructed them to save seating space for Harry and Sylvia.

Felicity frowned. Would even Harry have the temerity to come here if he had killed a man under the stage? "I didn't think Sylvia was speaking to him after the porn film revelation."

"I get the idea she made his giving that up a condition of her taking him back."

"But the drugs?" Felicity insisted. "We saw him."

Cynthia nodded. "He agreed to cooperate with the prosecution. I got the idea that was why they let him out on bail. And, by the way, I invited them to the wedding. That's all right, isn't it?"

"Of course it is. It's a church service everyone is welcome." Although Harry Forslund wasn't her favorite person—she certainly wouldn't want him to bark 'cut' in the middle of the ceremony—and she was far from convinced of his innocence. But the police would get to the truth soon. It wasn't her problem.

In the meantime, Felicity had responsibilities of her own. "I'd better get backstage to see what I can do to help." She glimpsed just the head of the camel in Nick's pen above the quarry rim. "Oh, good. Looks like all the animals are in place. At least the four-footed ones." She gave Antony a quick hug, then hurried on down to the back of the stage.

It was organized chaos. Gwena thrust a pile of surplices into her arms. "See what you can do to get everybody in some sort of costume. I swear half these youngsters never turned up for a rehearsal. Now they think they can go on stage." She shook her head and hurried on.

Felicity threw herself into the task at hand, moving from one uncostumed youth to the next, demanding, "What role?" If they didn't know, she pulled a surplice over their head and sent them to the corner where Kendra was assembling her angel choir. If they said shepherd, she found a charity shop dressing gown for them and tied a dark bath towel around their head. Corin or someone had even supplied a collection of small tree limbs to be used as shepherd staffs. "Shepherds on the hillside," she pointed to the western slope of the quarry just below the sheep pen.

By some miracle Gwen and Kendra had everyone in place

by the time the instrumentalists concluded the last strains of "In the Deep Midwinter" and Tanya began the narration, projecting just as Felicity had instructed her. "In those days, a decree when out from Caesar Augustus that all the world should be taxed."

"And everyone went to their own town to register." Balram's mellow voice came in. "So Joseph also went up from the town of Nazareth in Galilee to Judea, to Bethlehem the town of David, because he belonged to the house and lineage of David."

"Taking with him Mary, who was pledged to be married to him and was expecting a child," Tanya concluded.

Now the angelic choir began "O Little Town of Bethlehem" and Felicity knew Mary and Joseph would be beginning their descent from the back, down the sloping stairs through the center of the audience. She shot up a brief plea that the donkey would be in a cooperative mood.

This would perhaps be a good moment for Felicity to slip unseen up the side of the quarry so she could circle around and take her seat beside Antony after the holy family had completed their trek onto the quarry floor.

She made her way as unobtrusively as she could around the shepherds, keeping to the shadows of bushes, so as not to attract any attention. A swift glance over her shoulder, though, told her she needn't worry. All eyes appeared to be glued on Mary and Joseph who proceeded at a stately pace, encouraged by the slices of sugar beet Joseph had stashed in the satchel he carried slung over one shoulder.

"We hear the Christmas angels/ The great glad tidings tell/ O come to us, abide with us/ Our Lord Emmanuel." The choir concluded as Felicity gained the rim of the quarry.

Below her the narration continued with the familiar story of Joseph and Mary being turned away from the busy inn and settling in a stable for the night. Felicity knew that, leaving the donkey tethered below, they would be ascending the stairs at the side of the stage to begin forming the tableau beside the rough manger Corin and Nick had been required to construct on their own without Alfred's help.

Had Harry Forslund really killed the handyman over a drug deal gone wrong? She forced the whole thing out of her mind with a shake of her head. No. Pageant, then wedding, then the rest of her life. The police could worry over such gruesome questions.

"And she brought forth her firstborn son and laid him in the manger," the narration continued and the next carol floated up from the quarry floor, "Round yon virgin, mother and child/ Holy infant, so tender and mild/ Sleep in heavenly peace..."

Felicity shivered. She was in the dark now, beyond the reach of the torches, and it was noticeably colder up here out of the shelter of the quarry and the company of the audience. She just started around the outer reach beyond the sheep pen when a harsh voice made her stop.

"I told you I won't have it. You might think you've shown me up by borrowing a few beasts and carrying on with your scheme, but I won't have it." Felicity recognized the speaker's voice and the theme of the argument. Apparently Stanton Alnderby had changed his mind about boycotting his son's production. "After everything I've done to keep your inheritance safe, I'll not let you turn your back on the heritage of generations."

"And there were in the same country shepherds, abiding

in their fields." Balram's voice had taken on strength as the pageant progressed. The choir began "While shepherds watched their flocks by night..."

"That's my cue, Dad. We'll have to continue this later." The gate scraped the side of the pen as Corin opened it and whistled to Shep to send the sheep down the inclined path along the hillside to where their shepherds awaited them, then followed himself, costumed as a shepherd.

"I will not be balked in this." Stanton's voice followed his son's descent of the quarry side, ringing with angry determination. But what chilled Felicity more than the night air was the note of frenzied obsession. Of mania.

And with that came the certainty of the suspicion that had been roused when she and Antony found the family tree. This was a man who would kill to preserve what he saw as his own. Insane as it seemed, Stanton Alnderby had killed again and again to keep his great grandfather's secret hidden and a slice of the Duncombe estate in his possession.

And there was no doubt in Felicity's mind that he would kill again if he thought it necessary.

She couldn't get to her seat continuing on this way without being spotted. And if Stanton suspected she had overheard he would also suspect she might figure out the meaning of 'everything I've done to keep your inheritance'. She began backing away. She would have to go the long way round, past the steep end of the quarry, but that was better than risking an encounter with a crazed murderer.

Felicity took three steps back, almost beyond the spill of light from the nearest torch. Two more steps and she would be well hidden under a cloak of darkness. Once on the other side of the quarry and well out of range of being heard, she could ring the police.

The next step was her undoing. In the dark she failed to see the pile of stones. The top one turned under her foot and sent her sprawling sideways into a bush. She managed to stifle her cry, but not sufficiently to keep from alerting Alnderby.

"Who's there?" He took a long stride toward her.

Felicity tried to burrow deeper into the bush, but succeeded only in breaking several branches. To her ears the snapping sticks sounded like gunshots.

"Come on. You won't get away." She more felt than saw Stanton grab for her, but the darkness made his aim uncertain. She rolled sideways. A jagged limb scratched her face and she felt a trickle of blood on her cheek. She scrambled to her feet and began running toward the end of the quarry.

Felicity was fast. But Stanton had the longer legs. She could sense him closing the distance between them. Below her the choir sang "Angels we have heard on high..." the "Glo-o-o-o-r-ria" reverberating around the quarry walls below them.

She had reached the far end of the quarry when she felt Stanton's vice-like grip on her arm. He spun her around. "What do you mean by spying on me?" In the wavering light from a torch he examined her face. "You're that friend of Corin's, aren't you? One of those encouraging him in his mad scheme to be a priest."

Felicity wondered if she should try denying it, but knew nothing she said was likely to make any difference. Stanton pushed her closer to the rim of the quarry to see her better in the light. "Wait a minute. You were with that reporter, weren't you? I saw you when you came in the pub with her. What did she tell you?"

"Nothing," Felicity managed, but it came out barely above a whisper. She knew where they were. The deepest bend of the horseshoe that formed the quarry. Above the sheer precipice. With a drop of a hundred feet below her. And she knew what Stanton meant to do.

But she also knew that she was close enough to the edge to be visible to those below. Surely Antony would be wondering where she was. He knew she should have joined him by now. He would be looking around for her. If he spotted them up here he would see the danger. Call the police. Summon help. If she could stay here long enough for any of that to happen before Stanton hurled her over the cliff.

"Tell me. Don't think lies will save your pretty neck." Alnderby gave her a rough shake.

Felicity realized denial would get her nowhere. She needed to stall. "It's true. She didn't tell me anything. But she did give me a copy of her notes." Felicity's voice was gaining in assurance. "Which I gave to the police."

For a moment her words halted her captor. He stood frozen as Balram's announcement echoed from below: "Behold, there came wise men from the east." The pageant was nearing its climax. If her threat didn't make Stanton capitulate now she would truly be in dire straits. There would be little hope of help from the audience now. Every eye in the theatre would be glued on the entrance of the magnificently clad wise men accompanied by their entourage of camel, camel-drivers and llamas. Even Antony would be distracted from looking for her. A breeze carried the chime of the llamas' bells to her ears.

Then her blood chilled as a maniacal laugh drowned out all other sounds. "How kind of you to warn me. Now I'll be prepared when the plods come."

"What will you do? Burn the police station like you did Father Paulinus's hermitage?"

"That fool monk!" Stanton spit. "No one ever suspected. Four generations of clear sailing. Then he started nosing around. I thought I'd settled that. Then Corin tells me some noddy at his college has taken it up."

"The fireworks outside Antony's window. His car accident." Felicity tried to keep her voice level, in spite of the rising terror inside her. "The loose wheel on the camera dolly."

"Lame, I know. But I thought it would end it when that tart hung herself."

"But she didn't did she? You hung her." Felicity couldn't believe she was saying that to a killer holding her inches from the edge of a precipice.

"It was all part of that film they were shooting practically on my property. Filthy. She pretended to hang herself. Stark naked she was. As near as. Just her and that director fellow. And you should have seen the way she flaunted herself when he wasn't holding a camera. The slut deserved it.

"When they slipped off behind the caravan it was easy enough to fix the rope. She came back later for her clothes— just like I thought she would. The tart was even pleased when I told her I lived near and had been watching. A little flattery was all it took to get her to show me how she did the scene. Only this time she didn't get to pretend."

"O Star of wonder, star of night/ Star with royal beauty bright/ Westward leading, still proceeding/ Guide us to Thy perfect light." The increasing gusto of the music reaching up to the torch-encircled rim told Felicity the pageant was concluding. The wise men would be laying their gifts at the feet of the infant Jesus, then everyone would join in singing "Joy to the World" and there would be nothing to stop Stanton Alnderby from finishing the job he had in hand.

"But Alfred. Was he dealing drugs? Or did he try to stop a drugs deal? Why did you kill him?'

For the first time it seemed she had said something to perplex her captor. "Drugs? Surely you aren't suggesting I'd stoop to anything so sordid. When I realized Corin had helped himself to my best carpentry tools along with a pile of lumber I came to retrieve them. That clod of a gardener accused me of stealing. My own property. One shove did for him." The wavering light of the nearest torch twisted his features into an evil dance.

Felicity knew time was running out, but she would press her luck for just one more. "And Zoe? Why harm a poor dog?"

"Inquisitive, aren't you? A dumb dog should be the least of your worries." Felicity felt Stanton's muscles bunch. He reared back to give his thrust more impetus. She closed her eyes and stiffened. She would resist for all she was worth. "Now then—"

Stanton's words were cut off by a sharp cry of "Cut!" from the center of the audience. Stanton's thrust toward the cliff edge halted. Felicity followed his gaze to the astounding sight of Harry Forslund standing in the middle of the quarry pointing up at the pair on the rim of the precipice.

A woman shrieked. Cynthia, perhaps? And Felicity was certain she identified a cry from Antony. She had a fleeting glance of the entire audience surging toward the path along the side of the quarry. Help was racing toward her.

Until Stanton jerked her sideways with one hand and put two fingers in his mouth with the other. A long, piercing whistle rent the air, followed by two short, sharp notes.

Felicity twisted enough to be able to see Shep herding sheep and llamas to block off the path while the camel lumbered on its long legs and enormous hooves into the middle of the crowd and the donkey brayed.

An evil hiss in her ear brought Felicity's focus sharply back to her peril. Antony had seen her. As well as the more than one hundred people in the quarry below. All struggling to scale the wall and break through the animal barrier to come to her aid. But there was little hope they would reach her in time. Nor would the fact that there were more than a hundred witnesses stop her assailant. The frenzy of insanity had taken over.

A dazzle of light caught the corner of Felicity's eye. She extended her free arm in a lightning *port de bras* and grasped the flaring tiki torch. Thrusting the flame toward her captor, she forced him to release her arm and recoil.

He lunged at her with a manic snarl. With split-second timing Felicity did an *élancé* to the side. Alnderby's momentum, calculated to push Felicity over brink, carried him forward. Flailing to stop himself plummeting, he lashed out and grasped the hem of Felicity's coat.

She screamed as he pulled her toward the brink.

The world spun. She fell to the ground, grappling for a handhold. Strong hands grasped her wrists. With a jerk that she thought would pull her arms from their sockets her rescuer pulled her back from the edge, freeing her from her captor.

In the next moment she was engulfed in Antony's arms.

# CHAPTER 27

## Epiphany Eve

Felicity awoke to brilliant sunshine. She looked out her window and blinked in surprise. It had snowed during the night. The familiar green hills were dusted with white, sparkling in the morning sun. Felicity hugged herself. It was her wedding day. Her dancing day.

Finally. All the mayhem was behind her. All the puzzles solved. Finished. No more murder. No more mystery.

For just a moment she let the dark back in as she was once again on the edge of the quarry, looking down with Antony's arms securely around her.

In her memory it was dark and cold and yet the night filled with warmth and light because she was with Antony. "Don't let me go. Don't ever let go," she had cried. And she knew he wouldn't.

The emergency services had come. They had pulled Stanton's broken body out of the bushes and carried him away—whether to the hospital or the morgue made little difference. Nosterfield had been satisfied with all she told him.

For only a moment her confidence wavered. It must have been as Alnderby said. And yet, could he really have done all that unaided? Been in all those places without being seen? He must have been. After all, he confessed. Yet not so much a confession as a boast. As if he wanted her to think he did all that. All a credit to his own cleverness.

Then the uncertainty fled as Cynthia came in with a breakfast tray. "Happy is the bride the sun shines on." She fluffed the pillows and put the tray on Felicity's lap. "Even if it is bitterly cold. I had hoped for sunshine, but I didn't think to ask for warmth." She kissed her daughter and laughed.

Felicity had never realized before what a beautiful laugh her mother had. Musical, full-throated, like a woman half her age. "Mom, you and Dad—" Cynthia's smile was sufficient answer.

"Enjoy your breakfast, but don't dawdle. It's going to take ages to make those romantic little curls around your face. And then all those self-covered buttons to do up."

A short time later Judy arrived and Gwena returned from the train station with the aunt who had raised her and Antony. Cynthia embraced Beryl and turned her over to Andrew for company. His quiet attention would be the best possible comfort for the elderly woman who had so recently buried her husband of sixty years.

Meanwhile the rest of the cottage was swept up in a flurry of curling irons and flowing dresses. Felicity closed her eyes and set her lips, determined not to complain when the long row of fabric-covered buttons lining the way up her back caused Cynthia repeated fumbles as she hooked the tiny loops over each one. Then a single button at the wrist of each long, pointed sleeve.

Cynthia held Felicity at arms' length, a hand on each shoulder. She bit her lip and Felicity saw the tears in her mother's eyes. Cynthia held up a finger in a 'wait a minute' gesture and turned to a florist box in the corner. She rustled through a pile of tissue paper. At last she extracted a wreath of Syringa and held it aloft. "To hold your veil in place—the Idaho state flower. I don't want you forgetting your roots."

"Never, Mom." Felicity took a deep sniff of the heady, sweet mock orange, then leaned forward and gave her mother a kiss on each cheek.

The Church of the Transfiguration was incandescent with clear winter sunshine pouring through the high clerestory windows. Banks of candles made the carvings of wood and stone come alive. A bouquet of white flowers filled one corner of the nave—the only decoration especially for the wedding. Felicity, waiting in the sacristy with Gwena and Judy, the choir, clergy and servers, felt her heart beating in time with the Bach prelude. In her mind's eye she saw Jeff and Charlie seating Cynthia and Beryl on each side of the aisle. Cynthia had raised an eyebrow when Felicity explained that in an English wedding the mothers didn't make a special entrance but she didn't fuss.

Now Felicity imagined she could hear the gentle rustle of fabric and scrape of feet on stone as the church filled with their friends from the college and community, including the youth of the centre still flushed with their success from the night before. She wondered how many from the Studio Six crew had come.

Then all other thoughts were swept away when the choir began its procession down the north aisle behind crucifer, thurifer, boat boy and acolytes, singing the Palestrina introit she and Antony had chosen. Four priests in cloth of gold vestments concluded the liturgical procession.

When clergy and servers were in place before the attar

Felicity took a deep breath and clasped her father's arm. Choir and congregation began singing "Praise to the Lord, the Almighty, the King of creation..."

"That's our cue, Dad." Head up, smiling behind her veil, Felicity let her father lead her forward, followed by her bridesmaids. "Praise to the Lord! O let all that is in me adore him! All that hath life and breath come now with praises before him!"

They halted at the top of the aisle as Felicity's eyes sought out Antony standing with her brothers to her right. He was so handsome in his cutaway coat with ascot and vest. And so intent as he followed every word and gesture of the liturgy he had chosen from the most traditional prayer books.

The choir sang the "Gloria" from Palestrina's *Missa Brevis.* "We praise thee, we bless thee, we worship thee, we glorify thee, we give thanks to thee for thy great glory; O Lord God, heavenly King, God the Father Almighty..." The high altar gleamed, incense billowed, angelic music soared. It was all Felicity and Antony had dreamed of for so long.

Bride and groom sat side by side before the altar for the readings and wedding sermon. Father Anselm talked of commitment and quoted Bonhoeffer, "It's not love that makes the marriage, but marriage that sustains love."

And then, the Rite of Holy Matrimony. Bishop John, splendid in gold mitre asked, "Who giveth this woman to be married to this man?" The answer was not in words, but actions as Felicity's father stepped forward and placed her hand in Antony's, physically giving her to him.

"I, Antony Stuart, take thee, Felicity Margaret, to my wedded wife, to have and to hold from this day forward..."

"I, Felicity Margaret, take thee..." Her voice rang with an intense timbre before her throat closed.

The bishop blessed them with holy water. Then the rings. "With this ring I thee wed, with my body I thee worship..." Felicity's hand shook. She had always thought those the most beautiful words in the wedding ceremony.

The Bishop wrapped their hands together with the end of his stole and thundered the proclamation, "Those whom God hath joined together let no man put asunder." The message echoed from the stone arches: anyone who makes trouble incurs the wrath of God. They knelt for the Nuptial Blessing.

During the anthem *Exsultate justi* the bride and groom, accompanied by best man and chief bridesmaid, slipped to the side chapel to sign the civil registers.

And then, the Liturgy of the Eucharist. Bride and groom processed with the bread and wine to the high altar. "At the name of Jesus Every knee shall bow..." the congregation sang. Feeling so transported she could hardly breathe, and yet knowing she would never forget this moment, Felicity took Antony's hand as they stood at the foot of the golden altar while clergy and servers prepared the royal banquet, the food of angels, *Sanctus, sanctus, sanctus, Dominus Deus saboath pleni sunt caeli...* "Holy, holy, holy, Lord God of hosts, Heaven and earth are full of thy glory..." the choir sang in Palestrina's Latin.

"Gracious God, may Antony and Felicity, who have been bound together in these holy mysteries, become one in body and soul. Let their love for each other be a seal upon their hearts, a mantle about their shoulders, and a crown upon their foreheads."

Singing "Ye Holy Angels Bright" bride and groom led the

procession out the great west door as the community bell pealed joyfully over their heads.

They paused only briefly for photographs. Warmed by the fire of her joy, Felicity hardly felt the cold, but she could see Gwena and Judy shivering even in the faux fur stoles Cynthia had provided. Only a few steps down the hill, the college hall welcomed the wedding party and guests with cups of hot punch and a bountiful buffet.

"Do you have a speech, Dad?" Felicity asked, knowing her soft-spoken father wasn't one for much public speaking.

"It'll be short," he said as he rapped a fork on a glass for attention. When the room quieted he smiled at the couple beside him. "I know it's traditional at this moment for the bride's father to say 'we haven't lost a daughter; we've gained a son.' In our case, however, it seems that we haven't lost a daughter; we've gained a country." The room rang with applause as Andrew shook hands with his English son.

The rest of the time seemed to go in a whirl. Felicity moved between the long tables glimmering with tea lights shining on Cynthia's decorations, to greet their guests. Felicity felt she was reliving her entire life on this side of the Atlantic as she chatted with former classmates from Oxford, friends from London, Willibrord St. John and his wife from the retreat house on Lindisfarne, Sister Pamela from Julian's Centre in Norwich, Ryan and Nancy from their pilgrimage across Wales, Sister Gertrude from Fairacres...

Felicity had worked her way to the end of the long room when she was surprised to see Corin and his mother there. How must they be feeling after the events of last night?

She greeted them warmly. "Thank you so much for coming." She didn't know what else to say.

But Corin didn't dodge the topic. "I thought it would be good for Mum to get out of that dreary hospital. Besides, the police won't even let her near Dad's room."

Felicity was still trying to think of a reply when she glimpsed Antony talking to someone in the vestibule. What was DI Nosterfield doing here? Had he actually come to their wedding?

She stepped into the anteroom to greet him, then overheard enough to understand that the Detective Inspector was there on duty. Stanton Alnderby had died. She started forward but was stopped by an hysterical outburst, "No! No! No!"

Before Felicity could spot the source of the cry she felt herself slammed against the wall. A pair of strong hands seized her shoulders and began shaking her. "Murderess! You killed him! You killed—"

Antony and Nosterfield pulled Sylvia Mountbank from Felicity before she could bang her head into the stone wall again. Felicity shook her head to clear it. Had she understood the implications of Sylvia's hysteria correctly? Sylvia and Stanton?

"You were working with Stanton to secure his inheritance?" Felicity struggled to keep her voice level, to sound calm in the face of such frenzy.

"Inheritance? That didn't matter. Not to me. I loved him. And he loved me. I was worthy of him. I could make him happy. That poor man, stuck for all those years with that drab Elsa."

Corin and his mother entered just in time to hear Sylvia's words. Elsa strode across the foyer, pulled back her arm and landed a resounding slap on Sylvia's cheek. "'Helping scout filming locations,' he said. How stupid did you think I was? I suppose you thought you were the first? My husband used the women he made fall for him just like he used everyone else. Yes, I put up with it all for years because I fell for the 'saving the inheritance for Corin' line. But now that Corin doesn't want it, I would have blown the whistle if Stanton hadn't done it on himself."

Elsa paused and shook her head. "It's just a shame I didn't do it sooner. What a pity so many people had to die." She looked at the now-sobbing Sylvia. "Did you kill for him, or just help cover it all?"

But now that a more complete picture was forming in her mind Felicity had other questions. She stepped forward. It was her turn to grab Sylvia's shoulders. "Did you know about Harry's porn operation?"

At that Sylvia's tears turned to anger. "Of course I knew. Harry ogling naked women. This was the perfect way to get back at him. Two birds with one stone, so to speak."

"You brought the soap from the B & B, didn't you? You were in on the whole thing."

Sylvia's shoulders slumped. "What difference does it make now that Stanton's gone?"

"And you drugged your own dog?" Felicity's voice rang with incredulity.

"I wouldn't have let her die. It was a lucky touch that your mother happened along."

"And Harry wasn't the one dealing drugs, was he?"

Sylvia shrugged. "He was happy enough to make a delivery to Syd for me. I didn't actually intend to stitch him up. That was an added bonus."

"But why didn't Harry deny the charge?

Sylvia gave a smug smile.

"He loved you that much?" Felicity shook her head. "But why do all that to sabotage the film? Once you thought Father Paulinus's notes were gone?"

Sylvia almost spit. "Harry's precious mini-series. You heard him—there was no money in it. If it failed Harry would have had to accept that offer in Australia and I'd be free of him."

Felicity frowned. "Free of Harry? Why not just walk away?"

"And walk away from the company as well? And leave it to Harry? Never. He had to go and leave it to me."

"And if that didn't work framing him for the drugs would work just as well." Felicity was still shaking her head as Antony slipped his arm around her and led her away. "Did you hear that? She must be insane."

"Or far too clever for her own good. It sounds like they had some sort of agreement that if either one left Studio Six went to the remaining partner."

"Like a prenuptial agreement?" Felicity struggled to understand. "Only they weren't married."

"I think it's called a tontine—last man standing."

Felicity nodded. "And Sylvia was determined to be that man."

Behind them they heard DI Nosterfield charging Sylvia with conspiracy to commit murder. It would take the police a long time to sort it all out, but Antony and Felicity were free of all the entangling questions and shadows.

Cynthia, Andrew, Beryl and Gwendolyn met them at the back of the hall. Beyond them Felicity could see their guests laughing, visiting and enjoying the remains of the buffet and thick slices of the marzipan and fondant wrapped wedding cake.

"Don't worry, I'll save you a big piece of cake," Cynthia said as she wrapped Felicity's long, green woolen cape around her shoulders.

Gwena handed Antony his silver grey top hat. "On to the future, Squib," she said.

He grabbed Felicity's hand to lead her to the waiting car. "Let's go!"

# About the Author

Donna Fletcher Crow is the author of 45 books, mostly novels of British history. The award-winning *Glastonbury, The Novel of Christian England*, an Arthurian epic covering 15 centuries of English history, is her best-known work. She also authors The Lord Danvers Mysteries. *A Tincture of Murder* is her latest in these Victorian true-crime novels. The Elizabeth and Richard Mysteries are her literary suspense series of which *A Jane Austen Encounter* is the latest. *An All-Consuming Fire* is the fifth of Felicity and Antony's adventures in the Monastery Murders. Donna and her husband of 50 years live in Boise, Idaho. They have 4 adult children and 14 grandchildren. She is an enthusiastic gardener.

To read more about all of Donna's books and see pictures from her garden and research trips go to:

www.DonnaFletcherCrow.com

You can follow her on Facebook at: Donna Fletcher Crow, Novelist of British History

# Read all of Felicity and Antony's adventures:

**A Very Private Grave** Felicity is devastated when she finds her beloved Father Dominic bludgeoned to death. When Antony is accused of the murder they are propelled to a quest across the north of England in the steps of Saint Cuthbert, following and being followed by murderers.

**A Darkly Hidden Truth** Felicity can't possibly help Father Antony find the valuable missing icon. She's off to become a nun. Then her overwhelming mother turns up unexpectedly and a good friend turns up murdered. From the misty marshes of the Norfolk Broads to the domains of the Knights Hospitaller in London conflict and danger dog Felicity's steps.

**An Unholy Communion** The body plummeted from the tower, rolled down the hillside and landed at Felicity's feet demolishing her plans for a quiet summer holiday. The sinister events increase as Felicity and Antony guide a youthwalk along an ancient pilgrimage route in Wales turning an idyllic pilgrimage across the land of saints and legends into a life-and-death struggle between good and evil.

**A Newly Crimsoned Reliquary** Oxford's muffled bells toll another death. Could the Medieval Latin document Felicity is translating for the good sisters at the Convent of the Incarnation have anything to do with the repeated attacks? Can Felicity prevent the next tragedy when Murder stalks the shadows of Oxford's Hallowed Shrines?

CPSIA information can be obtained
at www.ICGtesting.com
Printed in the USA
LVHW052021030321
680485LV00014B/2170